CONTEMPORARY AMERICAN FICTION

WHITE HORSE CAFE

Roberta Smoodin is the author of *Ursus Major, Presto!*, and *Inventing Ivanov*. A native of Los Angeles, she graduated from UCLA and studied fiction in the graduate writing program at U. C. Irvine, where she received her MFA. Aside from writing and teaching fiction, she is a fine journalist whose work has appeared in *Esquire, Redbook, Mademoiselle*, and elsewhere.

ALSO BY ROBERTA SMOODIN

Ursus Major
Presto!
Inventing Ivanov

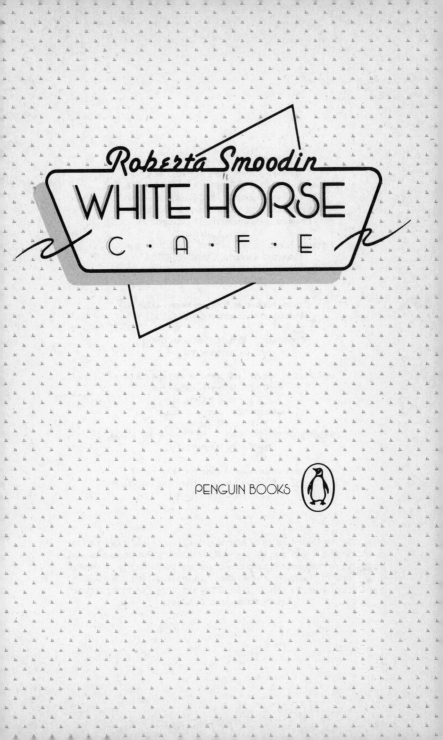

Roberta Smoodin

WHITE HORSE
C · A · F · E

PENGUIN BOOKS

PENGUIN BOOKS

Viking Penguin Inc., 40 West 23rd Street,
New York, New York 10010, U.S.A.
Penguin Books Ltd, 27 Wrights Lane, London W8 5TZ
(Publishing & Editorial) and Harmondsworth,
Middlesex, England (Distribution & Warehouse)
Penguin Books Australia Ltd, Ringwood,
Victoria, Australia
Penguin Books Canada Limited, 2801 John Street,
Markham, Ontario, Canada L3R 1B4
Penguin Books (N.Z.) Ltd, 182–190 Wairau Road,
Auckland 10, New Zealand

First published in Penguin Books 1988
Published simultaneously in Canada

LIBRARY OF CONGRESS CATALOGING IN PUBLICATION DATA
Smoodin, Roberta, 1952–
White Horse Cafe.
(Contemporary American fiction)
I. Title. II. Series.
PS3569.M647W45 1987   813'.54   87-11904
ISBN 0 14 00.9838 0

Printed in the United States of America by
R. R. Donnelley & Sons Company, Harrisonburg, Virginia
Set in Garamond Book

For
Ralph,
Pat,
Don,
Catherine,
Gene,
Judy,
Mark:
My friends, who make life possible.

One
SASHA

This mania for finding your real parents, I've never bought it. I mean, once you're over eighteen, your family is who you decide it should be. Then, you adopt people yourself. You let them into your life, you love them, you lose them, you grieve for them. Just like you would for real family. In many ways, I consider myself lucky, because it's much easier to abandon an adoptive mother and father than your real ones. My adoptive mother was short and dark and plump. My adoptive father was tall and dark with thick glasses always making a swollen red scar across his nose. And there I was, Sasha: this large, blond, blue-eyed child with big bones I always seemed about to grow into, but never did. I could never have been theirs except for the fluke of adoption. The craziest bonding of genes, the most outlandish freak of conception, couldn't have caused me to come from them. When I ran away, they wrote me letters for a while, and then stopped, as if I'd been a dream to them, too. A bad dream. The only thing of theirs I have kept is their last name, because it makes me vaguely exotic, Sasha Berlin. Everyone thinks I made it up to attract attention from agents and directors and casting people. Then I get to say no, I didn't make it up. It's the name I was born with. My little lie, because of course

I have no idea what name I was born with. Or, rather, I was born without a name, more purity than most babies. No name, no mother, no father. Papers with lawyers' names scrawled on them my only real heritage. And that's okay. I take contracts seriously. Read everything twice before I sign. This makes me one of the few smart actresses in the city.

Tomas, on the other hand, has more family than he knows what to do with. He's mired in family: family restaurant, sisters, brothers, aunts, uncles, and two mamas. Names handed down over generations, stories handed down too. The time his father's father, a diplomat in Germany, took the child to a lunatic asylum. One of the crazies sat hunched in a corner, fetal. A doctor suggested to this crazy that music played. The crazy cocked his head, heard the music, rose, and danced. The crazy was, by this time, a little out of shape, a little chubby, but he still danced like some unearthly thing, or something earthly, but not human. A panther kept too long in a cage. A tropical bird trained to say only tiresome things. Captivity does this to you. Tomas's father told him, Tomas, this story, and Tomas told it to me. The crazy was, of course, Nijinsky. One of the reasons Tomas loves me is that I am empty of stories. He tells me the saga of his family, fills me up with it, and I memorize it, because I have none of my own, nothing epic about me.

Tomas is my family. In bed, at night, I feel the gravitational pull of his body. He says I hurt him with my big bones while we sleep. That I try to lodge my knees between his legs, stick elbows in his ribs. Tomas never bruises, so it's hard to know if this is the truth. But I believe it. Whatever hurts Tomas hurts me, because he is like a piece of myself, only somehow separate, in the world. Like another limb, an arm, a leg. I believe, too, that amputees feel pain in the limbs they no longer have, because of the way I feel about Tomas. And I understand the worried looks on mothers' faces when they see their children, over a fence, across a playground, fall and hurt themselves. Having a detached piece of oneself at loose in the world is a dangerous thing. You risk more, everything.

Since I've known Tomas, been sleeping with Tomas, I've only had two nightmares. This from the child who always woke up screaming in the middle of the night. I was hardly a prize package, ever, to my poor adoptive parents. The two nightmares I had, I don't remember them. But instead of waking up screaming, alone, I woke up to Tomas holding my face, smoothing my hair, speaking to me softly, sweetly. This is not to say Tomas is some sort of angel. I talk in my sleep too, and I have awakened, a couple of times, to myself having some sort of conversation, asleep, with Tomas, awake. He soothes me back into sleep then, because he makes me feel so safe. Nothing bad can happen while I'm sleeping with Tomas. But in the morning, I have vague memories. He was saying to me: "Who is Alan?" or "tell me his name," or "how many times have you seen him?" But these words are like words in a dream, thin, feathery, like smoke.

Now, I look at Tomas asleep, and I love him completely. He seems violently alive, always, even with his face smashed into his pillow. When he wakes up, he will make love to me. We will be, briefly, one being, which is how it should be. We should not be separated by more than a few hours, a few miles, sleep.

The living room's atmosphere is dense and layered as a Tequila Sunrise. Basketball season, and one of those pro games on the television, on a delayed feed, magnetizes Tomas's, and Lonny's, and Bud's attention. All I wanted was to go to sleep, after six hours of being polite to people ordering expensive food, expensive wines with names they can't pronounce, sloppy expensive desserts. Too much pink and gray and abstract art in that restaurant. I prefer, in some ways, the funk of Tomas's place, though I would never tell him. He'd want me to work there then, and I'd make shit in tips. But now it's after one, and I wish I'd been home for a couple of hours watching television and getting loose with the guys.

"*Corazón,*" Tomas says, rises, hugs and kisses me as if we had not seen each other in six months: our ritual. I glue myself to him, as Lonny and Bud watch television, send plumes of yellow and silver smoke to rebound off the ceiling and settle in strata in the low room. "Baby," Tomas says. I run my fingers through his dirty hair, kiss him again to feel the allover warmth of him.

"What's on?" I ask, ready to settle into the couch, smoke the gourmet weed the guys pride themselves on, turn jelly, butter, custard next to Tomas.

"Lakers just won," Tomas says. "C'mon, sit down." Now Lonny and Bud can look at me, at us. We are no longer incendiary and dangerous to men who do not get laid regularly.

"Hey, Sasha," Lonny says. I lean down to field his brief kiss.

"Hi," Bud says.

"What can I get you, my poor baby?" Tomas puts on a show of looking after me, though no one will notice his largesse in the smog and fog. "A glass of wine? A massage?"

But the television picture leaps out at me as a study in depth and surprise. In the foreground, an announcer interviews a still-sweaty player. They talk about the game, trade jock banalities. But in the background, in the locker room, clearly visible, a man gets naked. A player. Unaware that a camera watches him. Studiously exhausted, he removes his jersey, his trunks, stands in his jock strap to remove his shoes and socks. I can't believe it.

"Look at that!" I say, and point at the television. But, because of the dope, the pinprick focus it brings, Lonny and Bud, and I guess Tomas, though I can't see him behind me, think I'm enjoying the interview.

"Fucking Lakers," Bud says appreciatively. "They really kicked ass tonight. Man, I love these dudes."

"No, no," I say. "Look."

"What is it?" Tomas says. He appreciates my perceptions, thinks sometimes that he and I have an extrasensory link, knew each other in former lives. It's possible.

"Right there," I say, and advance, with my index finger held out like a divining rod, toward the TV screen. I stick my fingertip to the man who now removes his jock strap on national television. The man stands there, naked, wondering what to do next. His beautiful body, muscles, planes, in the repose of fatigue. "A naked man," I say. Everyone leans in, looks closer.

"Fucking Robisch," Tomas says. "Look at that."

"I didn't even see him," Lonny says.

"I can't believe it," Bud says. "Right behind Norm Nixon talking about the fourth quarter."

"Hey, man, this is history," Lonny says.

Tomas hugs me, turns me around away from the screen. "Don't look," he says. "I don't want you getting ideas." Lonny and Bud laugh, but I know he's serious. It's in his hurt/jealous tone of voice which anyone else would think to be a joke. Tomas fears I'd like to sleep with basketball players. "Come here, talk to me," Tomas says, and pulls me into the kitchen, where the clean air and smooth white paint make my head feel better.

"Linda didn't come in again tonight," Tomas says. "Man, were we short. I gotta find a new waitress."

"What's going on with her?" I'm always solicitous about Tomas's business problems, especially when they involve waitresses. Partially because I'm one, a waitress. Also because we, waitresses, share one other characteristic: we're women. That always interests Tomas, and I keep track of what interests Tomas.

"I don't know, Julio says she'll be in, tomorrow, for sure. I don't know, man, I'd like to get rid of her. It's going to be a heavy Friday tomorrow, and if we're short then, we're really in trouble."

"What does Concepción say?"

"Mama says not to worry. That's easy for her to say. She's eighty-four, the old bag. What has she got to worry about?" But he says this so lovingly, the way he always talks about his grandmother. I remember the time he beat up someone in the alley behind his restaurant because this guy, in an argument with Tomas, made some obscene reference to Concepción. Tomas beat the shit out of him. Then, Tomas said, apologetically, "He can't say that about my granny." A mixture of sheepishness and pride.

"Hey," Lonny calls from the living room, "they just realized they've got Robisch naked behind them. You gotta see this."

Instead, though, I'm sitting on the sink with my legs wrapped around Tomas's waist, he presses his body against mine. We make out like teenagers, all tongue and mouth and sweaty bodies languishing under the restraint of clothes. No tiredness now, no pain in my calves and insteps. I fill myself up with Tomas, suck him in, sip him, eat him, and the world disappears.

The story of Concepción and the General fascinates me. I don't know history, not the history of this country, not, at all, the history of Mexico. So it's like a fairy tale, blurry and romantic, and even the unhappy ending can't ruin it. Actually, I like unhappy endings. They seem right, final, in a way happy endings never can.

So Concepción was this young girl, living on her parents' farm in Mexico, where there were constant wars. Not wars with other countries, but internal wars. Civil wars. Revolutions. The whole country like one big pot continually boiling over, boiling over. Everything always shimmying around, no semblance of neat politics like we have here, but politics like one of those parties where everyone has a switchblade in his pocket and is just waiting for some guy to say something crude about his girlfriend. That's the picture in which to place this young girl, Concepción. Maybe she was eighteen, maybe sixteen. Numbers are fuzzy to me too.

One day a ragtag group of soldiers rides through, on their way either to one war or from another, maybe both. But her parents agree with the politics of these soldiers, and take them in, feed them, house them, tend to their wounds. Their leader, General Santiago, shines, with the starry light of myth. Concepción thinks, this man will become famous. Secondly, she thinks: He's handsome. He's not that much older than she is, at most ten years, but already he's a general. In civil wars and revolutions, everyone who lives through a couple of battles becomes a general, a reward for the capacity to survive. We don't have those kind of rewards any more: survival is just expected. The General, it soon becomes clear, thinks that Concepción, too, shines. Perhaps he sees in her the tough wisdom I see now, or the strength. I can't believe she was beautiful, although that could just be age. I know her now, in her eighties. But Tomas's father was beautiful, and Tomas. I hear people call Concepción a beautiful old woman, but the word old obliterates the word beautiful.

Soon enough, then, the General courts Concepción, I guess within a few days after his arrival. Within two weeks, when the soldiers become healthy and rested and ready to ride off into this glorious uncertainty which sets men free from society and women (the reason men love war?), Concepción goes with the General, quickly married to him. She never sees her parents, her home again.

Unlike most warriors, though, the General depends completely upon his woman, trusts her intelligence, her deep true emotions. She goes with him to every battle, camps with him and his men. Twice, she walks through the ranks of men lined up, cleaned up, for inspection, and points to the one with the bullet in his gun marked for the General's heart, the one, with connections to the rival camp, who has been sent to kill the General. "I don't know, honey," she says to me when I ask her how she knew. "When you look at a rattlesnake, you don't think you want to take it home as a pet."

"But Mama, these were men, not snakes," I say. I want this information, not just because it's an important part of the story.

"Honey, the General was all I had. His life was my life. You know how dogs get these intuitions about people? How they never like some people, and how it always turns out that the people they don't like meant their masters some harm?"

This comparison I don't like one bit. Nothing romantic in it. Concepción is nothing like a dog, though I can imagine her citing her qualities in a doglike list: loyalty, fidelity, devotion. But in her wiliness, her craftiness, she can only be a human woman.

"You're more like a coyote than a dog," I say.

She laughs, that great laugh no other old woman could duplicate because it is so much bigger than her body, so much younger. "Yes, yes, honey, you're right. I wish I could tell you I smelled danger on them. But I just looked into the eyes of each man who might be able to harm the General, and in the eyes of assassins, I could see fear."

This means something. "Their eyes," I repeat.

"Yeah, sure. For all the good it did me. You don't get to look in the eyes of everyone. Then, I had the General. Now I have a restaurant, and Tomas." She sighs, and her body contracts from the largeness of the laugh into the smallness of age-old grief.

But, in the old days, nothing stopped Concepción or the General. She saw him through many campaigns, campaigns embroidered with the mythical names of Emiliano Zapata, Pancho Villa, the men who had movies made about them. The General became very powerful, and was a good, fair man, always. So good and fair he might have become president. At this point, his rival for the presidency, a not good, not fair man who wanted power more than anything, started another war, and Concepción went on another campaign of battles with the General. This was, I guess, in the early part of this century, at the point where war got really dirty, where you no longer got to examine the eyes of your General's men for signs of fear.

Two
TOMAS

Tomas loves daylight saving time. Then, when he arrives at El Caballo Blanco to open the place up, it's still light outside, and in this light he feels strong. In the dark, in the alley behind the restaurant, he feels as if he's no longer in the middle of Los Angeles. Instead, the alley's darkness magically develops qualities that darkness in the wilderness has: a feeling of enclosure, as if the darkness is a black velvet shroud hung around one's being. One can reach out and feel the purring softness of it, but whatever exists outside of it must remain unknown. Complete lack of depth perception. Anyone, anything, can hide in this kind of atmosphere, harboring evil intentions. When Tomas leaves each night, with the muslin sack of money and checks, this closeness stifles his breath, makes him pant like a frightened dog.

Now, four in the afternoon, the alley looks sad, decrepit, dusty. Tomas and his old black Ford pickup screech up behind the restaurant. A gentle grazing kiss between front fender and wall, the wall bruised by many such kisses. A swirling tornado of alley flotsam encircles the truck, an apocalyptic storm of dirt and handbills for the laundry on the corner and napkins and panty hose and beer cans and indescribably shredded bits of unknown objects.

The alley as post-Armageddon civilization. All Tomas sees is the restaurant. His restaurant. His grandmother's restaurant, family tradition in this one building since 1929. He jumps out of the truck without hearing the groan of the truck's door as he swings it open and swings it shut. Tomas is comfortable in his world, and perceives only change, differentness, keenly. Sameness is all a well-known song, Muzak, to him, the background soundtrack to his life. In a yard where there wasn't a dog yesterday, a dog now barks. This Tomas hears: maybe a Doberman's bark. Worth noting. Tomas remembers the story some guy told him about the woman returning home late at night to find a dead burglar in her bedroom, blood everywhere, his hand a bloody fingerless stump. And no sign of her pet Doberman. She calls the police, the police come, everyone in complete confusion. Then they hear the small mewing sound of choking coming from her closet, like a kitten swallowing milk wrong. They open the closet to find her Doberman having trouble breathing. She rushes the Doberman to the twenty-four-hour vet, the vet operates, and finds lodged in the dog's throat the burglar's fingers. Tomas smiles: a good story. He'll have to remember to tell Sasha. Maybe it's even true.

Holding his key chain full of too many keys, Tomas strides to El Caballo Blanco's back door, in control of his world. He must have been very handsome as a younger man, but perhaps too pretty. His fine, vaguely exotic, dark features, the large eyes, long nose, full mouth might have been slightly effeminate. But now, as a thirty-five-year-old man who has battered each day of his life into submission, wrestled with many angels and serpents for his soul, those features look well-used. The lines in his face express emotion rather than age. He smiles broadly, laughs loudly, furrows his eyebrows together into one stern line when he is angered. Excessive emotion, generally considered a feminine trait, has made his face more masculine, and more attractive. This large, expressive head might dwarf most bodies, but Tomas's shoulders and chest are massive, a Rodin torso, to support all the emotions written on his big face. Hips and legs an afterthought, slender but unimpressive. Nothing about him looks Mexican, except, perhaps, for his imperial, the dot of facial hair below his lips, above his chin. Darkly European, perhaps: Italian, Portuguese, Spanish, in a decadent aristocratic mode. A friend had once taken a photograph of Tomas dressed as a priest, in clerical collar, hair slicked back, eyes stern and pious: This worked too. Tomas's favorite photo of himself. Just the thought of celibacy can make him laugh aloud. Tomas a priest? Impossible.

Tomas unlocks the door, steps into the well-known darkness, throws a light switch. The hard light of the kitchen, instantly too hot. For years Tomas and Concepción have spoken about overhauling the kitchen, but it remains full of gleaming, ancient machines. An antique dishwasher still in full use, an archaic and enormous stove blackened by decades, chrome counters scarred by knives and tempers, teardrop lights for keeping plates of food warm. Empty of workers, of food, this kitchen would be indecipherable to an alien just landed on earth. To Tomas, the kitchen cannot be separated from its function. He feels, as always, the pleasure of proprietorship, and moves on to the dining room.

The murals on the dining room walls might be the work of a demented Grandma Moses, or Henri Rousseau on LSD. Perspective disappears, or never existed, as tiny men and women like gingerbread cookies in human form, dressed in traditional Mexican garb (sombreros, rick-racked skirts, baggy white pantaloons) are menaced by enormous smiling burros. A scene, perhaps, out of the Mexican version of Godzilla. When Godzilla is enmeshed in power lines, hovering malignantly over Tokyo. Only cheerful. Farther down one wall, a collection of too-orange Aztecs hang around a lopsided pyramid's steps, looking upward with happy expectation. Though all they could be expecting would be the ritual human heart freshly cut from the chest of a sacrificial victim. But no one is unhappy in the murals on the walls of El Caballo Blanco. If diners could see the victim, he too would be smiling.

On the opposite wall, an immense and vaginal cornucopia overflows, at its open end, with tacos, burritos, enchiladas all done in earth tones accented with a bloody red representing salsa. The paint job underneath the murals looks dirty-white rather than creamy beige, impossible to tell how old it is. Empty of customers and conversartion, the murals menace, their pervasive themes of goodwill and nourishment all too bright, too strong, a primitive Darwinistic message.

Tomas throws on the light and doesn't see the murals. After all, they've been there for nearly ten years. He focuses on the cash register, zeroes in on it like an aircraft coming in for a landing, takes the muslin sack full of change out of his shirt, where he's been holdiing it next to his heart. He switches on the stereo, loud rock 'n' roll on the radio, and places the ones, fives, tens, twenties in their correct slots. Quarters, dimes, nickels, pennies: a universe in perfect order.

One more official act: Tomas flips another switch next to the register, then goes to the front door, opens it, leans out. To survey his sign. The neon buzzes into life: El Caballo Blanco, very large sparkling orange letters up over the door, making Tomas happy, as they do every day, by their continued existence. Last month, a restaurant only a block away burned down because of a short in its neon sign, revenge of the name. But El Caballo Blanco has always brought good luck: The General always insisted on riding a perfectly white horse. Beneath the large letters of the name, in smaller, orange neon script, two more words: Continental Food. Concepción's idea. After all, their family isn't really Mexican, not Mexican Indian. They are Spanish, with a dash of French, Portuguese, perhaps even some Murano Jew (Concepción claims). Concepción thinks this Murano Jew part accounts for the ability to survive catastrophe in the family, the ultimate practicality. In the face of persecution, one alters oneself, but one remembers. So that later one knows whose throat to cut in revenge.

Hollywood rush hour in full gear, but Tomas sees Artie Vega on his cycle, dodging between lanes of cars which don't move no matter what color the traffic lights may be. The vrooming of the motorcycle Doppler-ing toward Tomas cuts through the low drone of unhappy car engines, sound of aggressive movement. Tomas does not think how small and slight Artie looks astride this macho machine, as he sees Artie riding it every day. Artie lifts one hand in Geronimo greeting, Tomas raises his right hand. At the corner, Artie turns, will pull up into the alley, then behind the restaurant. The smoothness of the opening makes Tomas feel powerful. Nothing will go wrong tonight, he is in control.

Artie re-creates the alley storm around himself and Tomas, who pulls the previous night's ominous black enormous trash bags from the kitchen to the dumpster out back. Neither shields eyes, nose, mouth from the tangible air. Though Artie scowls, furrows his forehead, the perpetual Artie-expression when he's not looking blank and pensive. Artie's face would be an interesting combination of mature intelligence and youthful hostility, a James Dean face, except for the acne scars that pit his skin, wizen him into chimpish agelessness. In black jeans, he also has the skinniest legs this side of an ostrich.

"*Hola, hombre!*" Tomas shouts, happy to see Artie. Blissfully unaware of his environment as he may be, Tomas loves people, loves the people who are regularly, daily, in his life.

"Hey, man," Artie says.

Tomas smacks his hands together to free them from garbage-bag bacteria, then throws one arm around Artie's narrow shoulders. They walk, bound this way, toward the restaurant. Artie makes a half a joint, lit, appear from his cupped hand.

"Want a hit?" Artie asks, already handing the joint to Tomas. Even when he knows the answers to questions, Artie will be polite, will ask. He is gracious in a formal, diplomatic way. And he is a philosopher who enjoys testing the rules of the universe. Will the sun rise in the morning? Will the next blackbird I see flying by be black? Will Tomas want a hit of my joint? These are all questions Artie momentarily entertains, to keep his mind rigorous, to take nothing for granted.

"Sure, dude," Tomas says, attaches the joint to his lips and fills his large chest. Artie wonders if a larger chest means a larger capacity for smoke, hence a quicker, better high. His own skinny chest would then make a terrific high impossible for him. But Artie already knows that life is never fair. This tenet he does not have to test.

"Keep it, man," Artie says. He inspects the kitchen for dirt, dust, fondles the warming lights. "*Cómo está La Señora?*"

"Mama's fine, mean as ever." Tomas lids his eyes, leans against a kitchen wall in opium smoker parody. "Fine weed, bro'."

"Please send her my regards," Artie says as he kneels to light the giant stove's pilot.

"You got a crush on my granny? Come on, man, you'll see her Sunday."

"Yes, but I want her to know that I think of her. She is such a fine woman."

"The old broad's tough," Tomas says.

"You do not know tough," Artie says, firing all the burners, eight of them, on the stove. Tomas laughs, loud and full, a laugh like his grandmother's.

With the dining room half full, its primitive acoustics making conversation a ricocheting, pinball possibility in which diners get to know the people in the next booth as well as their chosen companions, the murals fade to invisibility. The place *is* cheery. Paco, the fat cook, and Pablo, the older, skinny cook, turn the kitchen into a clattering, sizzling, well-oiled machine, too hot, as always, full of thick pungent smells, as always.

"Welcome, *amigo*," Tomas says to a lone, business-suited man, a regular.

"Hey, good to see you," to a young couple with a sleeping baby.

"How you doin', babe?" to an attractive young woman with a woman friend. He hugs the young woman, and she kisses him on the cheek. Tomas's skill as a greeter and organizer is apparent. "I've been saving a booth for you," he says to the two women, and leads them to it. He makes everyone feel welcome, special. The prices are low, the food good. This may be a thousand-dollar Friday night. Tomas's pleasantness, though, seems strained. He watches Julio, the one waiter, struggling with too many tables, too many customers raising their hands for his attention, wanting another beer, another tray of chips, another cup of salsa. This may be the first time Tomas has ever seen Julio sweat. Julio always looks as if he took his last shower thirty seconds ago, and washed his clothes just before that. His black hair is always perfectly combed back. Tomas suspected Julio to be gay, but a few months ago Julio married a very young woman who speaks no English, from the same Indian tribe, in northern Mexico, as Julio. Now they have a baby daughter. Sexual surprises of this sort, of every sort, always delight Tomas. He teases Julio about the "premature" arrival of the baby whenever possible.

Billy, the genetic mutant of El Caballo Blanco, eighteen and surfer blond, blue-eyed, tries to help. He distributes chips, but he has no idea how to be a waiter. He likes being a busboy, no responsibility, can think about waves and board waxing, and doesn't resent the fact that the other supposed busboy, Artie Vega, doesn't seem to work, to do a thing. Artie lounges, oversees, dislikes touching dirty dishes. Artie serves some unknown, spiritual purpose at El Caballo Blanco, this much Billy perceives. Artie's cool.

Tomas throws the swinging door from the dining room into the kitchen with such force that he nearly knocks over Julio, with a plate full of tamale, another with chile relleno, another with a taco/enchilada combination. He doesn't apologize. Julio scuttles around the boss, weaving his shoulders and arms to keep the plates balanced, a virtuoso performance.

"Shit, man," Tomas yells at Artie, who watches Paco prepare a chicken enchilada in green sauce. "I'll fire her if this happens one more time, I swear I will."

Artie examines Tomas's face, anger visible in the alignment of well-worn grooves around mouth, between eyes, like rubber laid out by a skidding sports car. "You do not have to worry about it," Artie says.

"One more chance," Tomas rants. "I'll kill her if she was out late last night with that gringo rock and rolly boyfriend. If she wasn't so cute I'd fire her as soon as she walks in."

Artie leaves overseeing the enchilada, lounges next to Tomas, betraying no emotion but a powerful self-assuredness. Artie seems to be wearing sunglasses even when he isn't.

"Do not worry about it, man," Artie says.

Tomas realizes Artie knows something he doesn't which makes him even angrier. "What'ya mean?"

"Linda is not coming in tonight. She is not coming in no more." Artie reaches into his windbreaker, takes a paperback book out so quickly, and replaces it as fast; Tomas cannot see what the book was. A gesture of someone who suddenly believes he has forgotten, left behind at home, an essential part of himself.

"Yeah, sure," Tomas says. This tic with the book indicates that Artie has a life separate from his shadowy hanging about at the Horse. Tomas finds this hard to believe. The thought has never before occurred to him. What does Artie do in his off time?

"Okay," Artie says evenly. "Do not find a replacement. I warned you. You know what happens when your grandmother becomes upset, man. If she should come in tonight and find you one worker short, she will need her pills real quick."

Julio pushes through the door, nearly bumping Tomas. "So sorry," he says. Smiling, "I just seated a party of five at the big booth in back. It's okay?" En route to picking up the chicken enchilada in green sauce, which will be delivered along with an enormous beef and bean tostada.

"Sure," Tomas says, without taking his eyes off Artie. "You're not shitting me? The feds get Linda?" Artie ramains inscrutable as a snake.

"Trust me," he says. "She is not coming in no more. Get it?"

Tomas has known Artie Vega for three years, since he hired him off the street one day when the kid came in asking for employment. Tomas liked his attitude. Cocky, but without an edge, without arrogance. Maybe some gang connections in his past: Artie has that kind of toughness. But he was so little and skinny he would have had to get out of gangs fast. Or use his brains to survive. That would take considerable brains, and Tomas found that hard to believe then, that this Arturo Vega might be some kind of mastermind. At this moment, however, it seems much more likely. Tomas hates readjusting his world view, furrows his face even more.

Artie says, "*Desaparecida*. Like in Argentina, you know? Accept it."

"The feds. Shit."

"Not the feds. *Desaparecida*. That is all I can tell you."

This is more than Tomas can stand. "You little asshole," he yells. Artie doesn't flinch, or show anything. He puts one hand to his heart, where his book nestles under his jacket. "What the fuck do you know?"

Artie considers, then speaks in a voice useful for convincing children it's time to go to bed. "Plenty of things. Things I tell no one. You talk too much, you lose power. Like you. *You* talk too much."

Tomas laughs. Truth always pleases him. Then he says, "Linda was like family to me. I've known her since she was fourteen." Paco shrieks a single syllable, stomps on a paper napkin which has spontaneously caught fire and floated to the floor like a meteorite. The unpredictable life of the kitchen seems separate from the rest of the universe, a constant in the face of stultifying predictability everywhere else. Both Tomas and Artie relax.

"Jesus Christ," Tomas says, "what a foxy fourteen she was, you know? Granny's gonna want to know what happened to her. If you tell Granny, Granny will tell me. She tells me everything."

Billy pushes through the swinging door with a tray full of dirty dishes. With heavy sauces, thick textures, Mexican food makes plates dirtier than any other cuisine.

"Shit, why didn't Granny open a Japanese restaurant?" Tomas crinkles his face up into an approximation of Toshiro Mifune. "So, you want California roll? No need for busboy. Zen exercise to pick rice off plates and tables with chopsticks." Then, "Hey, Blondie. Everything cool out there?"

" 'S cool," Billy says, "except for old Julio."

"La Señora does not tell you everything," Artie says. "And you are still short a waitress."

This depresses Tomas, who can charm himself out of bad feelings with his own performances. The imitations, the ethnic accents, mock-Swedish gibberish and mock-Japanese gibberish good for imitating Bergman's and Kurosawa's films are his specialties. He leans back against the wall next to Artie. Then his face turns free of lines, looks newborn, innocent. A bright idea.

"No prob," he says, and throws the swinging door open. He pats customers on their shoulders, asks how the food is, but doesn't stop moving, cuts straight through the dining room to the register, where the phone is. He dials a number he knows very well.

Three
SASHA

Whenever there's an open audition advertised in the trades, I go. These days, the ad usually says something like, "Tall, blond female, 18–22 but looks high school age, needed for featured role in major motion picture. Some dancing ability." I'm tall, I'm blond, I'm female. On good days, meaning on days after long night's sleep, days after nights off, maybe I can look twenty-two, though officially I miss by seven years. But it's always worth a try. So my friend Claire and I go. She's an actress and a waitress as well, and is younger than I am, by a few years. Her problem is dark brown hair. But she still goes to the auditions. "Hollywood discovered peroxide a long time ago," she says. A sort of a mantra, to be said over and over before every open audition. I should make one up for myself. Something like, "You're only as old as you think you are." Or, "You're only as old as your makeup." For auditions, Claire makes me up, and I do her. We sit at her multi-bulb-lit bathroom mirror, with colors and tubes and sticks and wands in front of us. We change ourselves. We become younger, tanner. We grow flying cheekbones. All in all, it's a very satisfactory process. It makes you feel as if you have control over your life, or at least over your wrinkles.

Today's open audition looks more promising. The age group slid up for it—20–25—"for featured role in serious dramatic production." A little vague, could be a play, film, or television, but Claire and I decide, what the hell.

"This could be my lucky day," Claire says. "They don't demand an albino for this part." She fluffs her hair as she watches herself in the mirror.

"Blondes have more mental illness," I say, pulling her hair as she watches in the mirror. "It's all those recessive genes."

"At least you're natural. Bleach causes brain damage."

"Natural," I say, holding my own long thick hair out from my head, its natural yellowness glinting unnaturally in Claire's bathroom light. Blond hair never looks natural in Hollywood. "I still don't get parts."

"You know, I've always wondered," Claire begins uneasily. "Why weren't you doing this ten years ago? You must have been a teenaged knockout. Just what they're looking for."

"But nobody knows what they want when they're nineteen. When you're nineteen, you want to get high and have fun and see how long you can go without sleep," I say. A lie. The truth is, at nineteen I was doing the same thing I am now. Going to auditions. Taking acting classes. Waitressing. The problem was, ten years ago, kids weren't in. Ten years ago, there weren't any parts for nineteen-year-olds, except for awful parts on family television shows. I played a friend of one of the Brady Bunch in one episode of that show. Then, for a short time, I became the stock blond friend: I stole boyfriends, I cheated on exams, I flirted with fathers. Each for about five minutes per show. Then the star of the show got to humiliate me, by playing fair, doing all the morally correct things. Then they got tired of blond friends, decided all friends should be brunettes, and that stars should be blond. I was out. Claire and I have known each other for about three years, since she graduated from college and decided to give acting a real shot. We met at a real Hollywood party, full of agents and producers and actresses. She can't comprehend how someone might have skipped college, might never have thought about majors and minors and sororities and class schedules. Since I was sixteen I've known I wanted to be an actress. Yet she and I are here, together, now. The same place. Except I'm blond and a little too old. And I've had this thing, this wanting, inside me for a longer time, making it much riper, much more painful. But nobody wants to hear how much more you've suffered than they have.

"Yeah," Claire says. "When I was nineteen I wanted to be tan."

"When I was nineteen, I wanted to have the blackest eyeliner and the shortest skirts."

"When I was nineteen I wore Lacoste shirts, with the little alligators, and thought I was really hip."

"When I was nineteen," I say, "I fucked Mick Jagger one night at the Holiday Inn on Sunset. Right after 'Exiles on Main Street' came out."

"Really?" Claire loves this. I must be a good actress; she believes me.

"Come on, kiddo," I say. Enough primping. Putting on makeup is like binge eating. Enough is never enough. The only way to stop is to stop. "This is as good as it gets."

"You look great," Claire says as she rises from her boudoir chair. "I wish I had your mouth."

"Yeah, I wish I had your nose."

The truth is, together, with our best features combined, we'd make one great beauty. Claire's curly hair, with my yellow color. My mouth, her nose. My bright blue nearly lavender eyes, but with her slanting, kind of almond shape. We'd be dynamite.

We leave Claire's apartment, squinting in the bright sun. With such perfect makeup applied, we don't dare risk sunglasses. That sweaty little line across the nose, smudged through layers of paint to real skin. Casting people must look for stuff like that. We'll squint all the way to the audition, then spend a minute meditating in Claire's car's front seat. Thinking about cool.

"Cucumbers," I'll say.

"Ice cubes," she'll say.

We keep our eyes lightly closed, careful not to damage the mascara.

"Margaritas."

"The Pacific Ocean."

"Eskimos."

We say these things to one another, as we sit with our eyes poised delicate and trembly as butterflies. Then, we're ready.

The whole Disneyland parking lot scene. Women hugging and kissing one another, without really touching. Honking, waving, screaming. Everyone so pretty, so perfect, as if the world has turned into one big television commercial. Lots of the usual blondes, but, because of the ad, a lot of brunettes, some black women, oriental women, Latina women. This makes me happier. I don't feel as if I've been cut out of the same Daryl Hannah cookie cutter as everyone else, that the world is full of big, athletic-looking blondes, my lost sisters.

We get in line, against the cool brick of the building, trying to forget the traffic on Olympic Boulevard, protecting our serenity. Actresses should appear serene. Only stars can have temperament.

Claire and I hold our portfolios carefully, so we don't get any smudgy fingerprints or marks on the margins of the resumé, or, God forbid, on our eight-by-tens. My resumé is one big lie. I can't list the work I did ten years ago, because then they'd know my real age. So I can list only a couple of extra spots in commercials, some little theater work around town. Embarrassing. Except that actresses are never embarrassed—I must remember that. I pull in my stomach, allow my shoulders to relax, my diaphragm to rise, my spine to be perfectly aligned with the top of my head as if an invisible wire holds me, dangling, like a puppet.

The line of women stretches around the building now. I see its tail coming around, about to overlap where it begins. Remember when, a long time ago, people joined hands around the Pentagon, thinking they could levitate it? Send it into space? That could happen here. Except for the fact that each woman here thinks only of herself, tunes inward rather than outward. Each woman feels that invisible wire straightening her body, allowing her to relax. The air hums with so much tuning inward, like the hum of many fine machines just oiled. The tail of the line reaches where Claire and I stand, and I see someone I know, not a friend, but someone who I always see at auditions.

"Janey!" I say. She leans over from her position in the second ring around the building to pretend to kiss me. I lean in toward her. Like two magnets we repel one another when we should be coming together. A good show. "Looking good," I say. Jane is the type of blond I could never be: wispy, fragile, an ash blonde rather than strong peasant yellow.

"Just got back from Europe," Jane says. She does look rested, healthy, shining.

"How'd you manage that?" I ask. Claire nudges my foot with hers.

"I try to go a couple of times a year. You know, buy some clothes. Shoes. You can't get shoes here like you can in Italy." I look at Jane's shoes, and they are beautiful. Made of some gleaming, scaled reptile twisted into many small perfect straps around her feet.

"Yeah, great shoes," I say. Claire remains silent, even hostile.

"So," Jane says, after a pause. "Have you gotten any work?"

"About a month ago I did a Coke commercial. I was part of this enthusiastic crowd of roller skaters. Filmed down on the board-walk. They made me wear these tiny shorts, a bikini top, the works."

"And how about you, Claire?" Jane asks, chilly. Next time Claire and I do our pre-audition meditation on cool, I will remember Jane's tone of voice.

"I just finished a play at the Odyssey Theater. It ran for sixteen weeks," Claire says, not to be outfrosted.

Then we move, and the line expands and contracts. We lose Jane, who winds up about fifteen feet behind us in her orbit.

"What was that about?" I ask Claire. I've never seen her so catty before.

"She's one of those trust-fund starlets," Claire says. "Daddy left her a bunch of money, so she dabbles. Acting in between shopping sprees. Or shopping in between acting sprees. She's six or seven years older than she claims to be."

This hurts. I just look at Claire, my whole body numb with anger which can find no words. This is how I get angry at everyday things, things other than Tomas. Only with Tomas does my anger find words, and then my hands do things.

"I'm sorry," Claire says, and she touches my shoulder, delicately, avoiding wrinkling my pale blue silk jumpsuit, or staining it with a smidgen of human finger sweat. "It's just that, she beat me out for a part in a movie once. It was the closest I've gotten. It was actually down to the two of us, and she got it."

"I hardly know her," I start to say, but Claire wants to go on.

"Then I heard all the usual stories. You know. That she was fucking the assistant director. That her mother knew the producer. Who knows? Maybe she was just better than me."

We see a few women already returning to their cars. Their posture is still perfect, in case anyone important might be watching with binoculars. Lots of hip, lots of shoulder, great walks. *Dramalogue* under the arm. One of them is someone Claire and I know, a woman named Mary who calls herself Marya. We call her over.

"So what's the story?" I ask.

"Hard to tell," Marya says, examining her manicure, which looks fine to me. Does she know more than she's saying? She seems to hesitate. She's big, taller than me, with this mane of lion's hair. Tawny. Golden tan, making the whites of her eyes look silver, glistening. "It's one of those 'leave me your resumé and photos and we may get back to you' deals." She hesitates some more, runs her fingernails, which are about three inches long, through her hair, using them like Afro picks, until she looks like Rod Stewart.

"But there's a mob here," Claire says. "Even more than usual. Someone must know something."

"Okay," Marya says quickly, and in a fast low voice, "rumor is that it's Spielberg's new film, that this will be the break of a lifetime, like Jessica Lange got in *King Kong*. That's why every bit of female talent in town is here."

"Is Spielberg directing or producing?" I like to know the info.

"Sasha, you're so fucking literal-minded," Marya says. "Who cares?"

"What kind of film is it?" Claire asks.

"Jesus, call up Rona Barrett. Don't ask me. I'm just telling you what my agent told me." This is a blow: she's one-upping us, letting us know she's got representation. Marya must be twenty-one, maybe twenty-two.

"So what're you doing here if you've got an agent?" Claire asks, good cross-examination. Even she feels old next to Marya, and it pisses her off. She juts her chin when she gets mad, an unattractive gesture.

"My agent thought this was worth coming to, because of the Spielberg rumor. My agent will call up Spielberg's offices on the lot first thing Monday morning and pitch me to them." Marya fluffs her hair some more, tugs at the hem of her black leather mini. Fishnet stockings, high heels: the outfit is off, a little too MTV. But I admire its concept, its theme. Marya flounces away, but some damage has been done. The actress in back of us overheard. She tells her friends in line with her what she knows.

"Spielberg," Claire and I hear her say. Claire raises her eyebrows, but we do not speak. And we hear, in soft repetitive whispers which might be echoes if there weren't that distinctness to each new voice, being passed down the line, the two syllables. Spielberg. Spielberg. Spielberg. Finally it gets too far away for us to hear it, and the line moves steadily for about ten minutes. Then this phenomenon occurs, something which must be explainable in scientific terms. Some metaphor in physics. Because all of a sudden, the name laps around the edge of the building, and the second ring of the line which curls by those of us in the first ring whispers the sibilant password. Like a train coming closer, closer, louder, closer, louder. We hear it go by us, disappear into the distance. Spielberg.

* * *

When I get to the door, no surprise. I walk in, hand my resumé and photos to a little, very old woman with hair dyed frightening orange.

"I'm Sasha Berlin," I say, and stand still, wondering what should come next. Sometimes they want you to walk, sometimes to dance, sometimes to do nothing. I've gone to auditions where they shut the door behind you and ask you to remove your clothes. Then I open the door and walk out fast.

"Just wait," the old woman says. I wait, trying not to fidget, though the seconds grow long, elastic.

She looks back at me after studying my pictures, as if to verify it's me. Or that I'm them. That's what I look like, I think. She studies the resumé.

"They're taking a leak or something," she says while she looks at my resumé. More long seconds.

Two business-suit types come in, the kind of guy who always looks like he's just had a haircut that morning. About my age, my real age. Young for executives, normal for agents, old for writers. Hard to figure.

"Hello," the first one says, extending a hand for me to shake. I shake it.

"How do you do?" I say.

"Hi, there," the second one says. His hand is clammy.

They look at me until we are all uneasy.

"Well," I say, "what do you have in mind here?"

They develop looks of perplexity. We all become more uneasy.

"We have your resumé?" one of them asks. "And eight-by-tens?"

"Yes."

"All right then," he says. "We'll be in touch."

I turn to walk out, remembering the wire, making my body perfect. Behind me, maybe I imagine it, one of the male voices might be whispering: "Fellatio." I hear, not imagine, both of them giggling. Outside, Claire waits for her turn. She looks at me warily, wanting the news.

"Major league jerkoff," I say, and she looks as if she could cry. She wanted to believe it was Spielberg.

* * *

Home, I'm exhausted. The sun, the concrete, the envy, my old age all conspire to make my whole body hurt. Nearly five already, and my skin feels as if it's been baked in batter, tempuraed. With Tomas at work, the only thing to help a terrible mood is a bath and a magazine. Sometimes it takes a bath, a magazine, and a movie. Especially weekend nights, when Tomas doesn't get home until after midnight.

I start the bath, with two paper packets of bubblebath. I scrub my face. I take off my clothes, my underwear, feel nearly human again. The steam from the tub makes the bathroom a hothouse, a place where orchids thrive, and southern belles. A good thought. I slip into the tub and Blanche Dubois at the same time. I've always depended upon the kindness of strangers. A motto for actresses. The water coils up my legs, devouring tired muscles. Didn't even pin my hair up. Who cares if the ends frazzle from steam and water. Tomas will still love me.

Then the phone rings. No one calls me on a Friday night. I let it ring, six times, ten, twelve. It stops. A ringing phone kills relaxation. Once more I let my body droop and slide, feel only water. The phone rings again, and after twenty rings it's still ringing. No hope. I get out, wrap my bath towel around me like an Indian blanket. Drip all the way to the kitchen. Up to thirty-two rings.

"Hello," I say. Beaten.

But it's Tomas. "Hi baby. How was the open call?" He's too sugary. Something's up.

"A pain. Another 'we'll call you.' Listen, I'm exhausted . . ."

"Yeah," he says quickly, "we need help here. Linda's not coming in."

"She's probably just late again." I think of my bath. Bubbles disappearing, turning to that white scum floating on the surface of the water. Not nearly the same.

"No. Artie says she's not coming in, ever." He's whining a little.

"How does he know?" Now I'm starting to get interested. And to shiver. It's always cold here by the beach. House walls rotted by salt and wind. I want my bath.

"He just knows. Can you come in tonight, just to help out? *Corazón?*" I should have known this was what he wanted. Tomas is hardly ever sweet on the phone when he calls from the restaurant.

"You promise it's just for tonight?" I ask, wanting a firm commitment. Getting stuck at the White Horse would be a fate worse than death for me. Completely tied in with Tomas, with the restaurant, no other real life. I might disappear.

"Yeah, of course, babe, just for tonight," he says. "Maybe tomorrow."

"You find someone after tonight," I say, drying myself with the towel, getting ready.

"*Pobrecita*, your one night off," he says, syrupy sweet. "I swear I'll make it up to you. I promise."

"You better."

"Make it quick, okay? I think we're gonna be real busy tonight. Bye."

Simple as that. My bath, my magazine, my movie. My few hours alone, brooding over the audition. Sucked up by Tomas. But, really, I don't resent him. He's in a tight spot. What else can I do?

Four
EL CABALLO BLANCO

The kitchen of El Caballo Blanco is in full bustle, Paco and Pablo, the cooks, working on multiple meals, juggling utensils, sweating. Billy wheels mountains of dirty dishes to the dishwasher. Julio looks like a silent comedy version of a waiter, in slightly speeded up motion. And he perspires visibly, big darkened rings of fabric under his arms, a crescent on his back. An expression of wide-eyed animal fear, like a rabbit about to be shot. But, when Sasha walks in, through the back door, Tomas is nowhere in sight. Through all this chaos, through flying tacos and a rain of tortilla chips and splattering grease, she sees Artie, sitting in the corner near the swinging door, reading. Tomas is out front busting his ass, and this little jerks sits here reading, Sasha thinks. As she walks toward Artie, thinking about whether or not she should kick him, she can read the title of the book: *The Great Gatsby*.

"Good book, Artie?" Sasha asks, sarcastic. He sits on a low, broken chair from the restaurant, so she towers over him, feeling like a vengeful goddess.

Artie doesn't even look up at her. "I read it before. One day I will memorize it."

"Yeah?" Sasha is still looking for a fight. "What's so terrific about it?"

Artie looks up at her now, his face pensive, serious. "I would like to have shirts of every color," he says. "And I would really like to know how you go about fixing the World Series. I know people who would pay big for that kind of intelligence." He dives back into the book, unaware of Sasha's wrath. Where the hell's Tomas, she thinks.

Through the swinging door, the dining room is as crazy as the kitchen. Full of people, customers, waiting to be seated, already seated, in pre-, mid-, and post-meal. Still no Tomas. Julio scurries by, so harried he doesn't even notice her. None of the usual courtly greetings for the boss's *novia*. Then she sees Tomas.

In the middle of the crowd of customers waiting for tables, at the front of the restaurant, Tomas is being kissed (and kissing? Sasha thinks) by a pretty, tan, dark-haired young woman. Sasha sees Tomas's back; the woman's arms snaking around him. He bends to her. A short little thing, Sasha thinks. Sasha sneaks down the aisle, she's three feet from them, can hear them. Restaurant din disappears as Sasha focuses on the woman's voice, and Tomas's.

"I just wanted to see you before I left town," the woman says. "I'll write you postcards,"

"Sure baby. I'm glad you came by," Tomas says as he hovers, his face inches from the woman's.

"I'll be in as soon as I'm back," the woman continues. "I'll be really tan then. All over."

"Gotta be careful with that kind of tan, babe." Then Tomas, himself, leans down and kisses her, again. A brief one, but he is the catalyst. He is clearly the kisser here. The woman, after the kiss, backs away from him, smiling, so that Sasha can get a good look at her. Not really so pretty, but made up, dressed to kill. The woman leaves.

Next to Sasha, a party of two waits for their meal, their silverware shiny and unused. Sasha picks up the man's teaspoon and throws it at Tomas's back, striking dead center.

"Hey, babe," Tomas says as he spins around, surprised.

Sasha wants to murder him. At the same time, she does not want to make a scene. At the same time, she wonders if anyone listens or watches amid all this chaotic pigging out.

"I bet you say that to all the girls," she says. Tomas still has no idea what's going on.

"What?" he asks sweetly. "What do I say?"

"You're such a creep," she starts, voice raised only slightly. She does not want to cry. "You don't even hear yourself. Everyone's your baby. I'm giving up two hundred dollar tip nights to find out that everyone's your baby. This is what I left a nice hot bath to find out."

Tomas hugs her, pets her head, like he does when she has nightmares. It always gets to her, being near him, having his hands on her.

"That was nothing. Really, man. She just comes in a lot. She's with that nudist magazine, her whole family's nudists. They bring me in a copy every so often, you know, you've seen it." His voice in her ear, low. She wants to believe him, but she also still wants to be mad at him.

"Then how come you call her baby?"

"Did I call her baby?"

This makes Sasha furious all over again. "You called her baby the same way you call me baby." Nobody watches them. Amazing, Sasha thinks as she experiences the waxing and waning of her own murderous rage: we've become invisible.

"Shit," Tomas says. "I didn't mean it."

"Swear you'll never do it again."

"I swear. On my grandmother's head," he says, "I swear I won't do it again. It's just that I have trouble remembering names. It's bad business not to remember names."

Now he's mad again, she sees his eyes turn flat black, the force field up. But he doesn't get off the hook so easily, she thinks. "Oh, that's great. That's why you call *me* baby?" And they both smile, they could make love right here, now, because nobody's looking, because their bodies are emanating that magnetic heat, molten, disgustingly unstoppable.

"Gimme a break," Tomas says. "I've remembered your name for at least a year now."

"Okay," she says, trying to retain some baby sulk in her voice, to keep his attention. As soon as he knows it's really okay, she will have lost him. He'll be back in the material world, in the restaurant.

"Really okay?" He kisses her hair.

"Yeah. Really okay. Baby. I'll get to work."

"Great." Tomas already walks away, toward the kitchen. "Thanks, Sally," he calls back over his shoulder. He grins his "I know I'm cute" grin. She wants to kick him and fuck him at the same time: this must be love, she thinks. As she stashes her purse under the cash register, she hums. Julio tells her which tables he needs her to cover. Tomas greets and seats. The buzz of the restaurant turns to harmony. Everything is under control.

Five
SASHA AND TOMAS

Tomas, on the bed smoking a joint, watches Sasha begin to undress. By the light of their digital clock (1:30 A.M.), by hazy moonlight wafting in between the warped, curling blinds on the windows, she looks paler than in daylight, more delicate. Sasha unbuttons her blouse, pulls the sleeves off her arms with heavy gestures, fatigue making her limbs feel weighted by iron, lead.

"You're beautiful," he says.

She throws the blouse on the floor. Wash it in the morning and it will still have the residual grease and taco smells. Tomas says this is why dogs always love him: he smells like an enchilada.

"Not tonight dear" Sasha says, "I have a headache."

Tomas stubs out the joint, stands behind her, putting his large hands on her waist, below her breasts, appreciating the fine, soft, taut skin there.

"Baby, you don't get headaches," he says.

In slow motion, she unzips her pants, peels them down her hips. But with him next to her, something lights up inside her. His hands on her always affect her, radiating warmth from wherever

they are throughout the rest of her body. She knows this is seduction. Enjoys it.

"So what's my excuse? What *do* I get?"

He rubs her hips, playing with the elastic band of her white
cotton bikini underwear, teasing.

"Nothing! *Nada!* You're the healthiest gringa chick I ever
knew!"

Sasha bends down to pull the pants off her feet, every gesture
so full of languor he wants to throw her right on the bed. But he
too enjoys the game.

"Gringa chicks are sickly little things?" she asks.

He caresses her all over, massaging more than petting, smoothing dull pain from her body.

"Yeah," he says. Then he parodies a whining woman, a high thin
falsetto voice, a bad falsetto much funnier than a good imitation.
"Oh," he says in this mock-feminine pitch, "today my throat hurts!"
He puts his arms around Sasha tenderly, as if she were his child
instead of his lover, and kisses her neck, half vampire, half parent
making the sore throat disappear.

Still in falsetto, he continues, "Oh, today I've got cramps!"

He bends, kisses her stomach with the lightest, sweetest touch
of his lips. She stands absolutely still, as if any movement were
dangerous.

Still in falsetto, "Oh, I must have pulled this muscle in my poor
little thigh in aerobics class today!"

Now he kneels, kisses her thigh. As if in a dream, she messes
and straightens his hair, her eyes closed.

Still in falsetto: "Oh, no, I must have a yeast infection!" Tenderly
one large hand slips between her legs, preparing for the healing
kiss.

She laughs, pushes him away onto the bed. He sits up on his
haunches like a trained bear. The two of them glow in the wan
light of the room.

"But I'm never sick," Sasha says. "I can work six nights a week
waitressing more tables than any other waitress at L'Etranger, then

spend my off night working for peanuts at your tacky little dive."
Good natured, mocking, daring. "Can't I?"

Tomas rises again, embraces her.

"Yeah, and get home and still want to make love."

"How do you know?"

"Because you're also the sexiest gringa chick I ever knew."

They kiss, her nearly naked body in bold relief against his dark
clothes, his darker presence, until she pushes him away again, this
time just inches.

"You're certainly the world's most highly trained authority in
the matter of sexy gringa chicks."

He laughs, kisses her again. "Baby, you're dealing with the ex-
pert."

She unbuttons his shirt, slowly, her slow-motion fatigue transformed now into pure sensuality, pleasure. They sit on the bed,
kiss. Finally, they recline.

"I like a man who's directed," she says, "who has an interest in
science. Who has a definite field of specialization."

"Tacos and gringa chicks, man," he says, lightly. But then his
voice darkens, goes low. "Do you love me?"

She pulls him to her, covers his mouth with hers. Enmeshed in
one another instantly, through practice, used to one another not
in a machine sense, a technical sense, but instead because they
work so well together. Always have, and they become better together, become keenly aware, on some unconscious level, of one
another's responses. Neither has had this with anyone before, this
sexual synchronism and precision.

But in the middle of lovemaking, Tomas pulls away, apart from
her.

"Do you love me?" he asks again.

She can only whisper. "Yes. I love you."

"How much?" He is serious, frightening.

She hugs him to her, into her again, arches her neck, cannot
answer him. She does not know what this question means. How
do you measure love for someone you adore as much as Tomas?

No experience has prepared her for this question, for her life full of extremes. First no love in it, none at all, only unknown compulsions and curiosity and desire. Then full of love, too much love, a dream of love, with him. How could he, with his family always around him, understand this?

Later, more attenuated moonlight illuminates their bedroom. They lay in each others' arms, her head on his chest. He tangles her hair with both his hands.

"It was weird in there tonight," she says.

"You're just used to a different type of place."

"No, it's not the place. It's Artie. Sitting there reading as if nothing was going on, talking about fixing the World Series. Sounds like delusions of grandeur. Is he a little crazy?"

Tomas feels he must defend his employee. "Artie's great, babe. He's never late, and he never misses work. Three years now, he hasn't missed a day."

"But he doesn't do anything!"

"And he loves Granny."

"Well," she says, "he gives me the willies. Like he's working overtime on being sinister."

She curls her body against his now, on her side, so that her legs can hug his. Her arms, freed, stroke his chest.

Tomas, thoughtful, says, "Lately he's been involved in lots of shit. I hope he's not getting back into gang stuff. That could kill you, man. But Artie's smart."

"Tomas," Sasha says, adamant. "He's talking about crime. I mean, fixing the World Series!"

But Tomas seems unconcerned, doesn't want to talk about Artie, tonight, in bed. "Okay, you've got a point. Tomorrow at Granny's, when Julio brings his baby by for the blessing, we'll have her talk to Artie. He'll listen to Mama."

"I got a teddy bear for Julio's baby," she says, still petting him.

Tomas isn't listening. He stares at the ceiling, distracted. "That's nice," he says, answering without hearing her because he perceived her voice's tone, demanding response. Then he focuses on the content, a whole new idea. "You think we ought to make a baby someday?"

She moves so close to him nothing, no silk lingerie, no ray of light, no atom of separation, could come between them. "I do like buying teddy bears," Sasha says. Tomas feels full of enormous, expanding happiness. Again they begin to kiss.

Six
CONCEPCIÓN

My son, Tomas, the father of my grandson Tomas, was always crazy. Crazy like his father, the General. But the General had war, so at home he could be mild and pleasant. While my son was too young for one war, too old for the next. Because of this, he became bad. He ran around with women, and made his wife unhappy. He would be angry, sad, or happy without apparent reasons, so his children never felt they could trust him. When he was home. Most of the time, though, he wasn't home. Airplanes called to him from airports, foreign cities whispered to him across continents. Wine too seduced him, spoke to him in a secret and romantic language. And drugs. His blood longed for any excitement. Without war, men destroy themselves in wanton ways. Men seek their own destructions if there are not other men with guns and politics trying to kill them.

By the time my grandson, Tomas, was ten, he too was becoming very bad. Mexico City was a bad place for a crazy boy to be growing up. His mother would write to me about the wickedness she saw growing in this little Tomas. Already he knew how to steal cars, to pinch and kiss maids, to smoke marijuana. But I knew there was sweetness too in this boy whose father was always gone.

Tomas, my son, beat Tomas, my grandson, when he infrequently came home from his trips, his women, his liquor. If the boy remained in this atmosphere, I knew his sweetness would soon be gone. Because, he was the baby, you see. Born ten years after his closest sister. The two brothers, the other sister, married, out of the house, so Tomas, my grandson, grew up alone. Alone, crazy boys became even more crazy, because their imaginations tempt them as well as the physical world. Cars, maids marijuana, and a life full of lonely fantasy. I feared for him.

His mother wrote to me about a traffic accident she and my grandson, Tomas, saw in Mexico City. Mexicans are terrible drivers. Mother and son sat in their taxi and watched seven cars crash into one another. Much blood in the streets, like the French Revolution. They watched from their taxi, and saw that one man had been decapitated in the accident. She tried to cover Tomas's eyes, but he threw her hands away from his face. He wanted to see. Already, he enjoyed the sight of blood; it thrilled him, excited him. This, finally, was what frightened me most. I decided I must act. The mother, she was a pretty, charming woman, but she too drank wine, and spent too much time with her rich friends, with writers and painters. She had not intended to give birth to another child, would have liked to be free from raising children. Bringing up children no longer interested her. Tomas, my grandson, was loved by his parents, of course. But in a strange way, from far, as an object is loved and admired. A crazy boy like this, who needed much more attention. This boy was likely to do anything.

So I wrote the mother a letter, asking her to send me the boy. I wrote to her that I was lonely, and that the restaurant no longer demanded much from me. A lie! A restaurant demands much more than any husband, any child. But the mother, who always visited me briefly, passed through Los Angeles like a breeze, like a Santa Ana wind, had no idea what running a restaurant demands. I wrote her, a lyrical and charming letter, about how much better her life would be with Tomas safely in my care. Perhaps then, I wrote, she would visit me more, my son, Tomas, would visit me more. Our family would be both freer and together more often.

She wrote me back that she would think about this proposition. To be separated from her baby would be terrible. Such a handsome boy, those big dark eyes full of mischief, full of life. I knew what his eyes were full of, the things she would never see because she did not look long enough. I know how to read eyes.

I wrote to her again, taking care to make my handwriting old, feeble, full of little shaking lines. How could she refuse an old woman this final pleasure, an old woman alone? I wrote to her that she should ask my son, Tomas, what he thought about this idea. Because, you see, I knew what Tomas, my son, would say. He could not refuse me anything. Latin women have this power over their sons, an excellent cultural tradition. Also, Tomas, my son, knew how much I love children who are already formed, past infancy and into miniature adulthood. And Tomas, my son, did not enjoy being around Tomas, my grandson, though he loved the boy. Perhaps he saw too much of himself in this child. Perhaps he did not see anything at all.

No letters for a month. Then, finally, a letter from the mother. The boy would be sent to me. Now, there was another step. If the child thought I coveted him like an object of art, he would not want to come live with me. I wrote him a letter, full of the delights of Los Angeles. I thought for a long time about what a wicked child might enjoy, and put these things in the letter. The new shiny cars everywhere, the beautiful young women, the palm trees, the balmy climate. Boys played until late at night, because the evening air was so mild, I wrote him. I am an old woman, infirm now, and he would be left on his own a lot, even more than he was in Mexico City, I wrote him. He would perfect his English, a language he enjoyed because of American movies, and because his ability to speak it made him exotic in Mexico. We would have so much fun. And, when he grew up, the restaurant would be his. He would learn all about the restaurant business: an easy life! More lies.

Tomas, my grandson, perhaps because he was smart enough to know his soul was in danger if he remained in Mexico, perhaps because my appeal to his wickedness succeeded, wanted to come live with me. Or maybe he sensed that I understood him in ways his parents did not. It was arranged. When he was ten, Tomas came to me, became my only Tomas, because his father was, really, long lost.

Oh, I was in my own way evil. I sent him to Catholic schools, where the nuns hit him for his dirty mouth, for stealing things, for not coming to classes. But he was smart, clever, and made good grades without studying. He never loved books, or what could be learned from their pages. What he loved was the act of being alive. He learned that being alive was most pleasurable when the nuns didn't hit him, so he behaved better.

He gave me so much joy, this child. Because he knew I adored him, no matter what mischief he committed, he told me everything. I kept my temper, and counseled him. If boys must be crazy, they can, at least, not get caught by policemen. They can not kill themselves in drunken driving. Or get killed in fights. I never allowed him to have knives or guns, and he respected this. There was a gentleness in his heart. He really did not want to hurt anyone else. But he had the warrior's blood in his veins, this I understood.

Now, he is dearer to me than my own children ever were. We work together, in the restaurant, in life. We count money together after every night's business, with the television on, sitting side by side on my sofa, leaning over my little table. He kisses me and hugs me as he always did. He still has the devil in him, but, then, so do I. After all, I ran away from home at sixteen to marry the General and to go to the wars with him. I lived like a soldier for many years, hatched plots with the General for leading a whole army, a whole country. Most women don't know as much about wickedness as I do, because they don't see this mischief in themselves. They cannot look in the mirror and remember shooting at men who ran away like coyotes into the night, men who had come to kill the General, and me. As a girl, I too had dreams, fantasies, of living a wild life. And then the General came. Tomas has me to share his wildness with.

He also has his *novia*, Sasha, a strange name for an American girl. She stares at him with those blue gringa eyes which might as well be cow's eyes except for their color. Her eyes drip with affection for him. For her, everything he does is perfect, exactly right. True, she does not know his heart as I do. But maybe this will spare her grief. He has me to share his heart with. He can share everything else with her.

I like her, perhaps I even love her. For a number of years now, I'm not sure how many because I forget years as I grow older, she has been coming, with Tomas, to my house. She is a part of my family now. The fact that I cannot remember how long she has spent holidays at my dining room table, the fact that I cannot clearly picture Tomas without Sasha, tells me this. I remember everything. What I forget is the real event, the real clue to figuring out what things mean in my life.

But I do not see any devil in her, in this Sasha. Unless too much love is a devil. I do not think so.

Seven

CONCEPCIÓN

Tomas and his grandmother sit apart from the small group in her living room, the reigning monarchs of these people. Señora Concepción Alvarez de Santiago watches with pleasure. This is how it was sixty years ago, when she was at home with the General. On weekend afternoons, their home would be open, people would come and go with small gifts, flowers, cakes, candles, for the host and hostess. The General would be gracious to all; Concepción would be congenial, too, but more watchful. She would be aware of everything, and those upon whom her scrutiny fell found it uncomfortable, even if they were innocent of bad thoughts and bad deeds. Now, nearing ninety, she thinks her favorite chair, which she's had for over twenty years, has grown. The world is full of magic, she knows. She is very tiny, very wrinkled, and very beautiful, her patrician, Spanish features still fine, only a little hidden in the midst of this expanding flesh. The wisdom her face shows is not common old people's wisdom. Everyone with wrinkles is assumed to be wise, though most aren't. Concepción still has the uncanny ability to know what people truly feel. Not their thoughts, because what use are those? Thoughts lie, thoughts test boundaries which will never be broken. But their feelings: Feelings don't lie. Right now, she knows that Tomas is edgy, feels uncomfortable because there is something he hasn't told his *novia*. He watches Sasha as if he fears she is in love with another, that kind of nervousness that grows from inside one's own heart, then flashes out like a beam of light to falsely illumine someone else. Concepción can see that Sasha thinks of no other, only Tomas. So it must be within Tomas, this secret anxiety. Concepción will speak to him about it later.

All of the employees of El Caballo Blanco are there, their attention focused upon Julio, who leans on the Señora's grand piano, next to his wife. His wife holds their three-week-old baby daughter, a tiny bundle invisible in many bright pink blankets. Everyone, in turn, goes up to the baby, leans down into the pink blankets, and whispers silliness, whistles, squeaks, but the baby sleeps through it all.

Bored with watching the baby from across the room, Concepción looks instead at the wall behind the piano, in back of Julio and his little family. The wall of photographs. Of herself when young, strong, dressed in peasant clothes for riding, her hair plaited about her head and very black. Of herself with a handsome young Spanish-looking man with a handlebar mustache, dressed up, aristocratic. Of this young man alone, with bandoliers and a frighteningly large rifle, his face set in determination. Young Concepción again, together with this man, but this time with two children, very proper looking, serious for the camera, a boy and a girl. The father stands with his arms crossed on his chest, the mother puts one hand on the shoulders of each of her children. Then many more photographs, in sparkling black and white, crisp real color, instead of the fading browns, sepias, of the older photos which Concepción finds her eyes drawn to. The newer ones are too real, too present, without magic. The smoky earthtoned ones of herself and the General come from a place and time so separate, so distant, she hardly recognizes either of the people. They do not look like the people she sees when she closes her eyes and remembers herself with the General. These people in the photographs are stronger, stiffer, and their eyes are dead.

"Here's what we got for the baby," Tomas says softly, into Concepción's ear, and she opens her eyes. Sasha enters with an enormous teddy bear with a pink bow around its neck. She presents the bear to Julio with a polite formality which makes Concepción proud. Julio, shy, sinking back against the piano because of the proximity of the boss's *novia*, accepts the bear, bows slightly, shakes Sasha's hand, then dandles the bear over the baby's little body as if performing some ritual of Satanism. The baby awakens, sees the large grotesque bear face, and cries ferociously.

Concepción forces her lips into a false smile, waves to Julio to reassure him.

"I hate crying babies," Concepción says to Tomas, through her clenched smile.

"C'mon, Mama," Tomas says. "You don't like crying anything."

Concepción considers this. "You're right. I don't like noise. And I don't like babies at all."

"You liked me when I was little."

She laughs. "*Querido*, you were my baby grandson. And you were beautiful."

"Now I'm not?" Tomas teases.

"Now you dress like a hippie, and you don't get married to this nice girl you live with, who loves you so much." The closest to a chastisement she can come. She does wish Tomas would keep his clothes pressed. But Tomas must be above reproach now as he stands with her, behind her, surveying their diminished territory.

"Sasha and I might get married," Tomas says, trying out the sound of this. He has felt, for many years, that he was allergic to marriage. But now, when he says this, he feels no attack of hives coming on. This makes him proud of himself: Perhaps he's grown up.

"Oh, yes?" Concepción says, her voice becoming brittle because she tries to control laughter. "And what will you wear to your wedding? Blue jeans? Sandals? *Dios mio*. Bring Julio and the infant over here before I feel compelled to have a talk with your *novia* and tell her what you have planned for her wedding."

Concepción watches Tomas cross the room, approach Julio, bend his large handsome head to Julio's smaller, rabbity, frightened one. To be summoned to the matriarch is always a terrifying proposition, Concepción thinks. The responsibility and irresponsibility of power that everyone without power fears. Julio's wife hands Julio the squalling baby whose red flesh blooms in relief against the white lace christening gown emerging now from the blankets. Concepción wishes the General stood beside her, all fair, stern judgment. A woman's power is always suspect; a man only may be a hero. Julio would not look like a weasel if the General were still alive.

"Señora," Julio says, holding the now-quiet infant up toward Concepción like an offering. "I have come for your blessing for my daughter." Tomas and his *novia* stand behind Julio, full of love for one another. The others ring them in an amorphous, shadowy group. The Señora's eyesight is not as good as it once was, in the days when she saw the truth in other men's eyes. She puts her small, wrinkled hand upon the baby's forehead, the lightest of fingertip touches, as much repulsion as delicacy. She would hate to start the crying up again. But the baby remains quiet, looking out at the world with hypnotized, fishbowl eyes.

"Yes, yes, my son. I give her my blessing," Concepción says. Julio glows with happiness and pleasure, all trace of the rodent gone from his face. The old dragon did not eat his child, Concepción thinks. He can be happy until the next trial for this little one.

"Gracias, muchas gracias, Señora," Julia says, blushing.

"And what is this child's name?"

More fear clouds Julio's features, and his mouth moves before words come out. The English letter "j" confounds his Spanish-speaking mouth. "Jessica," he finally says, the first letter a milkshake combination of "y" and "g," both ice skated over trickily.

"Cómo no," Concepción says, swallowing her laughter. "Of course. Jessica." As if this might ensure that the child would grow up blond and rosy and without the smell of tamales about her. Concepción waves the hand with which she touched the child, and Julio and the group of onlookers recede like a waving tide con-

trolled by a goddess. Only Tomas and Sasha remain, the chosen.

"Jessica," Concepción whispers to them. "Pretty, for an Indian."

Tomas speaks in his softest, secret voice to her. Something to do with the *novia*, Concepción thinks. But Tomas says, "Mama, I wish you'd talk to Artie. He's been acting strange lately. Paranoid." Something wrong with his tone here: He is not saying all he knows. Sasha nods in agreement, though she could only have half-heard. Concepción suspects this has little to do with Artie, really.

"Send him to me," Concepción says, and the small crowd in her living room instantly separates into new formations, groupings. Straight ahead of her, on her couch, she sees Artie Vega, dressed in impeccably laundered and pressed black clothes, reading a paperback book. Black for the blessing of a child? Artie looks up over his book, and his eyes meet hers. He nods almost imperceptibly, comes to her, slipping the book inside his jacket, as Tomas and Sasha join the others. The neatness of her own universe, her control over its order, impresses Concepción. She straightens her skirt over her skinny legs and sighs.

"*Buenas días, Señora*," Artie says, his posture as perfect as that of a man who is about to be shot by a firing squad.

"Arturo, *cómo estás*? You look worried, my son." Concepción cannot read Artie's troubles. This boy has made an art of hiding and scheming, and is powerful in it.

But Artie relaxes, even allows his lips to curl in a semi-smile. "Señora, there are so many bad things in the world," he says.

"When the General was assassinated," Concepción says, "I thought the world was filled with evil. Before they smuggled me out of the country, so that I too would not be murdered, I made them take me to the jail where they held the man who killed the General. They disguised me, and took me in to see this villain, this hired murderer of my husband. I went to his cell and looked in at him. He was just a small, dirty man, but when he looked up at me, I saw evil on his face. This man's soul could be bought and sold. I spit at him, through the bars, and left. And never saw Mexico City again."

"Señora," Artie says in his most kindly voice, just a trace of irony coloring this kindness into condescension. "I already know this story."

Concepción laughs loudly, and everyone looks around at her, in pleasure and surprise. Has Artie Vega really told the Señora a joke?

"You think I'm just an old lady who repeats herself because she's forgotten everything? I know I've told you this before. But never the part about the soul. I saved that," she says.

Now Artie fidgets, turning him from a brave man facing death into a teenager in front of a high school principal. "Excuse me, Señora," he says, "but so what?"

"The soul of Tomas cannot be bought, because of his eyes. In his eyes, he's always laughing. Life is all a big joke. But he keeps his soul."

"Tomas talks too much," Artie says.

"That too. But he keeps his soul."

"You want to tell me about my soul?" Artie reaches into his jacket, caresses his paperback, a moment of security at the confessional.

"You're a smart boy, Arturo Vega," Concepción says. "Your eyes are like the assassin's. All surface. Good for hiding too many secrets. *Cuidado*. You could sell your soul without knowing it." She's certain this is a good speech which will result in Artie telling her some essential truth, some revelation. But he surprises her.

"I may have already, Señora," he says, with soft simplicity. Without guile now, testing her compassion.

"Then come to me when you feel you need to. I may be able to help you. Don't go to Tomas. Tomas has enough troubles with the restaurant. Come to me."

Artie nods, lowers his head, recedes into the group, so small and thin he seems to fold himself into it, like a paper doll in a three-dimensional world. Can this boy be in real trouble? Can Tomas already be involved? Tomas stands in the center of her living room with his arms around Sasha, radiating nothing but strong self-assurance and happiness. Life has been easy for him since he came to live with her, she has loved him for his prettiness and his humor, has given him everything. If he is in trouble, she will know about it soon enough. Concepción closes her eyes, leans her head back into her chair, floats on the currents of musical Spanish and English conversation which lap up to her, around her, a balmy ocean of sensation.

Eight
SASHA

How can I be so jealous? With all these blond genes in me. Lazy Swedish genes good for coal mining. Able to withstand whole days of light without the relief of night, darkness. Genes like that have got to be tough, imperturbable. Don't mention the suicide rate. That only goes for Swedes in Sweden. Or maybe Danish genes. Happiest people in the world. Baking coffee cakes, dreaming of the Tivoli Gardens and sex. Danes never even kill themselves. They go to porno movies instead. Or make porno movies. And how about Norwegians? I don't even know what Norwegians do. But they've got fjords, which I think most be beautiful, glassy pale blue stretches. Fjords must make for national mental health. What does genetics mean, anyways? Does it determine how we function in the day-to-day, or just in some vaster scheme visible over generations? (For a moment the idea of German genes occurs to me, but I don't want to even begin to think about it. German culture the only one that can compete with Latin culture in terms of death-worship. Germans want to think themselves to death. Call each other *Scheisskopf*. Latins want to fuck to death, or knife each other. The worst possible combination of genes must be German and Latin. Good thing the Germans and the Spanish are separated by France and other subtler countries, countries where knifing grades into thinking, like blue into violet on the spectrum.) I want some genetic relief right now, because something is up with Tomas, and I can't stand it. I think Tomas is having an affair.

Certainly not the first time. The first time, or at least the first time I knew about, was the ballerina. I never met her, so I could picture her perfectly, freed from snapshot reality. Tiny wispy thing, little pin head, long thin legs deceptive, actually full of steel sinew. A guy I was out with once took me to the ballet, and whispered to me through the whole performance. He said things like, "I'd like her to wrap those legs around me." This is what I thought of when Tomas talked about his ex-girlfriend the ballerina. The one before me. Supposedly it was long over. But I'm not so dumb. One Sunday morning in bed, reading the paper, I saw the advertisement for the ballet company she danced with, three nights in Royce Hall at UCLA, three different repertoires, expensive tickets. My stomach clenched, my spine came to antsy life. I swallowed hard and tried to forget about it, but you know how it is with things you try to forget. The dates were tattooed behind my eyes in Day-Glo colors. No surprise when, on the second night of those dates, Tomas called to say he had to work real late. Didn't know when he'd be home. Big night at the restaurant. Then he had to swing by Randy's, help him out with some rush developing of photos. Sure thing. At ten o'clock that night I took some pills, a glass of wine, to ensure unconsciousness. Dead sleep, until the tiny, tinny sound of the key in the lock pumped adrenalin through my veins like an electroshock treatment. Wide awake, forget the pills, forget the wine, at nearly four in the morning. I pretended to be asleep, Tomas got into bed with more delicacy than he'd ever displayed. Picking up the corner of the sheet, depositing his body at the edge of the bed. Not touching me at all. No touching next morning either. This was unheard-of for us, to go a night and a morning without making love. I was cement, I was granite. My anger hardened my blood into something pure and chemical and impermeable in my veins, synthetic diamonds. He pretended to be asleep.

I got up, showered noisily. Dropping soap, throwing soap against the shower walls. I even threw a cologne bottle against the wall, one of those free cosmetic give-away bottles, and it didn't even break. But it made a hell of a clatter. Wrapped a towel around myself and went back into the bedroom to see him either sleeping or pretending. Pretending was better. That demonstrated guilt. Real sleep only demonstrated that he'd fucked his brains out the night before and was exhausted. I went back into the bathroom, grabbed the industrial flashlight, one of those enormous suckers for camping or patrolling warehouses. We keep it under the bathroom sink for power emergencies. This counted as one of those.

Back in the bedroom, I held the flashlight about three inches from his face, and turned the beam on. Fry those eyeballs right through the lid. His eyes flickered open, instinctive gesture of hand to eyes like shielding himself from bright sun. Men. Give them baseball caps with visors and they'll always be okay. He didn't even know enough to act guilty yet.

"You fucked her, didn't you?" I said in my best Gestapo voice.

"What?" He started to sit up, avoid the light, but I moved it with him, keeping it trained on his suffering eyes. I could see the pupils turning into anguished pinpricks. All right, I thought. Take that. Burn.

"I know all about it. You fucked her last night."

"*Querida*. Put that thing down, it's killing me. I had a little too much to drink last night. You know how klieg lights affect a hangover?" Honey-voiced, sure sign of criminal behavior.

"You didn't fuck her last night?" Now I felt tricky.

"I don't know what you're talking about. I went over to Randy's, you know. And we started drinking wine, and we forgot all about the chemicals and the prints. And then we passed out. *Borrachos*. You know how guys are."

"Yeah, I know." I slipped into bed beside him, letting the damp towel slide away from my body. I pressed up against him. Good spies must learn to control involuntary spasms of nausea. Good actresses must learn how to kiss actors with bad breath and false teeth and make it look like true love. I wound my leg between his, and he recoiled like a delicate virgin. I stood up again in triumph, brandishing the flashlight, and for the first time he looked frightened.

"I know you fucked her, so you better tell me right now before I make a big hole in your head."

Now he looked sheepish, some complicated Latin code at work. "I respect you too much to make love to you now. I love you."

I moved the flashlight from my right hand to my left, so that I could grab a handful of his hair with my right. "Let me get this straight," I said. "For some reason, you can't fuck me because you love me."

"I got drunk last night, and I was unfaithful to you. I feel terrible about it. *Corazón*, I love you. When I got into bed, I kept myself from touching you. Even this morning I didn't touch you. It wouldn't be right."

This pleased him. He had it all figured out. Infidelity resembling athlete's foot, or some other itchy, contagious rash. You stay away from those you love instead of giving them itches. This made you noble. I wanted to murder him.

"You asshole," I yelled, and he cowered, because of the flashlight. "How long does this take to wear off? How long before the other woman's cooties go away? I'm just supposed to wait around patiently as if you're off at the wars, wondering when we get to make love again? Do you know what a jerk you are?"

"*Corazón*, it didn't mean anything." This in a weasel voice I'd never heard before. Maybe because I'd never held a deadly weapon over his head before.

"If it didn't mean anything, why'd you do it? If it didn't mean anything, why are you acting like you've got the world's most contagious case of clap?"

This made him angry. The thought of any disease infecting his beloved prick infuriated him, the prick being a pure and wonderful symbol of himself at his best. The prick being the image he wanted to cast in an emasculated world. Any death I could imagine was too good for him.

But he yelled at me, from the bed, "Look, I didn't have to tell you. I'm being honest with you."

"Muchas gracias," I yelled back. "I ought to crush your skull."

Now he stood up, making me feel weaker, smaller, unable to control the situation with my piece of steel and wattage. I needed a shotgun, or a magnum. He yelled, "My grandfather fucked around on my grandmother, and my father fucked around on my mother. But that didn't mean they didn't love them. And they were good women, and they forgave them. What the hell's the big deal?"

"You fucking make it sound like some family tradition, you know? Eat a turkey on Thanksgiving. Open presents on Christmas morning. Fuck around on the woman you love, then don't touch her for forty-eight hours. Give me a break."

Then he said this sinister thing, the first time I ever heard him say it, though by now it's become a staple of our arguments. His voice quieted, became icy and strained. And his eyes looked evil, mean and slitty like some jungle beast's. "I've got the blood of warriors in my veins," he said. I knew I'd lost. I didn't speak again, just glared at him as I dressed, went into the bathroom and threw some things into my purse, makeup, deodorant, toothbrush. Back in the bedroom, I grabbed a sweater and jeans, stuffed clean panties in with the makeup. By this time he'd gotten back into bed and was pretending to read an old magazine which I'd used to help me fall asleep the previous night, a *Mademoiselle*.

So I went to Claire's, and she was great. Didn't answer her phone all day, even when it rang for fifteen minutes straight. Next morning he showed up at her door with a dozen red roses, and we went home together.

"It will never happen again," he said through clenched teeth, every word hurting. Because he knew it would, and Tomas doesn't like to lie. And I knew it would happen again, too. But I figure, now, in rational moments, he loves me. He's my home, my flesh, and I'm his. What difference does this one physical act make if you feel like that about someone?

It kills me. Now, with him looking sneaky, getting calls at home and all he can say into the telephone is, "Call me at the restaurant,"

I'm thinking about household weapons again. The heavy iron skillet. The two-foot-long carving knife. The enormous wrench. I have these little pains in specific parts of my body, my right toenail, my left elbow, the very base of my skull. But I'll wait for evidence before I act.

Maybe this is the Northern part of my being, genetics at work. Maybe because I wait before I commit mayhem, I can trace my heritage. No acts of passion for Swedes. Swedes think each step through. Like in every Bergman movie. How else could they come up with anything like baking in a sauna, rolling in the snow, back into the sauna, back into the snow? Mortify that body with careful precision. That's the kind of things Swedes come up with: premeditation. Then they don't have to feel guilty about anything they do, because they've thought it all through. While Latins, all those Catholics types, don't think. Crimes of passion, then into the confessional. Guilt, rosaries, candles, Hail Marys. Tomas acts without thinking, feels terrible, makes up for it later. Me, I scheme and plot to catch him and punish him. Because I love him. My violence of feeling when it comes to him doesn't even bother me. Who else should you want to kill but the person you love most?

In an orderly universe where cars stop for red and go for green, where automatic tellers at banks dispense just the amount of money you punched into their keyboards without ever surprising you with bounty or keeping that last ten-dollar bill stuck inside their metal lips, where the pastel seasons of Los Angeles shade into one another so that the pale green of April becomes, gradually, the gray of June, the butter yellow of September, the crackling beige of November, El Caballo Blanco remains a perverse pole of chaos, the rent in the perfect tapestry everyone knows Southern California to be. Opening time, a few customers hungry for enchiladas and margaritas made with wine and fruit rather than real hard liquor, and still Julio is the only waiter. Wiliness intermingles with worry on his rodenty face. He ducks into the kitchen, up behind the cash register, under a table to avoid Tomas. As he sticks his head out from under the front-most table, Tomas grabs his shoulders, stands him up. Julio wants to shrink, to become invisible, because Tomas exudes a dangerous smell that any small animal would recognize and run from.

"So where's your cousin, man?" Tomas asks, tightening his hands on Julio's skinny shoulders. Julio wriggles like a caught bug.

"What cousin?" Stupidity as a ruse works at some borders.

"The one who was coming in to help out until we found some-one permanent, *pendejo*."

No way out now. A specific question demands a reply, just as only one combination opens a lock. "Didn't I tell you?" Big-eyed movie-Mexican face.

"Didn't you fucking tell me what?"

Julio cringes, feels his feet rise off the floor because of his own attempts to make himself smaller and Tomas's attempt to stretch him into telling the truth. "She had to stay home with Maria and the baby."

"For Christ's sake, man, it's your ass. You're gonna be alone in here tonight and it's gonna be a madhouse. And I'm not gonna wait tables. I'm the boss." A group of customers, young parents with two kids, come in, smile, see Tomas engaged in some act of violence against their favorite waiter, and retreat. They'll go down the street to Casa Linda tonight, even if the peas are canned.

"Sasha would help," Julio suggests, deflating Tomas completely. Julio's feet touch ground again, the hands flutter off his shoulders.

"She'll kill me. She usually brings in about a hundred and fifty in tips on Wednesday nights." A couple enters, and the man waves to Tomas, who looks as if he's about to cry. "Sit anywhere," he says to them, none of his usual cordial greetings, ideal host's warmth.

Julio whispers, "But this is for love."

Tomas pounds both open hands down upon the table top, mak-ing silverware clatter in percussive cacophony. He's incredulous. "Who told you love and money were different things? That's why you'll always be a waiter." Julio again fears for his life, because of some theoretical nuance he hasn't grasped about commerce, but Artie enters from the kitchen, so cool, thin as a matchstick, a magnet for anger because of his posture, his impassive face. Tomas directs his musky glower in Artie's direction.

Artie says, "She said she would stop here on the way to work. To make sure everything was running smoothly. And to make sure you were okay." He pauses, in complete control over a conver-sation he had eavesdropped upon. "She worries about you."

"See?" Julio says, grinning.

But Tomas still pouts, dangerous in his sullenness. "That doesn't mean she won't kill me."

Artie stands up straighter, juts his chin, furrows his brows. "Are you afraid of your woman?"

Tomas spins around with his hands held over his head, and the whole restaurant becomes silent, molecules of air stirred up as if by a Cuisinart.

"Listen to this bullshit!" Tomas yells. "The natives are getting restless. You think you can insult my masculinity and my pride, you skinny little asshole?"

"You shouldn't talk that way to Artie," Julio instructs, smoothing his shirt, trying to erase the pawmarks from the fabric that covers his shoulders. "Artie has many friends."

"Shut up," Artie says. "You talk too much."

But Tomas's attention swivels to the front door. Sasha walks in, her face, one moment, still attuned to the order of outside, features calm. Then, the next moment, like a practiced mime demonstrating schizophrenia, her mouth, her eyes change. Her nostrils widen, like a horse smelling fire in the barn. A horrible sense of déjà vu: It's the same as over the weekend, no end to this chaos, and she knows she's about to be suckered. Tomas sees her sudden wish for flight, and rushes to her, trapping her, enveloping her in the warmth of his biggest loving smile.

"*Corazón,*" he says, "you look so beautiful tonight." He takes her hand, kisses it twice.

"Where's Julio's cousin?" she asks, slowly, as if speaking to a foreigner with only a rudimentary control of the English language.

Julio says, "She's home," but Tomas quickly interrupts the explanation.

"Get those people over there some chips, man," he says, and Julio scurries. But Artie remains standing next to Tomas like a malevolent shadow.

"How about you, amigo," Tomas says to him. "You heard of work? *Trabajar?*" He keeps hold of Sasha's hand.

"I am a busboy, the best you got," Artie says with great wounded dignity. Then he extends his left arm, so that his shirtsleeve creeps up his bony wrist, and he checks his watch. Sasha notes the watch: a solid gold Rolex. Nothing about Artie surprises her any more.

"It is only ten minutes since official opening," Artie says. "Not much work for a busboy to do in ten minutes. Do you want me to make some dishes dirty so that I can take them into the kitchen? Should I spill some water so that I can mop it up?"

"Go read," Sasha says, and Artie, looking triumphant, goes into the kitchen, leaving Tomas and Sasha in the restaurant which, without Tomas directing traffic, fills up haphazardly with people, two in the big booth in back which he always saves for six, college kids in the front throwing chips at more college kids across the aisle.

"The man's got an attitude," Tomas says, shaking his head.

"Yeah. You oughta know about that kind of stuff." Sasha thinks: What am I doing here, with these crazy jerks in this crazy restaurant? She imagines the pale pink and gray calm of L'Etranger, the tranquil neo-expressionist paintings, the soft hip rock and roll on the stereo system, the daily printed menus without years of fingerprints upon them. She thinks of Mike, the manager, who never raises his voice. It took her six months to discover he actually had an Australian accent. He likes her without having to utter oily compliments. Just the way he looks at her and then looks away too fast. She should be there, not here, with crazy people.

"What is this, pick on Tomas night?" Tomas says, baby-hurt.

"So I look beautiful?"

Tomas rallies, brightens. He's being asked to be charming. He gives her a big hug. "You look gorgeous, babe."

"Too gorgeous for L'Etranger, I bet."

Tomas sits down at the table, props his chin in his hands, utterly demoralized, chastened. He hates being found out. He hates realizing that all his charming scheming is transparent. Life hardly seems worth living if charm doesn't work. "We're shorthanded again," he says, in despair, "thanks to that *cabrón* Julio." Big hands smear his face, pushing and pulling features into silly putty until Sasha is reminded of the Richard Nixon masks teenagers used to wear on Halloween. She can't stand to see Tomas suffer. Without another word, she goes to the phone at the front of the restaurant, by the register, and dials L'Etranger. Tomas peeps out from behind his hands, watches, and listens.

"Mike? Hi, this is Sasha," she says, and pauses, smiles. "I know I'm late. I'm gonna be later." Another pause. Tomas can tell that this guy is pretty sweet on the phone, knows just what to say to Sasha. "Yeah, we've got a family emergency on our hands." Another pause, her face softens. And looks a little guilty. Obviously she's getting sympathy. "I know," she says, "if it was someone else, she'd be out on her ear. I appreciate your concern for me, Mike, I really do." During this pause, she looks like an alert dog trying to comprehend a complicated command, a new combination of sounds and words. "Yeah, you're terrific to me. But I don't know for how much longer. It's hard to tell with these emergencies, you know?" More Australian soft soap laid on, Tomas can tell. "Thanks. You're a great boss. Bye." Sasha looks relieved now, thinking she's pleased both her lover and her boss, though she should know this is impossible. Especially if the former has overheard a conversation with the latter. Tomas, surly, struts over, leans on the cash register.

"He's given me tonight and tomorrow if I need it to deal with this problem," she says. "After that, he's going to get in real trouble. And so am I. He's really taking a big risk for me. If the owner should come in."

"How terrific is he to you?"

Sasha closes her eyes, as if she's getting a suntan and doesn't want to expose eyeballs to dangerous rays, then opens her eyes. "You've got to be kidding."

"As terrific as I am?"

She thinks, guilty people project their own sins onto others. If he's jealous of me, must mean he's got something to hide himself. But she tries to display no evidence of thought on her face, tries to react quickly with genuinely hurt feelings to defuse the real argument she can feel welling up in her. No time or place for a real argument, with two more families just in the front door and Tomas glowering like King Kong chained on stage.

"Let me ask you one question," she says. "Who have I ended up working for this evening? In fact, let me ask you a second question. How much less money have I ended up working for?"

Tomas doesn't move, though he theatrically slits his eyes a little.

"Go greet, Kong. Make nice," she says, and shoves his shoulder as she passes him on her way to the kitchen to pick up her official waitress materials: her pad, her pencil, the tacky white apron she'll tie on over her pale gray slacks and white blouse, the required dress for the employees of L'Etranger.

Ten
SASHA

By nine-thirty, the rush is over and we can all relax. Tomas sits down with this tall, skinny surfer kid, tan, good-looking, not an unusual specimen in these parts. Not an unusual situation. But then Artie sits down with them, and they're all talking, real seriously, without even a decanter of wine between them. When Tomas has a friend come in, he always drinks with the friend. He says it's a Latin's responsibility to get his friends drunk, plus it's good for business. So, what does this mean? Is this kid not really a friend? If not a friend, what? And what is Artie doing in on it? In the kitchen, I ask Julio.

"Who's the guy talking to Tomas and Artie?"

And Julio, the height of subtlety, goes out the swinging door, stops, looks, puts his hands on his hips, scratches his chin, then comes back into the kitchen. Of course, I'm expecting zero info at this point.

"He comes in a lot lately," Julio says, a good little turncoat. "Usually late, like now. Then Tomas and Artie have time to sit down with him,"

"That much I can see," I say, and wonder even more what the hell's going on. I'm suspicious anyhow these days, but I never suspected the person I'd be jealous of would be tall, blond, cute, and male. I've got to find out.

"Let me take your table over there, those four low tippers," I say, pointing through the door at the back table nearest the booth where the fate of the nation is being decided. "They're about ready for dessert and coffee."

"I don't know," Julio whines, looking cagy. Everyone's a crybaby capitalist lately. When I first met Tomas, he didn't care a damn for the restaurant. Now he gets stars in his eyes when he talks about turning it into a multi-million-dollar industry, a chain, with frozen food in the supermarkets. If he can afford to renew the lease when it's up at the end of next month. The landlords have been threatening to triple the rent. Tomas says it would break Mama's heart to close or move the restaurant, but I think his heart is in jeopardy too. He's tied to this place now, like it's part of his family.

"Look, I'll take the table, and I'll give you the tip they leave."

"Sure thing!" Julio says, and claps his hands together like he's just gotten a birthday present.

So I go out to the table, and nobody even seems to notice they've got a new waiter. And I don't look at all like Julio. This kind of thing is bad for an actress's self-confidence. I can feel myself getting hostile as I recite the desserts.

"We have delicious home-made flan for dessert, and also chocolate and vanilla ice cream, Häagen-Dazs," I say. A flash of a thought: I could unbutton my blouse for a second, to assure them I wasn't Julio. But what if they still didn't notice?

At the same time, I'm trying to listen to the conversation between Tomas, Artie, and this blond kid.

"One scoop of vanilla," the first geek says. Real inventive.

"Same for me," the second geek.

The third one says, "Just coffee," but then gets an inspiration. "What's this flan stuff?" Making it hard for me to concentrate on what's happening at Tomas's table.

"It's caramel custard," I say, "you know, like pudding." This geek is thinking hard, trying to picture flan.

"No thanks, just coffee." Turns out the excitement of asking was enough for him.

The fourth guy sits there staring at the table in front of him, catatonic, and now I'm really hostile, because I've heard some of what's going on in the booth next door.

"How about you?" I ask. Drill instructor voice.

"Jeez, what pressure!" he says, but then buckles. "Okay. Chocolate ice cream."

I take a step away from the table, and write very very slowly, as if the order they've given is *Anna Karenina*, so I can catch the end of what has seemed to be something business-related, something serious among Tomas, Artie, and Surf City.

"When will the shipment be in?" Artie asks. I write on my pad, C-H-O-C-O-L-A-T-E, making nice neat block letters.

"As early as next week. But as soon as it comes in, we'll have to work fast to move it. It'll be plenty hot," the blond boy says.

"Don't worry," Tomas chimes in, officious. His in-control-of-everything voice. Which usually means he doesn't know what the fuck, and needs time to figure it out. "We've got it all set up at our end." I decorate my letters with curlicues as I feel something inside me get all tight with betrayal.

Artie doesn't like what Tomas said. Maybe he knows what that tone means, like I do. He puffs his chest out, tries to make himself larger, turn himself into the boss. "I have the contacts," he says. "You just get the stuff." Why is Tomas taking this shit from Artie? Now I'm pissed off at Tomas for a couple of things, and completely confused. I cross hatch the empty space between my letters.

The blond kid acts offended. "Don't be so uptight, man. Hey, this is, like, fun. This is for a little excitement. Get the cardiovascular system working. Like jogging."

"Artie's just concerned. He's a perfectionist, you know?" Tomas says, like a diplomat. But also as if Artie *is* the boss.

"I am a businessman," Artie says. "I am like the head of Chrysler. That guy with the funny-sounding name. Nothing ever goes right for a serious businessman, or at least that is the correct philosophy to have. That dude knows how to handle a crisis."

Blondie looks at Tomas for translation. "What's he talking about—Chrysler?"

Tomas's face lights up in a way I know well. He's heard a potential straight line. "It's a lot like BMW, or Porsche, kid. I know you've heard of BMW or Porsche. Only this one's made in Dee-troit." Silence from Artie and the kid. Tomas hates it when nobody laughs at his jokes.

And I've heard enough. I go to the kitchen, my hands clutching my pad and pencil so tightly they must be near shredding, tearing, snapping in two. I want to cry and to scream. I want to kill him. I don't want to go through more serious trouble. To be full of doubt and dread, full of waking in the middle of the night at the tiniest sound in the bushes outside, full of thoughts of sleeping with firearms under our pillows, again. Stopping by houses, on our way to the movies or dinner, that Tomas won't let me come in with him; I wait in the car then, wondering if Tomas will ever come out.

I lean against the kitchen wall, watching Paco and Pablo warming plates full of food that looks right now like squashed dead animals on a highway. Bill, our own blondie, is unlucky enough to wheel a cart full of dirty dishes in. I grab him by the arm and swing him around so that he's in front of me.

"Hey, you're strong," he says evenly. Right now I'm an amazon. I'm a heavyweight champion of the world. I'm a woman pissed off.

"Get Tomas for me," I say. Not letting go of Bill's arm.

"Like, he told us we shouldn't disturb him for any reason," Bill says. I feel my anger steaming out of my ears and nose like in some Cocteau film. But Bill acts as if he's being held by the regular me, regular Sasha, instead of a steam locomotive plummeting down a rickety track disguised as a woman.

I say, "What do you think that is out there, the Oval Office?" My voice careens around in my head, unable to rest on any tone or pitch, unmodulated, out of control. Years of acting lessons vanish. I squeeze his blond arm tighter. "Get him for me. Right now."

"Okay, okay," Bill says, rubbing his arm as I let him loose, send him out the swinging doors. I stand in the doorway and watch, and listen. Bill cautiously approaches the table where this seamy summit conference is happening. Artie scowls at him, but Tomas has always liked Bill, goes surfing with him sometimes, though he thinks he's a little bit dim.

"Hey, man," Tomas says, smacking Bill's arm where I've already mauled it. "Bring us some beers."

But Artie can't stand this interruption. I've never seen him like this, no shred of cool. "Disappear," Artie growls at Bill.

"Yeah, I'd like a Bud," the blond kid at the table says to Bill, who could be his cousin, they look so much alike to any eye untrained in California boys, a separate species. Bill stands there, shifting from foot to foot.

Now Tomas starts to get edgy. Nobody's listening to him. "You're not moving," he says. Bill still doesn't speak. He turns around and sees me in the door. I put my hands on my hips, to remind him that this is war, and he's my emissary. He may be scared of Tomas and Artie when they get hissy like this, but if he leaves that table without doing his duty he's got to be scared of me too.

"Your old lady's in back, and she's looking like she's about ready to start throwing things," Bill finally says.

Tomas rolls his eyes. "She's an actress," he says to Blondie Number One sitting at the table. "You know how that is. Very dramatic."

"That's pretty cool. An actress," Mr. Surf says.

Artie's heard none of this. "You are disturbing our talk." he says to Bill, in such a sinister, sibilant whisper I'm reminded of tea kettles forgotten on the lit stove. Clearly no one wants to make a move there. Bill turns around again to see if I've disappeared or come to my senses. No such luck.

"I'm really sorry," he begins, "but she said to get you, and I don't want to go back in there unless you go first. That chick's turned into a monster."

A flicker of awareness crosses Tomas's face, that only I would be able to decipher. When do I ever make any demands upon him, the fucker? He *better* move. As he gets up, he slips into another persona, slides his hands through his (imagined) greased-back hair, smiles without showing teeth. He's become his slimy Latino husband character, henpecked and macho. "*Chihuahua!*" he says, "*Momentito, por favor. Mi novia,*" and he shakes his head, points his finger at his ear as if it is a gun, then twirls the finger. That's right: I'm loco. This pantomime doesn't amuse Artie at all. His lips look like twin stainless steel razors as he watches Bill leading Tomas away, but the blond kid at the table looks cool as glass. This worries me even more than if the kid had looked agitated, or mad. The kid's a pro. I keep my eyes on him, can half-hear, half-read his lips across the room

"You're sure that dude's cool? 'Cause he seems kinda like a clown to me," Surfer Boy says. All business. He's got a future as a Hollywood agent.

Artie manages to spit out his words between those gunmetal lips. "This is his place we are doing business in."

"Yeah," Surfer Boy says. "And if anything goes wrong, I'll know who to blame it on."

I retreat into the kitchen, behind the doors, because I'm so pissed off all over again. Kitchen implements looks like weapons to me. Especially this gigantic iron frying pan, Paco's favorite. I snatch it from in front of him, not even noticing its weight. Paco and Pablo look at each other, don't say anything, begin to edge away from their counter, toward the back door. Abandoning a big-bladed chopping knife that smells of onions and looks more like a machete, good for vine-hacking in a rain forest, and for decapitation. I grab that too, just as Tomas comes in, with Bill shrinking away behind him, glad to be finished with his tour of duty.

I feel my heart pounding in my ears, feel tingly in my arms and legs. This must be what Tomas means when he talks about the blood of warriors flowing in his veins. We all have it. I have it too. No generals that I know about in my heritage, only pale ice, pale waters, pale people, but I am as alive as he with the urge to kill someone I love. Momentarily Latina. The weapons in my hand, perfect women warriors' weapons, kitchen tools for cooking and for murdering, come alive with my homicidal vibrations. I saw with the knife on the handle of the frying pan, anxious to get to work. Humming metal, like a good cook's song of delight at her newly created casserole, fills the kitchen. Grating, keening, a song that hurts my spine, the kind of song primitive tribesmen make before doing battle. All this comes naturally to me all of a sudden, making me more and more pissed off.

"Fuck you," I say to Tomas. But he thinks this is some kind of joke. He makes a couple of mock-karate moves, holding hands rigid before his chest, kicking straight at me, through the air, with one leg. He smiles, the doofus. I saw harder, my music louder.

"Put that stuff down now, babe," Tomas says. "What's the matter?"

I set my weapons down on the counter, knife over pan, knowing they will remain within arm's reach if I need them. Paco and Pablo lurk at the back door, ready to make a run for it. They understand that I am not through with their tools, see my strategy. Though I want to be strong, tough as Roberto Duran, filled with male anger which makes violence possible, I feel my lips start to quiver. Like a surgeon with congenitally shaky hands, I am not cut out for this job. Femaleness surfaces, the heritage I know and understand, and can't ignore. Shit.

"Come on," he says, coming too close, full dose of warm charm at work, his personal mojo. "I've got important stuff to handle out there."

"Yeah?" I say. "What kind of important stuff?" Trying to keep my voice soft, severe, giving nothing away. Voice as spine-tingling as the knife on the pan handle. But my lips betray, quivering. Tomas looks entirely puzzled.

"Oh, you know. The usual. Customers who want to pay with checks. Two drunk guys at one table who are yelling for the burro act."

Control the voice: any actress can do this. Play the role. Not Juliet, not Desdemona, not Blanche DuBois. Not even one of the wimpy heroes, like Hamlet. More like one of the guys from *Julius Caesar*, guys who put on metal breastplates and helmets with spikes and plunged their swords and knives into the flesh of a great man when they had to.

"I heard what kind of stuff you've got going on out there," I say. Then it happens. I'm not acting any more. My hands fly to my face, covering my cheeks, and tears come. And no voice control left at all, a bunch of words shaking and trilling out of my mouth. "You promised me this would never happen again. After that time you nearly ate it in that rich creep's Piper Cub, and you had to dump that ton of marijuana into the ocean. What's happened? Have all those years of smoking dope killed your brain cells and your memory? You came so close to getting caught then. You promised. No more drug scams."

He grips my upper arms with his hands, too hard, he's pissed off now, but there's something bogus about it. "What the fuck are you talking about?"

"You're just not smart enough for this kind of stuff. I love you so much, but you're not smart enough. You'll get caught, and that surfer kid will get off free 'cause his daddy will buy him a big-time lawyer. And you'll be the one to take the whole rap."

"I'm not getting into any trouble, really, babe," he says, but he's placating me, talking to a crying infant. "I'm not into dope smuggling any more."

Warrior resolve returning. I can't stand it when he lies to me. Now I can yell as I cry. "I don't want to visit you in prison! I don't want to look at you through bars!"

This impresses him, even turns him on. Any kind of passion does this, does this magic trick of turning into sex for Tomas. Hands off my arms, he's going to hug me, a moment between his gestures, from restraint to embrace. In that moment, I take one step back, away from him. I am large, strong, mean, angry as hell. My right hand turns into a fist, I swing my arm back. A real roundhouse punch. I hit Tomas as hard as I can on his chin, and he staggers, looking amazed. Through this pulsing, loud buzz in my head, I hear Paco and Pablo chattering in rapid Spanish. Then the buzz in my head dies, and everything becomes clear, Kodak picture focus, light beam focus.

"Don't go back out there," I say. "Please."

He looks at me as if I'm the most bizarre being he's ever seen, his first glimpse of an alien from outer space. "You're out of line, babe. I go wherever I like." In a voice without affect. Tomas, every bit of him always alive, speaks in this dead voice, a voice from a machine. Then he turns and walks back into the dining room, leaving the doors swinging.

I look at my hand, still fisted, and hurting. Fingers uncurl one by one, and as they do so, they shake. Then my whole hand shakes. Then my arm. Muscles turned to Jell-O. Airiness in my head, as if a space has opened up between brain and skull, and that space is filled with some dentist's anesthetic gas. From somewhere inside one of those cobwebbed and dusty parts of my brain, a bit of information surfaces: An epileptic having a seizure should have a stick or piece of silverware stuck between his teeth, to keep him from swallowing his own tongue. Paco's and Pablo's voices float into that empty space in my head. The world, the kitchen, exist again. I turn toward then, like a plant growing toward sunlight.

"You can come back now," I say, "the fireworks are over."

More animated than I've ever seen them, faces delighted and astonished, full of excitement. They think this scene has been great.

"What a *chingazo* you gave the boss!" Paco says, socking Pablo on the arm. Pablo laughs, socks him back.

Then the tears start again. I grab my purse from where I'd stashed it in a cupboard under the counter, and run out the back door, to my car.

Eleven
SASHA

I think of one night Tomas and I were together, when we were just dating. Though dating is hardly the word for what we did. We did not go to movies. Or out to dinner. Or any of the other inventive things people find to do to build up an evening's worth of suspense before they make love, as if they want to be unsure of the outcome of the date, want to dance around each other for a few hours pretending they're not drawn to that bed like paper clips to a magnet. No. Tomas would pick me up on a Monday night, the one night El Caballo Blanco closed, and take me to his place on the beach. A one-room apartment with only a huge water bed in it. At his place, we would drink champagne, smoke dope, and fuck. Over and over. And talk in between, our bodies touching in as many places as it is possible for bodies to touch. Usually, at the end of these evenings, very very late, we would fall into stuporous sleep without meaning to, sleep just another punctuation of our lovemaking. No getting ready for bed ritual, no toothbrushing, no good night kiss. Then we would wake up in the morning and make love again.

But this night I'm thinking of, I made Tomas take me home. The next morning he had to get up by six, to go downtown to

the wholesale market and buy the week's vegetables for the restaurant. This never bothered Tomas, having to get up so early
after a very late night of fooling around. Sleep, for him, just another
pleasure to be gotten when he could, like drugs, like sex. Thor-
oughly enjoyed when it comes his way, not missed when it doesn't.
But I'm different. Without sleep, I feel as if my head is stuffed full
of pink, sticky cotton candy, feel dumb, feel my IQ dive about
fifty points. Without sleep, I'll find myself driving along a busy
street and realize I've been unconscious for blocks, have seen
nothing. On days like that, I pray that no child or dog steps into
the street in front of my blind car.

So we'd smoked, and drunk, and made love, and at about three
in the morning I told Tomas he'd better take me home. We dressed
without showering, as we always did, because we loved the smell
of our sex. Even washing my sheets seemed wrong then. Wrong
to erase the smell of me and Tomas in favor of the chemical, bright
smell of detergent clean.

Outside, the universe had changed. When we went into his
apartment, the day had still been full of light, another pretty Los
Angeles day, palm trees swaying, air smelling of salt. With that
special cosmic lightness ocean air has: that it connects you to
places, people, far away, that it travels and yet binds you to that
far away-ness. Maybe it's because it smells woman-sexy, musky
and rich. But at three in that morning, one of those airport-closing
fogs had rolled in. A thick soup of it swirling about us, making us
feel that we were the only people left in the world. Air smelling
flat, dead, heavy. We couldn't see the gate to the little front yard
of Tomas's apartment, though it was only ten feet away. We couldn't
see Tomas's black truck. The ocean was gone, no sign of a horizon.
There was us, and there was fog, and it felt good.

"Let's go back in," Tomas said. I knew how he felt. This fog
made me want to make love again too. I pressed up against him
and kissed him, knowing no one could see us. We could make
love right there on the lawn, the fog covering us like a down
comforter.

"I've got to go," I said. "You know how cranky I am in the morning."

"Yeah," he said. "you're such a pain in the ass." Said sweetly, full of intimacy, all of me well-known to him, and still loved.

So we felt our way out of the yard, to the truck, and when Tomas had opened the door for me, locked me in, and begun to go around to his side, I got scared. The feeling you get when you're in an elevator jammed full of people, the door closes, and the thing gives a little jump, maybe the lights blink off for a moment. First you think, "This thing's going to break down." Second, you think, "I'm going to scream." The fog settled on the windshield of the truck, pushed in against the side windows. I couldn't breathe until Tomas opened his door, got in beside me. I slid up against him.

"This is dangerous," I said. Tomas was suddenly full of energy, all lit up.

"Come on, babe," he said. "This is great. This is going to be some cruise." He started the truck, turned the radio on to loud rock 'n' roll.

Traffic lights hung, invisibly suspended in the night, like the suit markings on playing cards. The red fuzzed into pink, the green into gray, the yellow into pure shimmer, like faraway stars. Other cars' headlights and taillights jumped out in front of us, out of nowhere. Brakes squealed, tires screeched, but the sound had an eerie, muffled quality, unreal, as if it was noise from another universe leaking through some warp in the fabric of things into ours.

The freeway was a fog desert, a vast creamy wasteland. As Tomas sped up, we seemed to be flying. Like when you're on a jet just rising through the layer of clouds, and you can see the texture of the clouds, the wispy white strands and clots of them, and they seem to be whooshing by you. The fog whooshed by us like that, turning into mottled, irregular stripes of fog instead of a blanket, while we seemed to be standing still.

L.A. closes down early. After midnight the freeways are empty concrete snakes, and you know that anyone out driving at three in the morning has got to be a lone weirdo. We raced along at sixty, and I knew that we wouldn't have a chance to see taillights jumping out at us. It would be a nightmare crash, the sound of metal on metal seeming faraway, the falling weightless, no knowing if the concrete was up or down. Tomas's truck didn't have seat belts.

"Slow down," I said.

But he said, "Scared, baby?" He turned his head to kiss me. I met his lips, knowing he closed his eyes when he kissed. I closed mine too. Everything sped up, a jolt of pure chemical in my veins, the drug not a drug of fear, but of thrill. This was it. We were in something real, something ultimate, together.

He pulled his head away and looked into my eyes. I looked back, feeling my pupils contract, expand, contract to focus on him in the strange night which was not black but a steamy white-gray. No nod, no expression, no words, but we agreed. He turned the radio up louder, looked in front of him, put one arm around me tightly. I gripped his thigh with both my hands. He floored it.

Now the fog was streamers around the truck, a ticker tape parade. I held his thigh, and struggled not to think, but to keep my eyes open to suck in everything I could. A crazed David Bowie song filled my head from the radio, Bowie screaming. Tomas laughed. We were in heaven, an absolutely still point at which nothing happens, but everything is full, waiting. Everything was possible. We could be James Dean together. We could hurtle through space together. If we died, it would be together, our blood commingling, one red pool on concrete. I thought, we were meant to be in danger together. Nothing was too scary, too perilous, that it wouldn't thrill us if we were in it with one another. The fog and speed erased time, erased distance, into a blurry, heightened eternity. I felt like screaming. But not with terror. With aliveness, with being alive in this moment with Tomas, close to the edge of life with Tomas.

"Do you love me?" he asked. He did not look at me. Only ahead, at the thickening clumps of fog hitting the windshield like a flock of thousands of sparrows.

"I love you," I said. This world without sound, without vision, encased by the metal of the truck and the joy of terror made me love him more than I ever had.

When we reached my house, he came in with me, and we made love on the floor, just inside my front door, with the door thrown wide open, my keys still in the lock.

Twelve
SASHA

Tomas does not come home. Eleven o'clock, eleven-thirty, twelve midnight. Sasha knew he would punish her, but thought it would be face to face. One of their yelling and screaming fights. Name calling. Swearing. Door slamming. She would find out exactly what was going on then, because eventually, ultimately, he told her the truth. But instead, he stays out, punishing her like an adolescent punishes a parent. She thinks of all the places he might be, and she calls each one. Calls Bud, Lonny, Bobby, Rich. She wakes up some of them, but they don't mind. They are the kinds of friends who are used to being awakened by a frightened or angry girlfriend or wife late at night. They are the kind of friends who are used to making up excuses for missing buddies. She realizes that Tomas hangs out with a bunch of flakes who find nothing unusual in the fact that Tomas has not come home. Not a good sign, she thinks. With friends like that, she thinks. She calls Randy last, because she knows he dislikes her. Randy the pornographer. Randy thinks Tomas should be with a more beautiful woman, beautiful meaning exotic. Randy likes to take photos and films of sloe-eyed women making love to black women. Randy thinks Tomas should be with the model du jour, a half-Japanese, half-Jewish dish named Tiffany.

Twice, Randy has been arrested, once for pimping and pandering (really only arranging models for an afternoon's shoot), once for using minors in his films (nobody told him the kids were only sixteen; Randy assumes eighteen unless somebody tells him otherwise). Both times Tomas bailed him. A couple of times, Tomas has helped out on a shoot, on camera, on sound. Tomas hangs out at Randy's darkroom a lot, raves about Randy's abilities there, calls him an artist. Randy gives Sasha the willies, as all guys with long greasy hair and bad posture do. She doesn't have to call most guys with long greasy hair and bad posture after midnight, though, to find out if her manfriend, her roommate, her lover, is there. Randy is this evening's official boogeyman for Sasha, the evil being standing between her and Tomas. She dials his number, lets it ring eight times before Randy picks up.

"Yeah?" Randy answers. He sounds sleepy, or preoccupied, or stoned.

"Hi, it's Sasha."

"What's hip and new?" He doesn't sound any more interested than before, except now she's certain he must be intrigued. He can't remember who Sasha is. But the name is interesting and foreign, the voice is female. It's enough to bring some life to his voice.

"May I speak to Tomas, please?" A clever tactic. Assume the fucker's there, don't sound alarmed, the most natural thing in the world.

"Tomas no está," Randy says, and laughs.

"Was he there earlier?" Now anxiety creeps into her tone, acting failing her yet again.

"Haven't seen him all day," Randy says. With his mouth farther from the mouthpiece of his phone, he says to someone, "Hey, don't touch the equipment. It's fragile. That's not what you're here for, darling."

"Okay," Sasha says. "Sorry I bothered you."

"We're having a party," Randy says.

"I bet."

"Join us."

"No thanks. I have to find Tomas."

"Try over at Concepción's. I bet he's there counting his coins and crying on her shoulder about how mean you treat him all the time."

"Bye," she says, and hangs up. Too late to call Mama and risk awakening her. Wrong to worry her, too. She'd fret if she thought Tomas was on the loose and angry. Sasha gets up, goes to the kitchen, pours herself a glass of wine, sets the bottle of wine and the now full glass down on the sink. Here's what she can do: She can drive by Concepción's house, see if Tomas's truck is parked out front. See if the lights there are on. See if there's any chance of solace there. She grabs her car keys out of her purse and rushes out the back door.

Willows, jacaranda, and palm trees make Concepción's street shady during the day, jungle black at night, perfect for growing fragile coffee plants at the base of the palms as is done in Colombia, if anyone had the urge. The combination of trees the work of some demented Hollywood gardener trying for the kind of botanical eclecticism that would have pleased Dr. Frankenstein on his way to monster surgery to graft strange body parts together. Small houses sit far back from the street, behind expanses of verdant lawns which never have to be watered because of the omnipresent shade and dampness. Most of the houses are dark as their front yards this time of night, but Concepción's bay window glows pale blue, a sign of life which encourages Sasha as she pulls her battered brown Honda up in front. Encouragement that doesn't balance the fact that Tomas's truck isn't there. Still. What if someone gave him a ride to Concepción's, Artie, for example? Tomas likes to ride on Artie's cycle. Then Tomas's truck might still be in the alley. Sasha curses herself that she didn't think of this sooner, didn't drive by the Horse to check out the scene there. Remembering the night she discovered Tomas and a buddy laid out, drunk, across two booths, at five in the morning. That night, though, she knew to go there because she had first roused Tomas with a phone call. When he picked up the phone and slurred a dog-like sound into the mouthpiece that was supposed to approximate hello, she hung up and got in her car. Tonight, no one answered at the restaurant. But that doesn't mean anything.

Sasha decides on espionage. She creeps up to the front door, stands there, puts her ear to its flaking, scaled paint surface. And hears, from inside, a soft, indistinct, monotone male voice.

"Are you feeling lucky, punk?" the male voice asks.

Tomas doing his Clint Eastwood imitation for Concepción! Sasha raps loudly on the door, says, "Tomas? I'm sorry, really I am." Tomas does a great Clint Eastwood.

Concepción opens the door, tiny, her white hair hanging down her back, her old purple chenille robe dragging on the floor. Concepción smiles, opens the door wider.

"Hello, honey," she says, before she sees the abashed disappointment on Sasha's face. Behind Concepción, Sasha can see the television glowing in the living room. Concepción has been watching *Dirty Harry* on the late movie. Sasha sobs. Concepción turns around to see what has inspired this sudden grief in her grandson's *novia*, sees Clint Eastwood holding a gun to a black man's head, puts her arm around the *novia*'s waist and pulls her into the living room.

Inside, Sasha realizes the whole tale cannot be told. Does Concepción know about Tomas's past escapades? How much? Sasha doesn't want to rat on Tomas, doesn't want to cause the old woman consternation and heartache. Shrink the story, personalize it into a lover's spat. As she sobs and settles herself onto Concepción's couch, Sasha's actress's instincts work overtime. Amazing, Sasha thinks, how do people get by without Strasberg?

"Mama, I don't know where he is," she begins.

"*Claro*. You had a fight?" Concepción sits in her favorite chair, holding the remote control wand. She jabs it at the television, and the sound disappears, though Clint remains, muted.

"I hit him," Sasha says.

"Marvelous, honey!" Now Concepción's really interested. She leans forward in her chair, face awed and reverential, and at the same time full of memory. "Did he hit you back?"

"He walked away, and now I don't know where he is." Sasha knows this answer will disappoint. Concepción leans back, thinking, her sharp black bird's eyes on the television.

"You know, honey, I can't count the number of times the General didn't come home at night." Concepción jabs the wand at the television again, and the picture changes from Clint Eastwood to David Letterman, still without sound. Only the clothing, the sports coats and ties and button-down shirts, mark the creatures on different channels of the television as the same species. "With men, it's like that sometimes. They forget where their home is for a few hours. Or days. Then, bam bam, their memories return to them. We must forgive them for temporary amnesia."

"Tomas has never done this before."

"Wait, you'll see. He's out getting drunk with his friends."

Sasha feels ashamed of all she's withheld from Concepción. They should be allies in this. "I already called all his friends. I woke them all up. They're all home in bed. And they don't know where Tomas is."

"Look at this *maricón*," Concepción says, nodding toward David Letterman. "Where does a boy with a face like this come from?"

"Mama," Sasha says, "I'm really worried. I'm scared."

Concepción aims the wand at the television again, and brings Clint back. Clint stands astride a freeway overpass looking like an angel of destiny, a monument to the fear of God one man can put into other men's hearts. "I'm sorry to ask you this," Concepción says, "but are there women we should call?"

Sasha's eyes forget their dramatic training again, and she weeps copiously. "Oh, God," she says, "I don't know. I've had suspicions lately. Nobody serious, I guess. Nobody serious that I know about."

"The General had women I knew about," Concepción says, a tuning fork of empathy vibrating in her chest. "It didn't matter. I knew I was the one he really loved, the one he would always come back to. The night he was assassinated, I sent messengers to three women's houses. When all the messengers came back without any news of the General, then I knew I would never see him again."

Sasha looks up at the old woman, wild-eyed. That was not the correct anecdote to tell, Concepción thinks.

"I'm sorry, honey." She puts down the wand and pats Sasha's leg.

"There are no women to call. No."

"Then this is very bad." Concepción punctuates the seriousness of her statement by snapping the wand smartly at Clint, who disappears into a crack of static, a diminishing speck of light. "Terrible things might happen to a man with a bag full of money if he's alone, in the alley, and has his mind on a *novia*'s anger." An imp exercises complete control of Concepción's imagination and words now. She knows that everything she says excites the *novia* instead of calming her. But this is a young woman who does not consider the real danger of life, Concepción thinks. She must feel the danger if she is to help Tomas, difficult boy, live to old age.

"Oh, God," Sasha sobs, pushing both fisted hands to her mouth.

A pang of consciousness stabs at Concepción's eyes. Crying is contagious, like nausea. Enough reality for the *novia*, she thinks. "All right. Arturo will know if Tomas left late. Or if Tomas left with someone. We'll find Arturo, and make him come over here right now. He will do this for me."

Sasha gulps, sucks breath. "What about calling the police?"

"Pendeja!" Concepción hisses. "Never call the police before you know where your man is. We'll find Arturo." She picks the telephone off the floor next to her chair. Finds her address book in the stack of magazines next to her chair. She knows the number is there, turns to the V's, hands the book to Sasha.

"Read me the number, *querida*," she says. "You know you're old when you can't read your own handwriting."

Sasha hears the growling of the motorcycle outside, and steps up to Concepción's front window to peek out. The old woman watches her with interest. In the brooding gloom of night and trees, Artie positions his cycle fastidiously behind Sasha's car, directly parallel to its bumper. He straightens his clothes after he gets off, smoothing pants, tugging at his jacket, a dapper shadow. Then she sees him run both hands over his hair before he starts up Concepción's walk. Sasha thinks, this is a guy on a date. No. Even worse, or better: a guy coming to pick up his high school sweetheart for their senior prom. What the hell is going on here, Sasha thinks. Concepción is calm, unmoved by the facts that her grandson has disappeared into some part of Los Angeles's unknown underworld, and Artie Vega does elaborate grooming rituals at two in the morning. And her eyes fill with tears, her chest heaves with heavy underwater breaths that come over her, like an illness, without warning. Life has become incomprehensible and terrifying for Sasha, because, as usual, of Tomas.

"Sit down, honey," Concepción says from her chair. "You should not appear anxious. Arturo is a tricky customer, and must be dealt with delicately."

"I could kill that midget," Sasha says. The old woman laughs, and Sasha has to control the wracking sobs again, because that laugh is so much like Tomas's.

"Later, we can kill him," Concepción says. "You don't want to kill anyone who might be able to give you information, at least not before they talk."

Artie's courtliness amazes Sasha. He bows to Concepción once he's in the door, makes all the correct small talk, asks after relatives and business. And ignores Sasha completely. More ritual. Then he sits down on the hard piano bench, folds his hands on his skinny thighs, and waits. The pre-interrogation ritual completed, ready for the next step. Ready for the electric cattle prods, Sasha thinks. She takes a deep breath, blinks, tries to find any vestigial traces of Scandinavian ice in her veins, any Gestapo heritage. Too much time around all this hot blood, she thinks, has made me an honorary hysteric. Or maybe I already was one: Remember the Swedish suicide rate. Remember Bergman movies. Bad thoughts: concentrate on here, now. On this skinny little wimp whose throat she wants to cut.

Concepción starts. "Arturo, you saw Tomas leave the restaurant this evening, after the restaurant was all closed up?"

"Yes, Señora." Not a twitch, not a flicker. Artie would make an ideal prisoner of war.

"And was he alone?"

"Yes, Señora."

"Do you have any idea where he might have been going?"

"No, Señora."

"Or who he might have been going to meet?"

"No, Señora."

"You creep, you're not going to tell us anything, are you?" Sasha's voice flies into a higher register, where air is thinner, where tears and sobs are a necessity. Until she realizes that she and Concepción are doing the traditional good cop/bad cop routine, so perfectly it's comical. This thought of theater in real life, of archetypal scenes played out eternally in life and in movies, calms her slightly. Artie, however, is impressed by none of this. He raises his eyebrows, says nothing, looks at Concepción for his next question which he can answer in monosyllables.

"For God's sake, Tomas could be hurt, and you're turning into Gary Cooper here," Sasha yells. But she cannot make him meet her eyes.

"He said he doesn't know where Tomas was going," Concepción says, as if explaining something rudimentary, like eating with a fork, to a retarded child.

"Come on," Sasha says, indignant, "he knows damn well where Tomas was going. Tomas goes to the same places every night, and this jerk doesn't even want to make an educated guess. Tomas either comes straight home, or he comes here for an hour or so, to do the night's receipts. Artie knows that." At this, Artie chuckles, a sinister little smile twisting his face. Which brings Sasha to her feet, transports her to Artie, where she looms nastily.

"You can ask me anything," Artie says.

"The trick in dealing with Artie," Sasha says, "is to ask just the right questions. Exact phrasing. Like in court."

"Arturo always tells me the truth. He's a good boy."

"Sure. But if you don't ask the right question, he's not lying. He's just being evasive."

"I will tell La Señora anything she wants to know."

Sasha plants her face in front of his, two inches away. "Tell *me*, Artie. You don't know where Tomas was going when he left."

"Correct."

Inspiration hits Sasha. "Do you have any idea at all where he might be, right now?"

"Yes," he says, and pauses. Sasha thinks she may have to haul off and slug him if he makes her ask where. But the pause is for dramatic effect. Artie continues, "I believe he might be somewhere with someone named Paul, who was at the restaurant tonight."

Relief washes over Sasha. "That surfer kid?"

"The one Tomas and I were discussing business with. Important business."

Sasha returns to the couch, excited and frightened. Now Mama has to know. "This is bad news. I didn't want to tell you about this. I don't want Tomas to get in trouble again. The thought of Tomas in jail . . ."

Concepción resumes questioning quickly, knowing the next line. "Did Tomas go with this Paul to make illegal business tonight?"

"No, Señora."

Sasha sobs again, all she can do if she can't kill Artie. "Then what the hell's going on here?" Concepción remains silent, studying both of the young people before her. Sasha thinks, she knows something about this, more than she's told me. A thought which chills her, frightens her. Leaves her without allies.

Artie says, slowly, carefully, "I believe that Paul wants Tomas to stay out of the way until our business with him is completed."

Quiet, then the possible horribleness underneath the immediate meaning of this sentence dawns upon Sasha. Concepción nods her head.

"Where has this Paul taken Tomas, Arturo?"

"I do not know," Artie says, though Sasha does not believe him for a moment. And her sense of theater grows alarmingly large, because she might be the audience now, the only one who doesn't know the script here.

"Can you find out?" Concepción asks, too cool, her old, birdlike, musical voice, the voice of someone who did not learn to speak English until late in life, composed, perfect.

"I will try, Señora. But I am certain Tomas is safe. It is all because he talks too much." Concepción smiles.

"How will you try?" Sasha asks, needing information, something to hold onto, something tangible, real. She is completely confused now, and even more upset, and more determined.

"I have a business acquaintance who knows where Paul lives. I will find this acquaintance first thing in the morning. After I sleep." He unfolds his hands, looks at them, puts them together and cracks his knuckles. As if everything has been settled.

"Thank you, Arturo. We will wait for news from you."

This is too much for Sasha. "No, Mama. I'll go with Artie." Surprising both of the other actors in the room. If indeed they are actors.

"Impossible," Artie says with finality.

Concepción enjoys this turn of plot, pats her chair's arms, curls her feet under her like a happy cat. "You shouldn't meddle in Arturo's business, *querida*."

"He's meddled in my *life*," Sasha yells. "Getting Tomas back into drugs, or something godawful connected with them. I'm going with him."

"No way," Artie says. "That would be unbusinesslike."

"You're not getting rid of me, Artie. I'll follow you wherever you go. I'll make your life miserable. I'll ruin any business you might have until you bring Tomas back."

Concepción seems to be trying to keep from laughing. "Perhaps she should go with you after all, Arturo. She is a high-strung girl, and she's worried about her *novio*. You can understand this." Sasha thinks: Is this what goes on between the President and the Russians when they talk about nuclear disarmament? Is the deck this stacked? Am I turning into a complete and total fucking paranoid?

"If you really believe this is the way we should operate, Señora," Artie says, his voice thick with irony and skepticism.

Sasha sinks into the couch, then sits back up, straight, resolute. No way she's going to be left out of rescuing Tomas, even if it means rescuing him from himself.

"You were one step away from finding the police at your door, pal," she says.

Artie and Concepción exchange a hard, steady look, which makes something in Sasha's stomach go cold. Put it away, put it away, she thinks, save the negativity, save the fear. In case, she thinks, I do have to kill this little asshole.

Thirteen
CONCEPCIÓN

Of course, I am no stranger to dealing with Tomas when he is in trouble. Then, he comes to me. Not to his friends. A group of *vatos locos*, crazy boys who are different from the crazy boys my son Tomas knew. Then, the crazy boys drank and took drugs to hide things, hide their pain, hide their flawed characters. If one couldn't make art, one became crazy in my son Tomas's group. This is why my son became crazy, because there is nothing artistic about our family, nothing at all. We live, we deal with adversity, we enjoy pleasure, we don't wear wristwatches. No art in any of this.

But these boys my grandson Tomas knows, they have nothing to hide. They are not deep. They are not phonies. All they are is what they show to the world. That is, all surface. Skin. They live in a universe of superficial sensation, say words like "feel good" and "party" and "get high" and "more" a lot.

I am not a deep woman. Part of the reason I was a perfect wife for the General is that I love the moment, can appreciate the fullness of life in each moment. And I know that moments are both good and bad, and that each is interesting because it passes. But these boys want their lives to be one long moment of pleasure, and that is a mistake. They are like those swimmers in warm seas who become lulled, seduced by the ocean's encompassing and weightless pleasantness and get sucked out into its middle, into a nothingness from which they cannot return. These are lost boys.

Tomas is different. He uses these lost boys as a drug, he pretends to be one of them. But he wants things, he suffers, he learns. Perhaps it is his appreciation of beauty that saves him. None of the others knows what beauty is, or they would wash more, speak better. All they know is sensation, thrill. Tomas wants more from life. But this split in him, this longing to kill the suffering, and this longing at the same time for the truly beautiful, makes him dangerous, gets him into trouble. Then he comes to me, and I must figure out how to save him. I stopped saving his father, because I saw in his father's eyes a loss of the knowledge of beauty, a depravity I could never comprehend. Tomas has no depravity. His eyes remain childlike, full of wonder. Because he is full of wonder, he gets into trouble. The wonder, too, is not a wise wonder. He is like a child who places his hand in the stove's flame once to see what happens, gets burned, heals, then does it again, just to find out if the pretty flame still hurts. Mothers may be wrong, though. This may be a valuable characteristic. Adults stop testing, limit their experiences, avoid pain. Not the General, and, because of his influence on my life, not me. And not Tomas. I see so much of the General in him, and grieve that these times do not permit him to shine, only to be misdirected, confused, and in trouble.

And he does not go to his *novia* when he is in trouble. Because he does not want to appear weak to her. Tomas, the big man, who can handle every catastrophe. I think she is a strong girl, that she could help him, as I helped the General. But he does not allow it. This is his flaw, and one of the few differences between him and the General. Tomas wants adoration only. One day Tomas may learn that women are smart, and capable, and that giving them power, and credit for intelligence, does not weaken him. Then he will be a formidable man.

Until then, he will continue to come to me for help. I am his only true resource. And I would be lying if I said that I did not enjoy this. Who else needs an old woman? Because Tomas is a boy smart enough to get into interesting trouble, because his friends have no soul, because he wants his *novia* to think he is like those bigshot movie heroes, like Clint Eastwood, he needs me. The comfort of my old age.

Fourteen
DOWNTOWN

"Get on the Santa Monica Freeway going east, toward downtown,"
is all Artie says when he gets into Sasha's car at ten the next
morning. She says nothing. If she talks, she'll have to threaten him
with all types of mayhem, describe in grisly detail what she would
like to do to his skinny little body. Reveal that she didn't sleep at
all, the absence of Tomas's warm body, her hovering fears about
what has happened to him. This would serve no purpose, and
might hurt her chances of getting Tomas back today. Diplomacy,
she decides, is all about keeping primitive urges out of conversation. Murder is not part of the language of diplomacy. Today,
she has the soul of a terrorist hiding beneath the facade of a
politician, all for Tomas. Anything for Tomas.

"I will give you directions when the time comes," Artie says as
Sasha works her way into the ubiquitous traffic on the freeway.
Then he takes *Gatsby* out of his jacket and begins to read. She
feels like shit, has trouble concentrating on the black Cadillac that
cuts her off without signaling, and on the orange Toyota pickup
with the "Honk if you love Jesus" and "No Bozos" bumper stickers.
Sasha honks anyway, to keep the guy out of her lane, and the guy

raises a hand in front of his rearview mirror and waves happily at her. The way to make friends in Los Angeles.

Heading east in L.A. is never a treat. You're driving into beige air, a blanket obscuring the tops of skyscrapers. The sound of police helicopters on an incessant search-and-destroy mission gives Vietnam vets freeway flashbacks. Sasha prefers to stay west of La Brea, and avoid the notion of East L.A. completely. So, of course, Artie would take her there.

"I deserve to know where we're going," Sasha finally says when they cross her mental boundary, past La Brea.

"MacArthur Park," Artie says without removing his gaze from *Gatsby*. "You know how to get to MacArthur Park?"

"The place with the little boats?"

"Yes," Artie says. Irritated now. He hates being interrupted.

"Yeah," she says. Guided by anger, she speeds up and slows down erratically, changes lanes at random, forcing other drivers to swerve out of her way. Tomas is God knows where, she thinks. Why should this little fucker sit here reading so calmly? But Artie seems unaware. He flips pages as regularly as he breathes, as if he's home soaking in a hot bath.

Junkies think MacArthur Park is a resort, a health spa. They hang out there in casual groups and singly, leaning on trees, gazing off toward the tiny man-made lake as if it's Lake Como and the Alps decorate the background. Every twenty to thirty feet, a very popular guy saunters, a junkie magnet. The leaners and gazers come to manic life when one of these guys comes near. Wordless commerce, clinging handshakes, and after each group reunion, the junkies disappear into bushes, into stands of trees, into the restrooms for a few minutes. Then they return to lean and gaze some more, radiating happiness of the blood.

In the park, Artie puts the fingers of one hand delicately onto Sasha's elbow to guide her. She slows her steps down to his rhythm, as he slows down to be inconspicuous among all the elastic bodies. They cruise toward the lake, where a couple of the tacky little motor boats putt-putt across the brown water, the boats full of single adults and numerous wriggling and writhing small children.

Sasha hates the feel of Artie's hand on her elbow. The lightness of his touch suggests that he thinks she's leprous. She looks down at him with utter loathing, focuses all the bad vibrations she can muster onto the top of his small head, until she sees him gesture, pointing with his oversized chin ahead of them. She looks where the chin points, and for a moment thinks she's either hallucinating, from lack of sleep and intense distress, or has stepped by mistake onto the set of a Fellini movie. On one of the benches by the lake, a man sits, dressed like Death, all in black, with a black bat-winged hat, black patent-leather shoes, and black gloves. Artie and Sasha sit on the bench closest to Death's, twenty feet away.

Artie yells, "Benny Mohammad!"

The man in black, his eyes obscured behind black-lensed shades, does not turn or acknowledge their presence in any way.

"Benny Mohammad!" Artie yells again. No apparent acknowledgment again. So Artie adds, "You owe me a favor!"

Benny Mohammad makes an elaborate twitch with his whole body, his arms and legs jumping in spasmodic motion. He sweeps his hands in front of his body, like a priest offering a mass blessing, or an orchestra conductor warming up.

"*Mais oui*, bro'. I'll help you out," Benny Mohammad says in a voice strained by his attempt at good humor. "Anything for you, Artie, man." Artie pulls on Sasha's elbow, and they both rise and approach Benny's bench. Artie sits between Sasha and Benny Mohammad. Sasha feels the pressure of patience in her sleep-starved and anxious brain, of having to wait to find anything out, having to rely on Artie Vega. As if her brain has grown two sizes too big, or her skull has shrunk in the wash. No perfect wire from the sky through the top of her head and neck, creating ideal actress's posture, today.

"Who's the bitch?" Benny Mohammad asks. Sasha holds her breath.

"A friend," Artie says.

"Since when do you have friends?" Benny Mohammad says, making mock-polite conversation.

"This young lady is directly involved in the situation I have come to discuss with you," Artie says after a moment's deliberation.

Benny watches a trio of little boys trying to lift the frothy pink skirt of a lone little girl. Once they succeed, after pushing her onto the grass, they lose interest.

"Wait a second, man," Benny Mohammad says, articulating each syllable with the perfection of someone who has gone to great trouble to lose a foreign accent, "just a second. The bitch looks familiar. Somebody better tell me what's going on, or there'll be no help from Benny Mohammad."

Sasha wipes sweaty palms on her pants, wonders if she should speak. But Artie's fingers trill a chord of warning on her arm.

"This is hightly unfair of you," Artie says. "I feel that you are questioning my integrity in a matter of business."

Benny Mohammad taps on his forehead with one black-gloved group of fingers. "I know who this is. Ba-ad news, man. This is Tomas's old lady. Word is that he's in trouble over at the Horse. Bodily harm type of trouble."

Artie stands up. "Benny Mohammad, how many times have you used my intelligence without charge? How many busts have I let you in on so you could conveniently be elsewhere? How many of your cousins have I kept out of the hole with my connections? I resent this attitude of yours. I owe a lot to Tomas, and he is in trouble. That is all there is to this visit. Now. Will you help me, or not?"

Who is this guy masquerading as one of Tomas's busboys? Sasha thinks. Artie's gold Rolex watch glints in the sunlight as he finishes his speech. She feels lighter, even optimistic. Maybe Artie *can* help get Tomas out of trouble. Even Benny Mohammad looks impressed, ashamed, with his head lowered in acquiescence, his profile hidden by the wings of his hat.

"Sure, man. Okay," Benny Mohammad says. "But, I don't know what I can do for you. I'm just a humble drug pusher, man. And I sold all my stuff already this morning."

Suddenly, Sasha thinks she understands everything. She blurts, "Is he part of that big deal you and Tomas were talking about?"

Benny sits up straight, no more shame. Artie looks like he wants to hit her.

"You talk too much," Artie says.

"Holding out on me, Artie Vega?" Benny Mohammad asks as he stands, rising to menacing height, full of black malevolence.

"This is out of your field," Artie says.

Sasha says, thinking only of Tomas, "But I thought you said he knew Paul?" She tries to make sense of the situation, but realizes as soon as she speaks that one understands through silence and watchfulness with men like this. Trying to get in on the negotiations is not the way to get Tomas back. Artie gives her a murderous look. Benny removes his sunglasses to glare at both of them, revealing reddened, avaricious little eyes.

"Okay, man," Benny Mohammad says, "I get it. You and Tomas and Paul. All thinking you could hold out on Benny Mohammad. That's dangerous thinking, bro'. I want to start hearing some explanations, pronto."

Now Sasha gets cagy, forgetting her vow of silence of a moment before. "So let's go get Paul and Tomas, so we can all talk." Artie's shoulders slump. He's beaten. He feels for *Gatsby* in his jacket.

"Yeah, yeah, all right," Benny Mohammad says. "Let's go get Paul and Tomas. You have a car here?"

Sasha nods. Artie, knowing he's momentarily been cut out of the planning, remains silent, alert.

"We'll take your car, then," Benny Mohammad says. "Mine's pig-magnetized."

Sasha nods again, thinking that the limit of her love for Tomas might have been getting into a car with this Benny Mohammad at the wheel.

He continues, "and if we get stopped, you don't know anything. You know no-thing, not a thing, *comprende*? You picked us up hitchhiking. Got it?"

As if Sasha would stop for any hitchhiker, let alone for a skinny little acne-scarred and motorcycle garbed Latino with greasy hair and a Robert Mitchum chin, and this MacArthur Park version of the grim reaper. The idea almost makes her laugh.

"There is no need for such extreme paranoia," Artie says quietly.

This does make Benny Mohammad laugh, a sound like a saw on metal, fingernails on a chalkboard. "That's right, bro'. No need. You and Tomas and Paul are into a deal without including your old pal Benny Mohammad. I find out all about it from this big-mouthed bitch. But there's no need to be paranoid, right? We're all friends, right?"

For a moment Sasha thinks the two men will get into a fistfight. The smell of danger, adrenalized sweat and something chemical, coming from Benny, fills the air. Though Benny Mahammad is larger, there's something brittle about him, like he'd snap in two. In a fight, she'd have to pick Artie, for tenacity, cunning. And, also, without Artie she'd be alone with this major league creep.

"Come on," Sasha says, weary of this petty macho stuff. She needs to rescue the man she loves, then get some sleep. With Tomas beside her. Artie shakes his head at this unprofessional conduct, but follows her. Benny Mohammad follows her too.

Fifteen
NEWPORT BEACH

A solid hour of palpable menace, skin-scorching ultraviolet rays floating from the backseat to the front as if the seat itself were the Berlin Wall. Plus Benny Momammad cannot sit still. He jiggles his knees, first one for fifteen minutes, then the other for another fifteen, against the back of the seat, giving Sasha's body an unwanted massage. He shifts positions on the seat, occupying first the extreme left side, pasted against the door; then the middle, one hand braced on either window; then the extreme right.

At least he knows the way. He directs her down the San Diego Freeway to the Newport Freeway, then down Newport Boulevard until streets converge into a tight little tangle of beachfronts, expensive postage-stamp lots with gently lapping ocean for back yards. Blond children play around the houses. Blond teenagers carry surfboards as if they're accessories. There's clearly no surf anywhere in the vicinity. Black rubber wetsuits, however, show off slender tanned teenaged bodies to perfection, create the perfect sexual tease, revealing everything while revealing nothing.

Artie reads, unaware, it seems, of the malevolent vibrations rebounding off the back of his head, until Benny Mohammad throws a pointing finger up and out so quickly it rams the car window.

"That's the one," Benny Mohammad says. The finger indicates a particularly beautiful, manicured, two-story New England style house with shutters, two chimneys, a gabled attic with round porthole windows. So Sasha parks.

Then she follows Artie, who follows Benny Mohammad, to the door. The only time she's seen Artie's attitude fail him. He slumps slightly, lets his mouth hang open, swivels his head to take it all in. He's never seen such WASP perfection, in such abundance, life in a television commercial for breakfast cereal which offers the complete minimum daily requirement of vitamins and minerals to assure that you will grow up male and blond and self-satisfied.

"Here we are in Aryan-land," Benny Mohammad says, voice full of cheerful jeopardy. "Put on your armbands. Get those immigration papers ready." Then he knocks. When the door opens a crack, before any human reveals himself, the cacophony assaults the neighborhood. Heavy metal music, animal moaning, and a Berlitz "Spanish for Beginners" tape at full blast, simultaneous, at odds with the white-bread ambience. The kid who materializes inside the house seems unaware of the strange juxtaposition of old Led Zeppelin albums and single-family beachfront dwellings.

"Howdy, Benny," the kid says. Sasha thinks, for a moment, that this is Paul. He's tall, thin, blond, tan, and strikingly good-looking. He wears few clothes, a pair of Levi's 501s hanging dangerously low on his hips, and a pair of aviator glasses. Paul does not wear glasses, Sasha's almost certain.

"Is Paul around?" Benny Mohammad asks, as if such a social visit happens regularly. Hard to imagine Benny dropping in on you for some good conversation and friendly companionship, Sasha thinks. What are these kids up to?

"Sure thing," the Paul look-alike says. "C'mon in." They enter single file, like refugees, or prisoners, or hikers on a narrow trail. This is uncharted territory for all of them. But the facade of privilege gives way to student decor inside. Garage sale furniture, one ratty sofa, one chair with stuffing popping out of its corners, a sparsely inhabited bookshelf made of bricks and boards, an Indian bedspread hung with thumbtacks over a large window on the backyard. Those noisy symbols of young male territoriality, huge black stereo speakers looking like children's coffins stood on their ends, loom in all four corners of the living room. Record album jackets are strewn about in such density they resemble a random, artistic tile flooring; no sign of the albums themselves. The chipped, dented coffee table has a topology as intricate as the Rocky Mountains, with its collection of stacked beer cans dotted here and there with full ash trays. A yellowing poster close-up photo of Bob Weir looking young and puckish, an antique from some older sister or brother's Grateful Dead period, is the only adornment on the walls. Most of the audio air pollution, the heavy metal and the Spanish, comes from upstairs. Somewhere in the house, incense has been burning for weeks without respite, an attempt to cover the stink of stale beer, cigarettes, and grass.

But the animal moaning, both lycanthropic and pathetic, comes from the corner of the living room. Sasha sees an Irish setter turning itself into a canine pretzel next to one of the huge speakers, writhing in such agony she thinks it must be dying from some godawfully painful disease. Only Artie's fingers on her elbow keep her from going to it. Watching it, she thinks of Tomas yet again, in a different way: Is he in pain somewhere, tormented by unseen forces? She wants to cry.

"So, where's my main man Paul," Benny Mohammad says, as if he thinks Paul's spectacled twin has forgotten the purpose of this visit during the time it has taken him to let the three of them in and close the door. Possible.

"Oh, yeah," the kid says. "He's upstairs doing his Spanish homework. I can get him if you want." The kid doesn't move. When he jams his hands into his pants pockets, the Levi's cruise another couple of inches down his hips, showing the blond beginning of pubic hair.

"What's wrong with the dog?" Sasha asks. Maybe the kid hasn't noticed. Maybe he's been made deaf from life in this house.

But the kid smiles, and says pleasantly, "Don't worry about Kelly, man. She's cool. We gave her half a tab of acid this morning, and, man, has she been tripping. She was okay until Paul put on the Van Halen."

"It's cruel to do that to an animal," Sasha says.

"Man, I know," the kid says, still smiling. "But the music helps Paul with his Spanish, and he needs all the help he can get. He's already on academic probation, and has to pass all his classes this quarter or he's out on his ass. His old man wouldn't like that at all." He suddenly seems to realize he isn't being a perfect host: a look of dismay, followed by cheerful dawning. "Hey, have a seat, get a beer from the fridge if you want. I'll go dig Paul up right now. I bet he could use a break." But Sasha and Artie and Benny Mohammad don't move as the kid goes up the stairs. The dog flops on her back, feet waving in the air like an insect turned upside down trying to right itself.

Paul comes right down, with the other kid following him, and Sasha can see the difference between them. Paul's face has some bones and style, a chance of developing character later in life if he can transcend blond as a lifestyle.

"Hey, man," Paul says. "Is this a party?"

"*Qué pasa*, bro'?" Benny Mohammad says. Even when he's imitating friendliness, he's sinister.

"Don't lay that alien tongue on me right now, Benny, man. I gotta pass a foreign language requirement. Fucking Spanish." Paul pauses. A thought only slightly alters his physiognomy. "No offense, Artie."

"This is business," Artie says.

Paul feels better. His face grows smooth once again. "Sure. What's up?"

"We need to talk to Tomas," Benny Mohammad says. Sasha feels as if she cannot breathe, will not breathe until Paul answers.

"So what's that got to do with me?"

Benny Mohammad gets a sly look on his face. Is everyone trying to scam him? "You don't know where Tomas is?"

Paul considers. He's been raised to be helpful and, besides, it's good business. "Whenever I want to see Tomas, I just go over to the Horse at night. You could try that."

Sasha swallows hard, to keep the sobs from happening. Her throat tightens into a length of hard rubber hose. Artie says, "We had reason to believe Tomas would be here with you."

"No kidding," Paul says.

Benny Mohammad throws his hands into the air as if he's about to utter a hallelujah. "Motherfuckers!" he says instead. "You're all in on this deal, and you're just trying to keep me stupid. No one out-cons Benny Mohammad and gets away with it. Little Paul and little Artie and the bitch here, and Tomas, all thinking they can out-con Benny Mohammad."

Paul looks stricken, disappointed, sneaky, and confused at the same time. "Come on, you guys. Artie, man, I thought there was some measure of confidentiality between you and me. I mean, you know I was a little worried about Tomas's part in this all along. But this shit at this moment makes me very unhappy. I thought Tomas would fuck up. Did Tomas tell Benny about our business venture?"

Benny Mohammad looks like a rocket about to blast off to the moon. His whole body goes into motion. "Paul, you are in bi-ig trouble, bro'. You double-dealing skinny little surfer asshole fucker. You think you can jerk Benny Mohammad around? We've done business before and I've never fucked with you like you're fucking with me right now. You are in bi-ig trouble." Unable to stand in one place, Benny paces from speaker to speaker around the living room, his head bent into his chest.

"Fill me in, man," Paul whispers to Artie. "What the hell's going on?"

"Tomas has disappeared," Artie says. Why doesn't Sasha believe him? His reading of the line is off, slightly wrong, lacking in sincerity. An actress notes these things, especially in non-actors trying to pretend they're professionals.

"That fuck-up," Paul says. "He's probably out getting drunk."

Artie shakes his head. "We have reason to believe he is not out getting drunk."

"Yeah? How would you have a piece of information like that?" Benny the Inquisitor asks.

Sasha moans, unable to control her tears any longer. "When he's out getting drunk, he either calls me late at night, or shows up with flowers in the morning." Ruining the businesslike approach of the whole scene.

To fix that, Artie says, monotone, "I saw him get in his truck to go home last night."

"You think this is related to our business?" Paul asks.

"Yes, I do."

Lifting his eyebrows to indicate serious thought, Paul keeps everyone in suspense while he figures things out. "Well, this could be really bad. I mean, just about the only people who might have found anything out about this would be federal cops. The feds are tough. But anyone else who might have found out, unaffiliated types in terms of the government, you know, would be even tougher."

"What does he mean?" Sasha asks. She's terrified now. A vision of Tomas being handed around as a captive by unaffiliated types or by federal agents makes something cold and hard happen in her stomach.

Artie remains silent, not wanting to be an interpreter. So Paul says, "Someone may want to get specific information out of Tomas. The thing is, Tomas doesn't have that information. They might be pretty rough on him until they find out he's telling the truth."

"Oh, God," Sasha says. She sits on the floor, leaning on the couch, trying to fathom what her complete attachment to Tomas has let her in for this time.

"All right. All right. I'm getting more and more pissed off at all of this," Benny Mohammad says in a hissing snake-voice. "Somebody better clue me in to this business, pronto."

Over the din of music and dog-howling and silent looks of hostility among the men, a woman's voice calls out from upstairs, "Paul! Are you coming back up?"

Before he can answer, a pretty young woman skips down the stairs into the snake pit. Her voluptuous figure, hidden only by tight jeans and a bikini top, bounces with each step, hypnotizing Benny and Paul. Even Artie looks surprised.

"Hi, Linda," Sasha says. The missing waitress, the one causing Sasha to work for less tips and put up with the constant reminder of Tomas's possible philandering at work as well as at home.

"Oh, hi," Linda says. "Is this a party?"

"What are you doing here?" Sasha wants some info, wants the universe to make some sense. Then she can believe she'll see Tomas alive again.

"I live here with Paul now," Linda says, then attaches herself to Paul's side with a gluey sexuality that makes Sasha's skin prickle.

"Yeah," Paul says. "Isn't that the coolest?"

Linda, with her long, coarse black hair, and her Latina-Indian pug face, and her natually darker-than-tan abundant skin, is all contrast next to blond Paul, as if the two of them were completely different species. Boy, do opposites attract, Sasha thinks. And then: Is this how Tomas and I look together? Are we a walking collage of clashing images?

Benny Mohammad can't stand the moment of tenderness while he's busy being angry. "Fucking Spanish," he says, mimicking Paul's voice with uncanny accuracy.

Sixteen
CONCEPCIÓN

I believe that cars become larger, and nights become darker, every year that I am alive. Probably a bad sign. Because of this I don't drive much anymore. So much nicer to be driven, to sit and watch the world without the responsibilities of turn indicators and horns and new stop signs growing from previously barren corners.

Tomas likes to drive me to doctors' appointments. These make up an old lady's social life. Tonight, though, I must go to the restaurant, although it is not Sunday, my usual only day there. Because the *novia* is running the place by herself, the first night in over forty years that a member of my immediate family has not been in charge, if I have not been able to take charge myself. Like a good general, I must visit my troops.

But my Buick is enormous, the door squeaks when I open it, the light inside the car no longer works. I find my way onto the seat in the dark garage, lean back. Then I realize how big the steering wheel has become, how high the dashboard. This business of getting old is one cruel joke after another. I feel like a child pretending to drive her father's car. I feel as if the world might easily harm me. Me, an old lady in a massive car in the dark, trying to see beyond dash and hood to the driveway, the street.

I fit the key into the ignition, pump the gas pedal three times, and turn the key. What a tubercular cough from my old car! An intestinal grinding! When was the last time I started it? Another joke: I can't remember. I remember dates from sixty years ago, the dates of important battles, the date of the General's death, the date when I escaped from Mexico carrying only one small valise, crossing the border right before sunrise as if I were a wetback Indian, the General's pearl-handled pistol tucked into my belt. The desert, gray and empty one moment, shimmering like the inside of a seashell when the sun began to light it, to display its detail, the saguaros all looking like dangerous enemies with guns drawn, the scurrying black snaking shapes of small animals searching for their daytime places to hide. But when did I last drive? This I don't remember at all. The dust on the windshield tells me it must have been some time ago. That Tomas! Didn't I ask him to start my Buick only last week? But Tomas forgets many things, and expects me to look after him. Tomas thinks I will never die.

I wait for a few seconds, and think calm thoughts of empty streets, wide and vacant lanes. I picture my old Buick maneuvering through these streets without difficulty. I turn the key again and pump the gas pedal at the same time, and the grinding and coughing turn into a promising sputter. The car comes to life, quivering. The garage fills with blue-black fumes which glow when I pull the headlight switch on, making me feel as if I'm in an old Humphrey Bogart movie. Emergency brake down, and the car lurches forward until I hit the brake with my foot, which barely reaches. How silly I would feel if I shaved the corner of my house on my way out, missed the driveway only because I want to make sure Tomas's *novia* has treated my restaurant with respect and care. I manage to miss the house, but the bushes on the other side of the driveway scratch like ghost-fingers at the car all the way out. This I don't mind. My dim eyes no longer register the quality of a car's paint job. Some aspects of getting old protect you from the mass of disturbing details in the world. Allow you to focus on what's important. Finally I hit the street.

By the time I can see the comforting lights of El Caballo Blanco's sign, my whole body hurts. From leaning forward, with my chin nearly touching the top of the steering wheel. From gripping either side of the wheel too tightly, my hands curled into claws. This business of driving is best left to strong giants, like Tomas's *novia*. That girl could manage my Buick without a single muscle twinge, without effort. Thanks to God, a parking spot right out front of the restaurant. Because it is past closing time, and only a few slow eaters and drinkers remain there. But scanning the customers distracts me. Though some ancient driving instinct makes my arms turn the steering wheel to the right, this instinct doesn't know when to stop, and my tires hit the curb. My Buick's rear end sticks out in an unseemly fashion into the street. I shut the headlights: Let someone hit this old tank. Any insurance company would pay a poor old woman a lot of money if her only means of transportation were damaged. I would like to shake my fist at some sheepish younger driver who had clipped my bumper, or shattered my taillight. There are not many good fights left in my life anymore, too little excitement. I used to look forward to the dawn of a day of battle even more than the General.

Inside the restaurant, I observe the tables. Three of them full, all with regulars whose faces I know. The *novia* sits in the back booth, a bottle of beer in front of her, another young woman sitting across from her. I relax, stand tall, smile. I know how to work the tables better than anybody, better even than Tomas. He learned all he knows from me.

"Hello, my friend," I say to a man at the first table. He's been coming in for fifteen years. "How are you?" I pat him on the shoulder.

"Fine, Señora," he says. "Good to see you." I pass on before conversation happens, though any other night I would stay and chat and encourage him to have more wine, coffee, or dessert. Tonight I want the place cleared out, locked up, safe from anyone not in my immediate family.

At the next table, "My you're looking well," to another man. I open my eyes wide to clear all thoughts from my head except for the vision of this man, and remember. "How is your son?"

"Almost through medical school," the man's wife answers, smiling. This is the secret of good business. Not remembering names, as many people think. Names can fool you. They all sound alike, these Anglo hard consonants and single syllables. But people's stories, the details of their lives, thrill them. People love to hear others recount their family histories. Remembering offspring, sisters, brothers, marriages and divorces, births and deaths, will keep customers returning. As if their own lives were one of my *novelas* on daytime TV. Which, of course, makes me the television, the instrument of presentation only. But, as long as they pay their bills, I am willing to record in my memory the moments of the lives of others.

At the third full table, "Señor, I haven't seen you in years! Is this your girlfriend?" In younger days, I might have risked a wink, to show I knew better. But old people cannot afford any cuteness that might be mistaken for a terminal palsy, a withering and sad disease. No one wants to eat around a diseased old woman. I count on my voice to carry just the right tone of good humor.

"No, my daughter," this customer says, pleased. The girl blushes.

"*Sí, cómo no!*" I say. "My old eyes!"

Now that I have made all the customers happy, I slide into the last booth next to the *novia*, where I can talk with her and still keep my old eyes on everything.

"Hello, *querida*," I say, and slip my arm around her shoulder. Which reminds me of my Buick's steering wheel, it is so high and wide. My arm hurts. This gesture of affection must be quick, but still she looks grateful. "A good night?" I straighten my skirt, rest elbows upon the table, sigh. I am at home. So many nights spent here, in this booth, smelling the sauces and lard and spices, watching people eat and talk and laugh.

"Too good," Sasha says, "You know my friend Claire, Mama?"

The young woman across the table smiles, though she looks as weary as the *novia*.

"Claire helped me out tonight. She works at the same place I usually work," the *novia* says.

"We did fine," Claire says. "Sasha knows this place like the back of her hand. She could take it over tomorrow."

"Jesus, what a thought," Sasha says. "Some guy slipped and fell and threatened to sue, so I gave him a free carafe of wine. A couple of broken glasses. Artie hasn't done a damn thing all evening. I guess everything's in order."

"Always exciting in the restaurant business," I say, and take a sip of the *novia*'s beer. "I wasn't worried, you understand. I only thought you might appreciate a little moral support."

"Thanks, Mama."

Then her face changes, when the young woman from the last table, the daughter of the old regular, comes over. A pretty girl, young. She stops a few feet away, hesitates, then steps up to the table.

"Where's Tomas?" she asks. "On vacation?" The *novia* closes her eyes hard as if she is trying to make the world disappear. I fear for a cutomer-displeasing phrase from her. Or even physical violence: The *novia* is so large, and so physical. Sitting this close to her, I am almost certain I hear a faint, pale-blue hum coming not from the refrigerators or the stoves or the air conditioning that has never worked but always makes noise, but from the *novia*'s body.

"Yeah," the *novia* says. "At the beach." I feel proud of her.

"Well, tell him Cindy says hi when he comes back. Okay?"

"Certainly," I say. Who would name their daughter Cindy?

The girl returns to her table. Sasha and I watch her walk, her round hips swaying, her thighs creeping around each other.

"If I ever see him again, I'll kill him," Sasha says, slamming her hand down onto the table so that the beer bottles jump. Her friend reaches across the table to pat that big hand.

"My *pobrecita*," I say, "this is very hard on you, I know. I remember how I felt when the General went off to the wars. Never knowing if he'd return. Never knowing who wanted to see him dead—his known enemies, or those who seemed to be on his own side." The *novia* shakes her head. Perhaps this was not the right thing to say.

The friend speaks quickly. "She's doing really well. You should have seen her run this whole place."

I say, "Oh, I knew she could do it. I'm not checking up on you, honey. It's just that, before Tomas took over, I used to come in every night at closing time. Just to see how things were, make sure everything was all right."

"I understand, really, Mama. I'm glad you came."

"And driving was quite an adventure! Everyone is so rude these days. Everyone likes to make noise with their horns, likes to play with their headlights. So distracting."

The friend, Claire, checks her watch. "I gotta go. There's that open audition tomorrow, and I want to look something resembling fresh. You're not gonna make it?"

Poor *novia*. She says, "I couldn't look fresh at this point if I slept in a refrigerator for a hundred years." And it's true: lines around her eyes, lavender circles under them. These gringas don't do well with adversity. Their skin needs tranquility to thrive. My skin, like a rattlesnake's, could always stand sun and wind and sand and sleeplessness and grief without revealing anything to the world.

Claire rises, then turns back to us. "You know, you could stay with me. It must be awfully sad for you to be in that house alone. We'd have fun, take your mind off all this."

But Sasha shakes her head. If she speaks, I can see that she might sob. "Okay," the friend says. "It's an open offer. Call me if you need anything." She bends over the table to stroke the *novia*'s blond hair. Which warms me. Affection between women is something I never knew. Women were competitors, were dangerous to me when I was young. One had to depend upon the world of men for affection, and the world of those related by blood. And sometimes, one or the other or even both would fail you. This new fraternity between women is a good thing, though I will never understand it. Claire leaves through the kitchen, and the *novia* shouts out after her, "Careful out back, in the alley!"

"You know," I say to the *novia*, "you could sleep in Tomas's old room, at my house." Her eyes fill with tears, and she hugs me with a strength and ferocity that surprise me. Is there real passion, apart from her brute strength, in her, deep inside that too pale exterior, inside those blue, cow's eyes?

"Oh, Mama. I feel like I'm never going to see him again. I can't believe he's gone." Her strong arms hold me so tight I have to take little shallow breaths.

"Everything may work out. Have hope."

"How can I? Artie sits in the kitchen reading and looking smug. All I can do is cry. And Tomas is still gone."

The middle table's customers fuss with sweaters and napkins, turn to wave at me. So I have an excuse to wriggle my shoulders free of the *novia*'s weightlifter's grip, and I wave back. She doesn't pay any attention to this, so I take a hard look at their table. It's okay. They left their check, and money to pay it, on the table.

"When Tomas was a little boy," I say, "he was too much trouble for his mother and father. They were always flying around, going to parties, drinking champagne. You know what I mean?"

"Jetsetters," she says. These are bad times, when a whole story can be encompassed in one word.

"Spoiled rotten," I continue, choosing my words more carefully, trying to remember if I've seen specific words on those newspapers at the supermarket checkout stands that might help me make my story racier and more concise. "Whatever Tomas wanted, he got. Eight years old and he was pinching maids, stealing cameras, driving motorscooters, sneaking out at night. And what a mouth on him! He learned every bad word in two languages." I pause, to see if she has a word for all this, but she remains silent, looking like a child hearing a fairy tale. "They thought about putting him in a terrible school. A Catholic military academy—nuns and guns. This was when I did my old lady act, and had him sent to me."

"What was he like then?" She brushes tears from her eyes. This kind of love makes me feel as if I've eaten too many milk chocolate candies.

"Oh, so cute," I say. "And a terror."

"What did you do to change him?"

"I loved him. In the right way."

The tears start again. "I love him in the right way too, Mama. This is killing me."

"I know. Have faith, *querida*, that all wrong things will soon be corrected. Now, will you come with me tonight?" And I'm thinking not only of how sad she seems, but also, if she comes with me, I can ask her to leave her car here and drive me, in my Buick, home. I can comfort her in the car, while she handles the steering wheel and the other drivers with her untapped power.

"I can't," she says. "I have to be there. In my real home. In case he calls, or needs me."

"Of course. Then I'm going. It's late for an old woman to be out. The latest I've been out in years."

But she's not finished. "Mama? Will you talk to Artie? Maybe he'll tell you something. He's been hiding out in the kitchen even more than usual. Just a wild goose chase. But I'd feel better."

"I'll talk to Arturo," I say, knowing that Arturo and I have nothing to say to each other. He and I understand each other now. He visited me this morning, before he went to meet the *novia*. When he knew we could speak together alone, in confidence. A good boy, Arturo: clearly he didn't tell the *novia* that we'd spoken.

I get up, my poor body feeling sore, feeling as if it might make the same noise as my Buick's door made when I opened it tonight. The *novia* reaches out for my arm, her face full of concern.

"Mama, take some cushions from the chairs to sit on. To help you see on the drive home," she says, and smiles. I bend over, carefully, to kiss her on the cheek. Sometimes she has more sense than I give her credit for, this *querida* gringa. I decide, this very moment, she can be trusted.

Seventeen
SASHA

Sasha gets home very late after closing the restaurant, counting the night's receipts, driving from Hollywood to Venice. She pulls into their rickety garage, gets out into the misty night, closes the garage door, walks through the alley to their back door. Without any twinge of danger or foreboding. In a daze of assumption of the usual rules pertaining. The usual rules would make any risk to her impossible, because this late Tomas would be up waiting for her, patrolling the house and yard, anxious to question her as to where she's been, and with whom. Tomas's jealousy makes coming home late from work perfectly safe.

When she gets to the back door, where she forgot to leave a light on when she left in the hazy afternoon, and reaches into her purse to hunt for the key chain she had already tossed back into her purse after locking her car, her hand shakes. She looks at it as if it might be a captured dove or rabbit, something fragile and foreign and imperiled, not a part of her stolid self. Then she hears a noise in the alley.

No: not really a noise. A stillness, instead. Someone or something had been moving in the alley, with stealth, trying to be quiet. The end of that movement, that attempt at silence in motion, alerts her, and makes her go cold all over, the mist of the beach at night now under her skin, in her veins, her heart. And the trembling in her hand infects her entire body, moving up her arm, down her legs. Her neck now so weak she feels she might not be able to hold her head up for much longer. She leans her head against the door as tears course down her cheeks, because of the sudden knowledge of the emptiness of the house. No one waits for her. No one patrols the scene with loving and passionate jealousy for her. No one cares who she has been with. Her aloneness closes in upon her, a dense hood like the one an executioner puts on the condemned after he's been asked what his last request is, after that last request has been pathetically gratified. A time, truly, of no hope, and Sasha gives in to it, because nothing else seems possible.

Until whatever it is stirs in the alley again, a tentative shifting of weight, more a vibration in the dense humid air than an actual noise, perceived by skin rather than ears, sound made palpable, as it must be for dogs and great cats seeking prey. Sasha's hand comes to life in her purse, blindly searching for keys. Sasha's other hand grips the door knob to steady the rest of her palpitating body. Keys in lock now, hand turning doorknob, door giving way into the dank mustiness of any uninhabited house, any house left alone for an entire day. Door shut and locked behind her. Now she turns and peers out the porch window trying to see what's going on in the alley, without turning the light on, the smarts of a woman living alone returning to her in a rush. No one. Or: is that a man-size shadow? Or a large foraging dog standing up on one of the neighbor's garbage cans? Now no one again, nothing, as dark shapes and shadows blend into consuming night. Bolt in place, shades in back drawn, and Sasha steps into the kitchen.

She throws the light switch on, and feels comforted by the sink full of dirty dishes. A sign that people lived here once, together, in a sensual existence, eating meals, people who enjoyed life. She grabs a paper towel from the rack, rips, and applies it to her cheeks, rubbing tears and makeup off together, enjoying the roughness of the paper fabric on her skin because it creates a tactile reality separate from fear and trembling and loneliness.

An ashtray on the sink, full of ashes, a roach, a silver alligator roach clip, right out in the open. Anyone peeking into their kitchen could have seen it. Another ash tray with drug-residue and para-phernalia on their small kitchen table. Sasha never realized before how messy Tomas is with his vices: nothing hidden about Tomas, until now. Dangerous, tears welling in her eyes and throat again. Leaving the kitchen light on, because she thinks that tonight she needs lots of light, all the light this house can muster, she scuffs, heavy-footed, heavy-legged, a waitress's signature walk, into the living room, and turns on the overhead light there as well. Then she turns on the small lamps on either side of their ratty old dirt-colored sofa, as if some old, married, comfy couple sat there read-ing mystery novels in preparation for their regular bedtime hour. Sasha and Tomas never sit at either end of the sofa reading novels. Tomas sifts marijuana under those lamps, and rolls joints. Sasha files her nails. No regular bedtime exists for them. Sasha closes her eyes hard, hoping that she can fuse the ghost-couple with herself and Tomas to make this moment feel safer, less extraor-dinary, but the readers remain faceless, and Tomas remains gone.

The day's mail lies scattered by the front door, under the slot. Sasha retrieves it and, numbed, sorts through it. A bill and an advertisement for a sale at one of her favorite clothing stores for her, three bills and a postcard for Tomas. Sasha can't read the signature on the card, but she's certain the handwriting is a wom-an's. Too many loops and swirls, all of it rounded, pert. She turns the card over: Cabo San Lucas. Over again, another attempt to read this handwriting, but her eyes won't focus, from tiredness and another welling batch of tears. Doesn't matter: nothing on the card could cheer her. What if the requisite "wish you were here" appears? Maybe that's where he is, the creep. Cabo San Lucas. Getting a tan, drinking margaritas, making love in the tropics. He'd always promised her they'd go to the tropics for a vacation, some-where where they could lounge naked on the beach all day, sleep in hammocks at night, make love in hammocks. This was at that unspecified point in the future when the restaurant would be doing so well it would run itself. "I'll have an assistant manager, then, *corazón*," Tomas would say. "No prob. We'll take a week off, so I can show you Mexico." Meantime, they'd never had a vacation together, not even a weekend. Not even a free Saturday night. That was when the restaurant was busiest.

"Fuck you!" Sasha says aloud, loud, and throws the card at the front door. The stillness that greets her outburst frightens her. No reciprocal drama, no engagement, no audience: an actress's nightmare, playing to an empty house. She separates the blinds on the front window to check out the small front yard: nothing. The only living thing in the vicinity is back in the alley, either looking for leftover scraps from someone's dinner, or waiting to break into the house and murder her. Fine, Sasha decides, fuck you too. She grabs the brightly-painted Mexican baseball bat they keep in the corner by the door and tucks it under her arm. Anyone messes with me now will be very, very sorry, she thinks. But even this does not comfort her.

More lights on in the hall, which appears curiously naked to Sasha tonight. Nothing on the walls. Why haven't they ever put up photos, like Mama has in her living room, chronicling the existence of a family, together? Why don't they ever take photos of the two of them? No photos, no record of the two of them. This thought makes Sasha gasp. She turns quickly to lean against the wall, and slaps the wall with the baseball bat she forgot was tucked under her arm, making a visible dent in the wall like a meteorite's crater in the desert. *Desaparecido*: like in Argentina, Chile, all those horrible hot fascist Latin countries where people disappear, where family photographs guarantee nothing. Her Tomas, vanished. How is she supposed to deal with this? No one vanishes in cold places, in clean blond places with stable boring governments continuing for centuries, and high level technology in every home, where philosophies of isolation rather than plans of genocide bloom in refrigerated brains. She wishes, for a moment, her eyes shut, that she had more of a taste for boredom.

That she wanted two color televisions and a VCR for her home. A phone-answering machine. A personal computer. All the things that make existence impossible to deny for all the mutant forces in the universe, that ensure the continuation of life against unknown noises in the alley. That negate the possibility of alleys. I've got a Mexican baseball bat, she thinks, and smiles. Maybe Tomas was right: If she had let him buy a gun for their home, she could have it out, cocked, ready, now. But she had become furious, insisted that there was something proto-fascist, cop-like, Charles Bronson-y, about owning a gun for your home, Miss Bleeding Heart Liberal. Tomas understands the dangers of day-to-day life much better than she does, she thinks.

Sasha flips the bathroom light on without going in, because she knows what she'd find there. Tomas's pile of very dirty clothes deposited, just as he'd stepped out of them, in front of the shower, waiting for the laundry genie to collect and wash them. Towels smelling of Tomas draped rather than folded on the towel racks. All of the most intimate of Tomas's belongings, the razor which he only uses two or three times a week, as he hardly has any beard; aloe shampoo; Old Spice stick deodorant; a brown plastic fingernail brush, to get grime and taco residue out from under his nails. All the saddest evidence of his past existence in this house. She decides to avoid using the bathroom for as long as possible, wishes she'd had the foresight to use the ladies' at El Caballo Blanco before leaving. The light on, at least, helps.

Then the bedroom, overhead lights on, night table lights on. Sasha sits heavily on the bed and removes her shoes. The silence is painful, humming in her teeth, inside her head. She removes her shirt, slowly, moving like a small child new to the concept of buttons, and throws it into a far corner, then undoes her pants waistband and zipper and works the pants down her hips and legs without standing up. A hunkering bear way to undress. No posture, no confidence, she thinks now, and no man. She tries to remember the words to any Billie Holiday song, but her brain is too filled up with silence. In her bra and bikini panties she sits on the bed for too long, with only the faintest yearning that she might become vertebrate again. Limbo isn't bad, floating in the ozone isn't bad at a time like this. What is there to wake up to?

Goose bumps all over her white flesh, skin telling her she's cold, without awareness of cold. A robot, she rises, goes to the closet, opens her half of it. Nothing interests her there, all of her carefully selected clothes like dead things, a garment morgue. Who do these clothes belong to? Then she opens Tomas's half: much better. These clothes make sense to her. All his worn, old, soft shirts, some floral hippie leftovers, some Hawaiians, some solid colors for work. She selects a faded flannel plaid, slips it on, buttons it. Like a dress on her, falling to her thighs. Sleeves need rolling up. This accomplished, however, she doesn't feel happier. The shirt smells of Tomas, though he hasn't worn it for months. This triggers more tears, a hopeless cycle. Sasha gets into bed, pulling the covers up, making certain the bat is on the floor next to her.

She dozes, a sleep the function of equal measures of fatigue and agitation, the sleep of a weak and wary animal always ready for flight from a world filled with larger, swifter predators. A sleep so superficial and attuned to the reality of light and sound that the tiny noise of the back doorknob being jiggled causes her to awaken in a sunburst of purple under her eyelids. Her eyes shoot open. Her fingers curl around the bat. All impulse, instinct, heart pounding a jangly creepy message through her body, she thinks nothing but feels like homicide.

Creeping into the hallway, the bat held out in front of her so she can read the royal blue scrollworked "Mexico" cutting through the red and yellow circling stripes, Sasha realizes all the lights are still on in the house. What kind of brain-damaged burglar would try to break into a house so blazingly lit? Stopping to consider this, some germ of conspiracy theory grows in Sasha's brain. She's been consorting with rough types, involved in the disappearance of the person she loves most in the whole world, putting herself into unknown peril. As she takes long, sliding, silent steps through the hall into the living room, her mind takes steps as well. Someone out to get her? Probably not. Living in Venice assures that there's someone out to get everyone, anyone. The maniacs ranting to themselves and God out on the boardwalk. The midnight drunk drivers leaning on their horns for blocks, or smashing into parked cars and careening off into the night, zebra-striping streets with burnt rubber. The fox-eyed leftover hippies, waiting for an open handbag or forgotten camera or unlocked car to karmically and cosmically come their way. Sasha steps into the kitchen now and sees the doorknob shaking, and realizes that anonymous violence and personal, purposeful violence come together in the moment of perpetration. She hefts the baseball bat like Reggie Jackson waiting for a high fastball, steps right up to the brightly lit spot where the door will open wide enough to allow a man to enter. This is the only real certainty about the intruder, the only smart bet Sasha would be willing to place at this moment: a bet on gender. Only a man will come through that door.

When the door opens into the abyss of alley and night, Sasha's eyes can't focus fast enough, can see only a large dark shape beginning to enter, someone crouched, wary, sneaking. But that's enough. Whoever it is must be up to no good, and deserves to be clubbed. She starts to swing the bat as hard as she can toward what she guesses to be the head of the interloper.

"Hey, babe! Wait a second! Don't be angry!" Tomas's voice and her heightened animal awareness cause her to pull her swing, throw the bat onto the floor. Tomas cringes as the bat thumps and pounds and slides across the floor into the kitchen cabinets, wood on wood. She is propelled into him by forces she can only compare, when she has time to think about it, to gravity, or plants growing toward light. Not sure if she's going to scratch his eyes out or slug him with her bare hands now, he puts his arms in front of his face for a moment. But her arms snake around him, trapping him in his defensive posture, and he realizes he's safe. Sasha could never hurt Tomas when she hasn't seen him for more than twenty-four hours. He embraces her by wiggling his arms free, begins to kiss her, when she stiffens.

"Who else is here?" Sasha asks, because at least one shadow lurks outside the door, one near, and maybe one farther away, in the alley, birdlike and watchful.

"It's just Artie," Tomas says, still holding her. Artie steps into the kitchen so he can be seen (does the *novia* have a gun? he wonders. The wisest thing to do if someone holds a gun is to come forward, appear familiar, unmenacing. Smile.). Another realization for Sasha: she's wearing only underwear and Tomas's big shirt, exposing vast expanses of goose-pimpled pale skin of thigh, even a little hip. She pulls at the shirt, frees herself from Tomas's hug to attempt seemliness. Artie looks at the floor.

"*Hasta* lumbago, man," Tomas says, glaring at sheepish Artie. Artie knows he's supposed to disappear.

"I am sorry if we frightened you," Artie says to Sasha and, still examining his shoes, leaves. No one notes that other winged waiting shadow. Sasha and Tomas embrace in the glare of thousands of watts.

In candlelight, Tomas and Sasha on the bed. Now a confusion of impulses for Sasha instead of animal monomania. She wants to make love to him, and she wants to scream chastisements at him, half and half, simultaneously. He unbuttons the first button of his shirt on her body, she strokes his head and kisses his neck. He unbuttons the second button, she draws back and her voice is ice.

"Where have you been?"

All charm and guile. "Baby, I'm sorry. I should have called. But you know me. I was so drunk."

Sasha sits up, crosses her arms on her chest. "Not this time." Tomas reaches for the shirt, to tug on one of its tails, pull her to him. But she slaps his hand away, holds the front of the shirt together chastely in her fists.

"I spent this morning schlepping around with Artie and your creepy pal Benny Mohammad. So don't lie to me."

Now Tomas sits up. "Shit," he says. "Nobody told me Benny Mohammad was involved. How'd he find out?"

"Benny was the only one who knew where Paul lives."

A look of confusion as Tomas tries to add facts up to a precise sum, and can't. "They shouldn't have let you get into this," he says, with such a real edge in his voice that the skin on the back of her neck prickles. The excitement of real danger. He's got her now, she knows. One of the basic reasons she's with Tomas, stays with him: Danger is sexy.

Proud of herself, she says, "I forced them to let me. I had to find you." The kind of line every actress dreams of uttering and making real, complete soap opera, full of heroic feeling.

And he responds with caresses, some corresponding spark rising in him in awareness of her agitation, the endless mirror trick of love. *"Corazón,"* he says, *"mi novia."*

Now anger and need intermingle in one of those surprisingly unappealing hybrids, like a donkey, a tangelo: a whine. "You can't just disappear, and then lie to me, and expect me to take you back without a word," she says, hating herself for losing the aliveness of the drama. Nothing squashes the life out of a scene like a whiney voice. But she can't stop herself. "I'm not some little Latina wall-flower raised to take whatever you dish out because you're the man, you know."

This time he's the one to sit up and away. Stern voiced, "Granny waited as long as she had to for the General to come home. He would be out on the battlefield, or in meetings deciding the fate of the whole country. And she never guilt-tripped him. What was he supposed to do? Call home to check in with the little woman?"

"I'm just so fucking sick and tired of your epic family saga," she says, her tone now a further refinement, whine and resignation.

Tomas yells, "I've got the blood of generals flowing in my veins! I'm not some henpecked WASP CPA working until I can afford a down payment on a house in the San Fernando Valley. Is that what you want? You want to fuck CPAs?"

Adrenalized, rushing, the top of her head full of bubbling gases, now Sasha feels passion fill her, anger burst from her. "You asshole! They told me you might be tortured for information! They told me you might get killed!"

"But I wasn't! Here I am!" he yells back. A still moment, the two of them crouching on the bed, eyes fixed on one another as the scene shifts into another reality, that of the corporeal truth of his return to the living. Simultaneously, they rise to their knees and embrace.

Instantly *in medias res*, bodies fitted tightly against one another. Tomas pulls one hand over her head, through her hair, down her back, over her ass. Pausing there, then continuing, down the backs of her thighs. None of the boredom that well-known territory has caused for him with other women, before knowing Sasha. Instead, the profoundest excitement, the certainty of great pleasure coupled with the possibility of some greater, as yet unimagined depth of sensation: This is what sex is for them. Not novelty, but process, progress, some true expression of their souls, of their closeness, as if in lovemaking they become one brilliant artist creating the perfect work of art. Sasha pushes against his body as his hand trails down her legs, then eases herself away as his hand flutters to the front of her thigh, begins to make its way back up. Until it reaches the crux of her, where she is already wet from the dangerous excitement of the argument, and the knowledge of what would inevitably come after.

"*Querida*," he says, as he caresses her, and she throws her head back, begins to give in completely. Only a moment now, a moment, she thinks, and, this is what I was made for, nothing else. Their ritualized caresses over, he rolls on top of her, into her, and she sucks a quick intake of breath, deep, as if by inhaling she could make more room inside herself for him, or pull him more deeply into her.

He grips her shoulders, kisses her as if he might eat her entire face. She finds the flat of the small of his back, above his ass, where her hands can rest and push, synchronized with his body's rhythm. Both of them now one smoothly working machine, moving toward one goal. All of them wet, Tomas sweating profusely, Sasha sweating too, but also bathed in Tomas's sweat until they seemed oiled, no friction, only glide.

Impossible to know who starts first. With other lovers, Sasha always felt a separateness in climax, a taking of turns, a holding back by one or the other to try to make everything work out equitably, as if sex were mathematics, or commerce. No thought of that with Tomas. Maybe the spark starts in her, in that place so deep inside her it seems spiritual rather than physical, a slow spark, slow warming in her torso which gradually works its way out, diffusing heat and light like rays of sun, like shimmering invisible waves on the surface of a desert. Or maybe her body perceives his subtle quickening, and responds. She wraps her legs around him, tucking her feet in behind his knees as he lifts his body up slightly on his elbows, still moving in her. Then a stillness, a tiny moment, when she pulls him down to her with all her considerable strength. Perhaps she moans, or perhaps the sound is inside her, or perhaps it comes from him, or from both of them. They come together, tears streaming from her eyes into her hair, mixing with her sweat and Tomas's, drenching the pillow.

Afterward, Tomas wants to smoke a joint, he's hungry and wants Sasha to make him a sandwich, he wants to hear about how the restaurant did without him, wants to know if the Lakers won last night. He fills the air with chat as she remains quiet and sullen, aware of the fact that he's saying everything except what she needs to hear.

"First thing in the morning, you gotta take me to pick up my truck so I can get vegetables for the week, babe," he natters, "we must be running low on tomatillos and lettuce, at least. And avocados. Did you check out the avocados at the restaurant? They could be going bad by now."

"I can't believe you're not going to tell me," Sasha says, with enough seriousness to deflect any possible joke he might make, any bit of buffoonery to throw her off course.

"*Corazón*," he coos, "of course. You know I love you."

Completely stern now. "You know that's not it." A pause, to see the hooded look descend upon his eyes, the transparent mendacity he gets away with, most of the time, because no one, least of all Sasha, wants to spoil his good humor at being alive and cute. "What's the scam? Where have you been?" She sees him about to talk, knows that what is about to come from his mouth will be pure falsehood, utter hooey. "And no crap, Tomas. I've been through a lot, and I need to know what's going on."

Mendacity now gives way to grandiosity as Tomas props himself up with two pillows, baring his enormous chest, flicking errant strands of hair out of his face, preparing to wax heroic. Sasha breathes deeply to control the tightening in her throat, the hard fist of anger in her chest. "I'm only here right now because you were stirring things up so much, calling so much attention to what's going down. Babe, there's heavy shit happening," he begins, voice low and urgent. She thinks, he should be the actor in this house, he's the one with the flair for the melodramatic. A movie actor, with his big head, his upper body that makes him appear to be taller than he really is. The Al Pacino eyes. Only the fluke of family got this guy into the restaurant business. And only his own laziness and pleasure in transitory things and complete lack of ambition keep him in that business. Do similar things keep Sasha in this relationship? No. What keeps her in is the same sense of peril that makes any good movie plot work. At any moment, she might lose him. To another woman. To illegal forces she knows nothing about. To unbelievable scams. Or she herself might become embroiled in shady activities because of him, with him. She knows that, whatever he will eventually tell her, and he *will* tell her the truth because she knows how to get it out of him, it will be stupid as hell, impossible, dangerous, and she will be enmeshed in it up to her ears, against all of her cool northern logic, her Scandinavian desire to see a steady and never-ending horizon of icy grays and blues. Tomas will engage her in his movie plot much as a toreador engages a bull in hopeless combat by flourishing that red cape. Tomas continues to do Humphrey Bogart, "and it could be a really big score. It could be an island for us, and running around naked on beaches, and making love all the time. Like, paradise, you know?"

She smacks him on the chest with her open hand. "It's drugs!" she says, despairing at his dumbness and lack of imagination.

But he's offended. "No babe, it's not drugs. I promised you, didn't I? No more drug scams. Give me a break."

"So what the fuck is it?"

Bogart again. He even picks up an already-rolled joint and sticks it into the corner of his mouth, feels around on the night table, then on the floor, then in the blankets, for matches. "I can't tell you. It's dangerous, and I don't want you to get hurt."

"Listen. I spent a whole afternoon chauffeuring Artie and Benny around. I visited Paul and Paul's twin brother. I know that Linda's been turned into a live-in Spanish teacher. Come on. You've got to tell me, so I can trust you again."

"There are people here I have to protect, people you'd never think were involved. The less you know, the better." He lights his joints, sucks in until the tip glows orange, closes his eyes. A wall between them, this drug, she thinks. He gets to go away, forget all about me.

Sasha jumps up from the bed, pulls his shirt on, pushes the sleeves up past her elbows, plants hands on hips. Then knocks the joint out of his hand with one cat swipe, forcing him to cough in surprise as he expels brown smoke.

"You better tell me a little bit of what's going on, right now."

He searches among the bedclothes for the lit joint, finds it, smiles. The scene has been played out for tension and drama, and maximum grandeur for him. He's been stoical, protective, brave, and now he gets to talk. He finds the joint first, and takes another drag.

"It's rubies, babe," he says, and pauses for effect. "I've always loved rubies."

Sasha sits down on the bed, next to Tomas, and leans her head onto his chest to hear his heart beat, the steady drum of it that always assures her everythings's fine. "So how did you and rubies get connected?" She feels beaten, deflated, a victim of his sense of narrative. Now she has to hear all of it.

"Burma, man. The best ones come from Burma, the deepest red. The color they call 'pigeon's blood.' Paul's father is some State Department honcho in Burma who's tired of logging all those flight miles in rinky-dink little single engine planes in the Himalayas. All that Republican shit work. But he wants to retire in style, you know? A big score. So he can afford a house on the eighteenth hole of the country club of his choice." Tomas strokes her hair, lulls her with this bedtime story. "This guy's always been mister three-piece suit. He could bring fourteen-year-old Burmese virgins into the country in that diplomatic pouch and no one would suspect him. Shit, in the Vietnam days, the best smack was brought in by State Department honchos. They all made a bundle. Diplomatic immunity, man. Those rubies'll cruise right in, no sweat. And this is where the bad ass son he wanted to disinherit five years ago comes in handy. Did you know I had to bail Paul out twice when his old man thought it would be a good lesson for the kid to spend the night in jail? Now the old guy comes to Paul to help him lay off the rubies." Tomas pauses, to appreciate the karmic justice of his tale, but Sasha only wants to get to the good part.

"So where do you come in?" she asks, exhausted by work, worry, anger, sex, and Tomas's sense of suspense.

"Paul's gone college, man. He doesn't have the connections anymore, he's so busy doing homework. So Paul comes to me and Artie, and we've got ourselves a deal." Slow motion, Sasha creeps up onto Tomas, sits astride him so she can look into his eyes.

"You really want to do this?" She searches for any flicker of doubt or fear, any sign that all this might be a con to disguise a more down-to-earth scam. Nothing.

"You think I'm some kind of dimwit," he says, hurt. "That I can't pull this off."

"You've already been disappeared."

His face relaxes into happy relief. "But, that was nothing, *corazón*. That was just to protect me, and to get some of our contacts firmed up. I can't get specific about it, but it's nothing to worry about. Trust me. This is foolproof."

Sasha shakes her head slowly, holds his face in her hands. "This scares the hell out of me, Tomas. We're talking big-time illegal here."

"Illegal never bothered me." Pure Bogart.

"Does dead bother you? Because this could get us killed. Last week in the newspaper, I read about these guys in New York who got involved in diamond smuggling. People like us, in over their heads, thinking they were smart. The cops found them bound and gagged, tied to chairs in some tenement. With one bullet in each of their heads. Professional criminals do this kind of shit, Tomas, not people like us."

"What's this 'us' shit?" he yells, his Bogart number disrupted by having a woman in on the deal. Bacall always hung around looking sexy and cool and uninvolved.

"If you're in, I'm in," she says, softly. "Anyway, Paul and Artie already think I'm in. And Benny Mohammad."

"Jesus Christ," Tomas says, twisting his body to start getting up so he can pace and think, but she clamps down on him with her legs, pushes with her arms, forces him to be still beneath her.

"Unless you forget all about this," she begins. But he grabs her shoulders and topples her onto the bed next to him, stronger than she is, and angry. He stomps out of the bedroom, into the hall. She hears him slam the bathroom door, and feels like making some retaliatory loud noise, like throwing their clock-radio at the wall, or through the window. But he's clearly upstaged her, hooked her, and instead she sinks into the bed, the tickle of danger deep inside her as if she were in the instant just before sexual climax. No obvious boundaries exist for her at this moment, no limits: sanity and insanity, responsibility and irresponsibility, recklessness and safety all hover as equal possibilities in her life, and in his, and in theirs.

Eighteen
ARTURO

The alley in back of the Horse resembles, on this perfect Los Angeles afternoon, the Disneyland diorama of the Grand Canyon in its seemingly thought-out assemblage more than any real alley. The dust stratum that always hovers two to three feet above actual ground level blends right into the smoggy air, connecting terra firma and air quality in a watercolor wash pleasing to the senses, harmonious, as long as you don't have to breathe. The junk always littering the actual floor of the alley seems to hover in this haze, like whimsical and useless objects placed inside an aquarium for the amusement of the human eye pleased by anomalous juxtaposition rather than for the comfort of inhabitant fishes. The visual distortion the haze affords, blurring edges, shapes, sizes, makes the alley appear liquid rather than solid and gas. A torn, discarded white shirt looks like an immense and pale carnation blooming. Beer cans look like squishy pillows. Artie's feet and lower legs appear to be an Indian beggar's elephantine limbs, ballooned by disease and the rags swathing it, perhaps double club-footed.

Above the knees, out of the aqueous layer of dust, Artie's cool. He leans on his motorcycle, which leans on the back wall of the restaurant, and he almost makes reading standing up seem to be a leisure activity. Artie's posture becomes an almost balletic feat: the curving back indicating relaxation, the slightly hunched shoulders wrapping the body around the book, the down-tilted head. As if Artie sits in a comfy Barcalounger reading. But, leaning on a motorcycle in an alley makes this body arrangement attitude, position, rather than letting go at home after work, makes it a willed act acknowledging the world as audience. Artie reads *The Great Gatsby* with studied concentration, mouthing some words, turning pages slowly. Perhaps just waiting for the boss to show up with the keys, as it's near opening time. But, Artie has his own set of keys, and Tomas is always late.

A scruffy, alley-regular dog trots by, enraging the invisible Doberman next door into howling, hungry-wolf barks. The dog thinks it knows Artie, or intuits that Artie has something to do with the manufacture of food, and approaches him, floppy-tongued, tail wagging. But Artie has no time for dogs. Head just emerging from the bottom-level murk, the dog stares up at him in that canine effort at psychic connection that in certain humans bends spoons, or in the Soviet Union moves untouched chessmen into strategic positions. The dog, however, fails to draw Artie's attention from the book, and decides to give up and hit the dry cleaner's garbage cans just down the alley. Now Artie reveals something: he glances at his Rolex. He is waiting for someone, and that person must be late.

A loud revving motor noise surrounded by a tremendous throbbing dust cloud careens into the alley, whips into a spot right next to Artie as tires whir and buzz in the dirt that muffles the possibility of a real squeal of rubber. Artie keeps reading. The dust laps away, settles, to reveal a no-longer-shiny silver Porsche, from which Paul emerges coughing effeminately and waving one hand at the dust as if it could be shooed away. Slowly, Artie notes the page he's on and slips the book into its spot inside his jacket.

"Artie, man," Paul says, surfer-friendly, *"qué pasa, hermano?"*

"Pretty good Spanish." Clearly a compliment designed to make a business transaction more efficient. Artie wastes nothing.

"Yeah, Linda's been helping me. Gets better every day."

"You can tell me now why you needed to meet with me," Artie says in a flat shrink's voice. Paul leans back onto his Porsche for the conversation, both men attached by their butts to their metallic machines for grounding and security, for the illusory comfort of a team effort.

"Well," Paul begins, slimy and earnest as a good salesman, "we're a little concerned about things at my end of the transaction."

"Dígame," Artie says, to no response. Then, "tell me."

"I'm confused, man. Was Tomas really kidnapped yesterday, or what?"

"Take my word. Yesterday does not matter," Artie says, in a dead-serious voice making false earnestness impossible. Paul shakes the coughing and sincere fop routine, and gets serious back, a jarring change. For a skinny little acne-scarred Latino man to talk tough makes sense. For a blond-streaked pretty-boy leaning, muscleless, on a silver sports car, tough seems as phony as earnest. Though true tough attaches itself not to appearance, but to some metallic quality of spine and soul.

"Yes it does, man. You brought crazy Benny Mohammad and Tomas's old lady to my house." He pauses to regain some of his false composure. "Where's Tomas now?"

"At home."

"He's not kidnapped any more?"

"Not any more. He is cool now." Artie's voice doesn't waver, but he hopes fervently that Tomas arrives later than usual, doesn't drive up in the middle of this negotiation and act like a clown. Artie, alone, knows he can handle Paul. Tomas becomes a dangerous wild card.

"So where was he?"

Artie says, "I realize that we are partners in a difficult business venture, and I respect your concern. But there are some areas in which you just have to trust me. You know my word is always good."

Paul gets so angry he stands away from his Porsche power base, straightens up to gesticulate. "Without me, there's no deal, man. I'm the one who knows when my dad's coming to town. So it's not a good thing if I'm worried. Or if I feel left out. This is not good psychology, man."

Artie doesn't like this yelling in the alley. So obvious. Everyone can hear. But he feels his own superiority in this situation growing, because Paul is no longer cool. "I take full responsibility. I will deal with Tomas, and with Tomas's old lady."

"And Benny Mohammad?" Paul yells. Artie perceives Paul's point now: Paul is afraid of Benny Mohammad. This is important information.

"Yes," Artie says.

"Benny could get nasty."

"I know."

Paul sinks back against his car, resigned to inferior coolness and lack of knowledge. Artie's complete inscrutability means no one else is going to get anything out of him, either. The perfect prisoner of war. "Okay. Soon as my dad's in, we go into action. We want this business taken care of quickly and smoothly."

"Of course."

"Great," Paul says, enthusiastic, as if closing a big real estate deal. "It'll be Wednesday at the latest. I'll call you when I've got the merchandise."

Now Artie abandons his studied posture. But instead of losing cool, he gains authority, seems to grow a couple of inches and a few pounds. "No," he says, "that is not what we agreed on."

Paul's face goes weak and weasely. "It isn't?"

Artie has this verbal contract memorized. "The agreement was that some representative of our interests gets to be there when your father arrives. Along with you. Because we are sole agents for this merchandise, and have an understandable interest in knowing how much arrives, and when, exactly."

"Come on, man, I wouldn't fuck with you. It's just gonna look strange as hell if I'm there to greet dear old dad with you and Tomas in tow. 'Hey, Pop, good to see you. These are my friends Artie and Tomas. They're glad to see you too.' Uh-huh. No way, José." Artie knows that Paul's point is a good one in terms of appearances, but a bad one in terms of ensuring fair business practices. And altering an agreement without discussion is never a good thing. Especially with Paul in full false-earnest whine. Especially the day after everything nearly falls apart because of Tomas and Tomas's old lady.

Artie says, "we made a deal. We get to see the arrival of the merchandise. Or we do not use our contacts to move it for you. These things are simple." Artie takes *Gatsby* out of his jacket, looks at its cover illustration, a blond man gazing wistfully off the book. Paul knows he's beaten for now.

"Yeah, yeah, all right. I'll call you when I know the day and time, and we can figure this minor difficultly out then."

"No," Artie says. "You know how we have done things up till now. Do not call. The telephone can be risky. Come in."

More whining. "It's a drag of a ride, man. All the way from Newport."

Artie's had enough, unexpected change being the most destructive element in disintegrating business relationships, but he musters all the friendliness he's capable of at the moment. "How fast does that go?" he asks, indicating the Porsche with his copy of *Gatsby*.

Paul's fooled. "Pretty cool, isn't it? It can do 160, easy."

Artie opens the book to his page, reads the first words of the paragraph he'd left off from, then looks at Paul and talks tough. "No problem, then, man. Speed."

"Swell," Paul says, adolescent anger. He gets in his car and whips out of the alley, beating the air into a brownish meringue that rises above Artie's head, making reading impossible.

After a very slow night offering Artie and Tomas too much time to think, the closing ritual. Everyone else gone. Artie does the kitchen, Tomas works on the dining room. He opens the front door and looks both ways down the street, checking for hoods, hangers-out, bums, suspicious people sitting in cars with windows rolled up and lit points of cigarettes illuminating the movement of dark shapes. Nothing. Tomas slams the door hard, pulls on it, jiggles the knob to make sure it's locked, throws the bolt. Then he pulls the shades down on the big front window, so that he can punch out on the cash register in absolute privacy.

Only someone as strong as Tomas can make the ancient cash register spit out its contents. No wimpy robber can succeed. Though it demoralizes Tomas that Sasha did it easily, or at least without complaint, while he was gone. She's strong, that gringa. Tomas collects the neat stacks of bills, rubber-bands them, and puts them in his muslin sack. Then he throws the coins in after them, to be sorted and counted later, at Mama's. The night's checks go in too, so that rudimentary books may be kept on business. Lucky to break $800 tonight, though. Almost better not to count, if it weren't for the nosy IRS.

Artie yells from inside the swinging door, "Kitchen is done."

Tomas pulls a joint from his shirt pocket, holds it under his nose to smell the *sinsemilla* a customer laid on him just as any connoisseur would do with a Havana cigar, then lights up. "Hey, man," he yells to Artie. A thoughtful pause. "You ever carry a piece?"

Artie comes through the door with a quizzical terrier look on his face. "What?" Sometimes he thinks that his universe and Tomas's intersect only at very peculiar places, a dangerous perception to have about one's business partner.

Tomas drags on the joint, holds the smoke with eyes closed Buddha-style, exhales an enormous waft of smog. "A gun," he says, as if language had been the communication problem rather than concept, and smiles. Because of the grass, Artie wonders? Or the pleasing notion of firearms?

"You are crazy, man," Artie says, fearing that this whole transaction may be getting out of hand. May have been a bad idea from the start. Should he have done it without Tomas? This notion of honor can be onerous: He'd felt he owed it to Tomas to let him in, owed it, in fact, to La Señora.

Tomas twists the open end of his muslin sack closed, so that the checks and currency crackle inside like a fire. "You have one at home?"

Must put a stop to this line of thought. "What would I need a gun for?"

"Protection," Tomas says. "What if some kid jumped you in the alley one night when you were the last one leaving here?"

Artie walks up to Tomas, stands a foot in front of him, close enough to make a stoned person good and paranoid, make him pay attention. "No kid would jump me in the alley. I know all the kids who jump people. They come to me when they are in trouble."

"Yeah," Tomas says, and tokes again. Now he'll get to what he really wants to say, Artie thinks. "What if Paul got cute on us?"

Artie shakes his head. "Paul is under control. He needs us." Tomas finally passes the joint, and Artie smokes it with great delicacy, just a taste rather than a drag, a desire for all knowledge rather than an obsession with altered consciousness or escape.

"How about Benny Mohammad?" Tomas asks, serious now.

Artie exhales dark blue smoke through his nose. "There will be no trouble with Benny Mohammad."

"Oh, yeah?" Tomas says. Artie pays attention: There's something he doesn't know. Tomas continues, "He's been hanging around, man."

Artie turns, neatens the arrangement of salt, pepper, sugar on one table, then on the table next to it. Not good to show someone knows more than you do; especially your business partner. Work on the voice: Show no inordinate interest in this information. "Where? Here?"

"My house, man. Like a cockroach—you see him, and then you blink, and then he's gone. He's standing outside in front, or in the alley, and then there's nothing there. It's fucking eerie, man. I don't like it. I worry about Sasha with that creep around."

Artie has forgotten how strange Benny Mohammad can be, because of too many drugs, or environment-conditioned sociopathy, or genetic bad brain chemicals. Artie knows the reasons people turn into weirdos, but he forgets, because he assumes everyone will be as rational as he is, that everyone is, at heart, a philosopher. The limits of his vast logic and interested disinterest. To forget that the world is full of irrationality negates personal philosophy for a businessman like Artie. Now two wild cards to deal with. This transaction looks worse and worse. "I will talk to him," Artie says.

But Tomas can't stop thinking about that birdlike, bat-winged shadow haunting his house. "The guy's really a creep, man. He's crazy." During this intense meditation on Benny Mohammad, Tomas has let his joint go out. A true display of serious thought.

"If it becomes necessary," Artie says, slowly, considering, "we will get him to do business. But no guns, okay?" Discourage criminal behavior at all costs. Tomas may have taken as many drugs, during the course of his foolish life, as Benny Mohammad, making him just as big a risk.

Tomas fingers the unraveling fabric at the opening of his cash sack. "Shitty night, man. Sometimes this restaurant business sucks."

"But it is steady," Artie says, avuncular. Tomas smiles at him, obliterating all trace of readable thought, turning on the charm. Then he proffers the joint to Artie again. Artie thinks, disgusted: other people! He has a sudden vision, unusual for him because of its whimsy: What if everyone had some sort of electronic hookup in their brains which sent a constant stream of subtitles across their foreheads, like at the bottom of French movies, revealing exactly what they were thinking? This thought of instant and accurate information makes Artie happy enough to go home without itching, antsy doubts plaguing him, leaving Tomas puffing his joint in the dining room of El Caballo Blanco with thoughts completely unknowable even to a student of Tomas-ness like Artie Vega.

Nineteen

CONCEPCIÓN

In my old bathrobe, my hair down, sitting like a lump on my old couch, I give only half of my attention to Johnny Carson. Instead of listening to what he says, I think about how old he must be now. He's getting old, that gringo. Gray hair, wrinkles. And the way his clothes never change, everything perfectly medium. Medium-width ties and medium lapels and medium-baggy pants legs. So that he will always be in fashion. So that his shows can be repeated next year and twenty years from now. He'll be making money from his old shows after he's dead, that smart gringo. I wish I had figured out a good deal like that, instead of just getting old without any obvious benefits. With just a restaurant in constant need of attention to fret about.

But I won't have to watch this Johnny Carson long tonight, because Tomas will be by, as always, to do the night's receipts. I did not ask what the *novia* did with the receipts while the restaurant was hers. Not that I really care. Let the tax men come after me! An old woman, clearly not living in luxury, a foreigner with a small business. For the tax man, I only speak Spanish, and I'm senile, and all the recipes at El Caballo Blanco have been handed down for generations in my family. I would have any judge in tears within fifteen minutes. Just let them try to put me in jail. Actually, I made up all the recipes sixty years ago when I needed to start a business to make some money. Me, who'd never cooked. The General didn't need a cook by his side during the many battles, the intrigues, the danger. So I invented cooking because of boredom and need, and named the restaurant after the General's horse. Who could have foreseen the way things have worked out?

When Tomas arrives he looks tired but, good boy, he kisses me and doesn't complain. Time off from work doesn't do anybody any good, especially Tomas.

"A difficult night?" I ask. He sits down next to me, sets the cash bag on my coffee table. The sound it makes is a little too hollow, too soft. I can tell it was a slow night tonight, and that the people who did come in didn't eat much.

"You shouldn't watch this shit, Mama," Tomas says, and puts his arm around me. "Fall asleep in front of the television with this on, and you'll wake up a WASP. How'll I explain having a WASP granny?"

I point the wand at the television set and Johnny Carson disappears into a shrinking white pinpoint of light. "*Cómo no*," I say, and laugh. "Me a WASP! But you, you should watch out! With your blond *novia*. Maybe it's contagious!"

"Then I'm in big trouble," Tomas says, "because I do my best to catch whatever Sasha's got."

Tomas empties the cash sack onto my table, coins and packets of bills everywhere. This always makes me feel comfortable and warm. Together, we look at our restaurant's money.

"Bills or change tonight, Mama?"

I look at my hands, flex and bend my fingers to test them. Your hands tell you when you're getting old. They turn into wooden replicas of themselves, and sometimes you have to think very hard to get them to do what you want, what they used to do naturally, without being asked. "My fingers feel a little stiff tonight. Give me the change." Tomas pushes the coins toward me, and collects the bills for himself. This is like a child's game now. I sort the coins, a little nest of quarters, collection of dimes, a corner for nickels, pennies off by themselves, more bother than they're worth. Every so often a Susan B. Anthony silver dollar, or a Kennedy half confuses me for a moment, then makes me happy. Something new and different! Tomas and I are alike in at least this one way—we become bored so very easily, and are delighted by such small things if these things surprise us.

"Is you *novia* glad to have you back?" I ask as I push coins around the table to their correct spots.

"Sure. But she was really pissed off at me first."

With her cow eyes. Hard to imagine her angry. "But that's better now?"

"Yeah." He stops counting a pack of tens, considers, then starts again, having forgotten where he was. And he thinks I don't smell the marijuana smoke on his clothes and hair and breath. The boy can't count when he *hasn't* been smoking that loco weed. "It just feels bad to have to keep things from her, you know?" he says.

"Sometimes things must be kept from people for their own good," I say, hoping to discourage any honesty trend. Young people believe too much these days in revealing all that their souls hold. I knew all I needed to know about the General from looking into his eyes the first time I saw him, when he rode onto my parents' farm with his uniform torn and shredded from battle, his horse bleeding from many wounds, his arm in a sling. But pretending to feel no pain, to be more concerned with his men and their wounds than with his own. We never needed to tell each other the truth.

"What a tough old broad you are!" Tomas says, laughing. I pat his cheek. Such a sweet boy! Tonight, even though he looks tired, he's so handsome. His eyes shine with as much mischief as they did when he was twelve, and he has those strong, dramatic cheekbones, just like the General did. Of course, the *novia* should learn to iron. Tomas always looks rumpled, his shirts always full of tiny creases. And his pants look a little grimy, as if he's worn them one day too many. But these are such minor things, especially for such a fine boy as Tomas. He is full of life and love, and enjoyment. I know that he looks tired because he spent all last night making love with the *novia* after their fight, after he got back home. Not from work, because hardly anybody came into the restaurant tonight. Tired from love. This is the way life should be.

We finish counting, a very very bad night: $787.54. Also bad, because the receipts from the checks add up to $796.35. Neither Tomas nor I know what to do when we come up short. Add our own money to the till? Lie in the ledger? On the other hand, when we come up over, there is no problem. Tomas always needs extra spending money. Tonight, we lie in the ledger, and hope the IRS never realizes that we exist. Until about five years ago, when Tomas really took over, I never kept books at all, never counted receipts, and did they ever come after me? No, those *estúpidos*. Tomas looks worried as he enters the numbers into the big green canvas book, though. Disparity in numbers makes him unhappy.

"The restaurant business is no business for you to spend the rest of your life in," I say as he closes the book, to reassure him.

"I know, Mama," he says.

"It's good that you are making other plans," I say. More reassurance. Instead, he only appears to be more worried.

"Mama, I'm thinking about getting a gun," he says. First, I think: Tomas and guns should not mix. He can be hotheaded, thoughtless, can act before he thinks. I remember how hard I worked to keep him away from weapons when he was a teenager. No Swiss army knife with all those little arms and hands that pretend to be for opening cans in the woods, fixing broken nails, but are really for stabbing other people in imaginatively painful ways. When all the other boys had Swiss army knives, a fad when Tomas was in junior high school, Tomas went without. One of the few times in his whole life with me that I refused him anything.

But then I think, life can be dangerous. Right now, Tomas knows some people who do not respect you simply because you speak firmly and well and can make them laugh. Respect can be bought with guns from people who never respect anything else but the potential for violence. I learned this from the General. And, as well, Tomas is now an adult. Now, I have to trust Tomas to know what he needs in life. I always worried that Tomas would not live to be thirty years old, he was such a *vato loco*. The rough boys he ran around with. His heritage of crazy behavior, of drinking and carrying on past all the limits of sanity and good health. Then, Tomas passed thirty, still crazy but in many basic, important ways very solid. For which I must give myself much of the credit, I admit. All the love I gave that boy! And he continues to count receipts with me every night, like a mature person. I must learn to trust him, and his instincts, trust him as much as I love him.

"Good," I say, but cannot stop myself. I must give advice, must tell some of my own story. Me, a real Ancient Mariner, always applying my sad and thrilling history to everyone else's troubles. *Dios mio.* "The General wouldn't go to sleep without a rifle by the side of the bed and a pistol under his pillow. Many nights I too slept with my own pistol in my hand, afraid. Because the General was a sounder sleeper than me."

"Great," Tomas says. "Don't tell me about the General and guns—remember all the good it did him." We both laugh. Even tragedies, if enough decades separate you from them, become humorous. And Tomas knows I can laugh at everything, especially myself. What good did guns do for the General?

"*Bueno*," I say. "Perhaps you should have a gun. Just don't depend upon it to protect you." *This* is good advice. No gun alone will keep Tomas alive and out of trouble. He nods, as if he understands, but then he picks up the television wand and, as if bored, or needing to forget, pushes the buttons, snapping the TV on and flying through the stations. And I have no idea if Tomas has heard me, or understood me. He is like his child-self still, too easily bored to be truly smart. This inability to concentrate on an issue, meditate on it, makes me worry about Tomas. How can he make intelligent decisions in times of risk? For the General, life was different. No chance to get bored, because everywhere around him was constant peril, war, enemies. So many possible deaths surrounded the General. For Tomas, life surrounds him with pleasures, so he can forget about guns and watch television when my talk becomes tiresome, the talk of an old and lonely woman. Life would do Tomas a favor by throwing some real and constant peril his way. Then he might exploit all the gifts I know he has in his soul. Then he could be, truly, like the General. That would make me very happy.

Twenty
TOMAS

Tonight, Tomas feels the pressures of business and family combined to give his life an underwater, slow-motion effect, as if air
were liquid, heavy, holding him down beneath its surface as if he
has stones in his pockets. Effeminate, suicidal, Virginia Woolf-ish
feelings, which disturb him. When he has thought of suicide, it is
male and romantic, with guns, and self splattered permanently
onto environs, dramatic rather than passive, Hemingwayesque.
Not that Tomas has given much thought to suicide. No sex, drugs,
nor rock 'n' roll after suicide, no seeing the aftershocks of one's
own drama. With a good drunk, you have a good hangover afterward, a continuation of sensation. Tomas cannot quite fathom any
event that does not present a soap opera of aftereffects for himself,
an ongoing ripple underlining not only his existence but his con-
sequence in the world.

It's nine-thirty, and the restaurant is still jumping, every table
and booth full, including the back one at which Artie and Paul sit
waiting for him to finish his host duties and join them to discuss
their own, private, business. Sasha, on her night off, has come in
to help out. Which would normally be great, more attention, more

stimulation, a kiss or squeeze from her added to the usual ladies who come in and act cute, the guys who want to joke or go out back and smoke a joint. But Sasha's seen the powwow in the back booth shaping up, and she glares at Tomas every time they pass on their way into and out of the kitchen, in the aisles of the Horse.

She wants him to tell Artie and Paul that they can smuggle rubies on their own, without him, but that notion makes him feel so unhappy, so out of it. All he wants is a little excitement, the chance to escape the restaurant business into something that suits him more, something that he himself can invent as a career rather than something his granny invented fifty or sixty years ago that he must fit himself into. Not that what he wants hasn't been done before. The life of a man of leisure and wealth. But he feels uniquely suited to it, feels he could give it newness and innovation. He knows he's got a flair in that direction. Why can't Sasha see that? Why can't she see that if he, Tomas, were happier, she would be happier? Because he's the kind of guy who shares his happiness, has a green thumb for good feelings, is a Johnny Appleseed when it comes to cheer and fun. One large table of six gets up after much discussion about how to divide the bill. Tomas rushes over to them.

"How was dinner, guys?" he asks, slapping one young man on the shoulder. Tomas can't remember any of their names, though they've been coming in for a couple of years. Do they go to USC? UCLA? Better not make sports talk.

"Great," the one in the Dodgers jacket says. "This place is really happening."

"And this is a slow night," Tomas says. They laugh politely, and Tomas does too. "You should see us when we're really on a roll. You know, on those special nights when Julio wears his tuxedo, and I answer the phone in my French accent. When we do nouvelle Mexican, really pretty plates with one tiny enchilada and a sprig of cilantro kind of thing."

"Yeah, on those nights the prices go up, too," Dodgers jacket says.

"The guy's a comedian," Tomas says. Then he remembers: USC

business school. Bunch of MBAs-to-be. "Let me know when you get your degree. I'll give you a job figuring out how I can become a millionaire on this place."

The nerdy one in the glasses says, "A liquor license." Which depresses Tomas, because that's what he's always wanted for the restaurant. But that costs a minimum of twenty-thousand. Before the bribes. If this rubies scam comes through, they could get a liquor license within six months, turn this place into a real money-maker. The business-nerds walk out, waving.

"Come back soon, guys," Tomas says, thinking, fucking Trojans. Hope your basketball team never wins another game. As if a liquor license has never occurred to him. Tomas rushes back into the kitchen to make sure Paco and Pablo are getting the last batch of enchiladas together, so that they all can get out of this dump before midnight. Then he stops himself. If he goes into the kitchen, he'll have to see Sasha, who's in there waiting for that last order of food. Jesus. Any other night like this, Tomas could take a break about now, go out into the alley, smoke a joint, look at the stars if they're out, at the smog if they're not. Meditate about things, empty his mind of all the chatter and bad jokes and unremembered names. Breathe deeply for a few minutes. Tonight, the only way out into the alley for dope and meditation is via the Scylla and Charybdis of El Caballo Blanco, Sasha and the cooks. Not to mention Paul and Artie glaring at him for his lack of priorities, restaurant before rubies. More perils than any mythical hero ever had to face. Paul looks cross, motions Tomas over as if Tomas were his butler. Tomas smiles at Paul, makes an elaborate Latin shrug indicating the chaos of good business all around him, and goes to the register. Looking at the money in there always cheers him up a little. Then, after checking out the night's take, Tomas struts back to the gem smuggling business, very casual. He sits down, motions for Bill to come over. The master of his surroundings.

"Hey, blondie," Tomas says, "another round of beers here." Bill nods, indicating he might have heard, or he might be in another universe where the sun always shines and waves are always ten feet high and perfectly shaped, tubular, cresting, endless. Where men become amphibious in their black rubber second skins, and women become blond, naked, and tan.

"Sorry, man. Business," Tomas says, but Paul shakes his head, angry, and starts right in where he'd left off. Tomas has forgotten they'd been arguing. This much motion, this many people, the increased air pressure, Sasha's scowl and Paco's and Pablo's taco sloth fill his head and kill his short-term memory. May as well take drugs if you have to spend your time in a place like this.

"This is ridiculous," Paul says, slapping the table. "You guys are being paranoid and impractical."

Artie struggles with the divisive forces of frustration and diplomacy with the seriousness of Rockefeller. "No. You do not understand. We are just being good businessmen. Even if what we are engaged in is illegal, it is still business, and a certain code of behavior must be enforced."

But before the argument can heat up, a pretty young woman strolls over to their booth. The sound of her denim thighs scraping against each other magnetizes Tomas's and Paul's heads. They have to look at her, like dogs hearing a midnight fire engine siren have to run to the nearest window. Artie, though, seems to be tuned to a different frequency.

"Good night, Tomas," the young woman says, and waits. Her over-large, loosely knitted sweater hangs on her body in a way designed to reveal the absence of underwear. Other women would register this fact, and keep the information in mind for some future occasion when they might want to give that effect, while at the same time judging her harshly for this mildly sluttish appearance. For Tomas and Paul, no fact or judgment registers, only the sensation of increasing distraction as she gets closer. If a lengthy conversation were to ensue, they might figure out why her body is more interesting than her face. But Tomas only wants to get rid of her now.

"Good night, babe," Tomas says. What the fuck's her name? Shelley? Sandy?

The young woman doesn't move. "Will you walk me to the door? I've got something I'd like to tell you." She shifts her body, more grating denim and movement inside the sweater. Ionization of the air over the back booth occurs, excitation in the atmosphere similar to what must happen inside a turned-on microwave oven heating up a frozen dinner.

"Not tonight," Tomas says. This will have to impress Artie—such a businesslike approach, such strength of character. "We're busy here."

"Oh," she says, sexual disappointment in her whine. Who invented women like this? Makes you believe in God and the Devil and the temptation of good men into evil ways to prove some obscure moral point important only to angels and saints. Tomas prays that Sasha stands waiting for her enchiladas, her back to the dining room, because from far, this delicate business of standing up against temptation will only look like a mundane bit of flirting. "Okay," she says.

"Next time, all right?" He smiles warmly, makes genial eye contact even though his eyes long to dart to other parts of her which act as magnetic poles, which call to his fingers.

"Yeah, sure," she says, and walks away, joining an also-pretty friend who giggles, shoots Tomas a look from across the dining room. Paul shakes his head in disapproval. This kid's no fun, Tomas thinks. He used to be fun when he was into getting fucked up and showing his old man that he was bad. Now that he's in business with the old man, he's turned into a younger, tanner version of him. People shouldn't grow up, Tomas thinks, ever. Look at this partnership. A beachboy turned entrepreneur, disdaining a little flirtation while he's got his waitress tucked away at home listening to Berlitz tapes, and Artie, who's wanted to be J. P. Morgan since he was twelve. Tomas thinks, am I the only one here who wants to enjoy my life? Maybe Sasha's right. Maybe I should get out of this deal. Who wants to play with grown-ups?

Paul says, "How businesslike was that, man?"

And Artie agrees. "Women are always interfering."

"Hey, it's my job to be friendly," Tomas says, laughing. He can make friendly sound like a very dirty word. "It keeps business up. I've got to think about the welfare of the restaurant."

"No problem," Artie says, back on track. "Now what are we going to do about Paul's father?"

"Look, I'm firm on this point," Paul says. "I won't take you guys with me to the airport. That's like alerting the cops, you know? That's just putting unnecessary bad vibes into the universe."

"Come on," Tomas says. "Parents love me. I'm cute. I'm cuddly."

"You guys are really dense," Paul says. Artie looks at him with complete perplexity. Social unacceptability and commerce have nothing to do with each other in an ideal business relationship.

"I'll wear a tie," Tomas says, and makes a face across the table at Artie, sending him a psychic message: Lighten up, man. "I'll polish my shoes. You can pick out my wardrobe for the day." No laughs. The decibel level of all the conversation in the restaurant and the silverware clanking against plates gets much higher suddenly for Tomas who, unused to signs of stress, thinks about soundproofing the ceiling.

"You guys just don't get it," Paul says, and sighs.

In the kitchen, Sasha waits for her dishes, which have been slowed because of an intense discussion between the cooks about an upcoming prize fight. Sasha drums on the counter with both hands, then kicks the bottom of the counter, turns, and goes to the swinging door to open it a crack. Through it, she can see Tomas, Artie, and Paul having their ongoing serious discussion. She watches Julio make the rounds of his tables, passing right by the back booth and approaching the kitchen. She blocks the door. Julio stops in front of her, waiting for whatever new surprise the *novia* has for him. These gringas, so unpredictable, so full of demands. Gringas shouldn't be allowed to work as waitresses, ethnically unfit for serving food and the teamwork of a restaurant, though blond hair certainly seems to help when it comes to tips.

"Can you hear what they're saying?" Sasha asks.

Julio makes a football running back's move around her, to expedite his trip to the counter, saying, as he sidles, "They are speaking very softly." Then, to Paco and Pablo, *"Cabrónes, dónde están los burritos con carne?"*

Surrounded by foreign men interested only in the slow production of food and the quick knockout punch of Carlos Palomino, Sasha feels the silvery rush of anger she seems unable to control lately, and the corresponding brimming of tears in her eyes, and the shortness of breath. She leans against the nearest kitchen wall without thinking about the greasy residue this will leave on her back, and tries to remember cool things, as she and Claire do when they go to auditions. But nothing cool comes to mind in this restaurant full of salsas and chiles and a broken air conditioner. Tomas makes jokes about Mexican air-conditioning in the middle of those hot, hot Santa Ana nights when she can't sleep. He blows on her face, laughs, and her skin prickles with the sexual tingle of contrast, cool breath on warm sweat. God damn Tomas, she thinks. Then she hears, as if for the first time, the loud rock 'n' roll music that's always on in the restaurant, and is particularly loud in the back of the dining room, under the two speakers.

"Let's turn down the music," Sasha says, "it's so loud it's giving me a headache."

Paco doesn't even look up from the burrito he's preparing. "No way, José," he says.

Julio concurs. "Only the boss is allowed to touch the stereo." As if they're talking about the bones of a saint, or the button that controls the missiles pointed toward Moscow—men and their fucking machines, Sasha thinks. Men and their need to symbolically pee on their precious territory.

"Tomas is such a fascist," she says, hoping to work up their Latin dislike of authority. Coups happen every month in some South American and Central American countries. Presidents are routinely shot or disappeared by ambitious generals, and vice versa. Latin America is turning communist. She thinks about all this as she realizes that nobody is paying any attention to her.

"He's the boss," Paco says, as he hands two plates with meat burritos to Julio, who smiles like a contented cat curled up in the sun.

"Hey, bud, I put in my order for enchiladas way before he got in his burritos," Sasha says loudly, and slams a frying pan onto the countertop. Then she goes back to the swinging door for another look at that back booth. As an actress, her lipreading abilities must surpass the general public's. An actress's nightmare, one of the many typical ones, involves going deaf on stage in the middle of a scene in which your memory for dialogue is already shaky. Most actors and actresses pay attention to the movement of lips because of this dream, which at least is a remediable one if this catastrophe were to occur in real life, and if one studied lipreading seriously. The dream in which you find yourself onstage and naked can't be helped. The dream in which you find yourself onstage, in period costume for, say, a Molière farce, and everyone else is in Harold Pinter contemporary English country clothes, leaves you equally helpless. Sasha squints at the back booth, but the lips of Tomas, the lips she knows best in the whole world through both conversation and their connection to her own body, move, and yet communicate nothing to her.

A standoff in the back booth, and Artie decides to take another approach. "Okay," he says, "I understand your point." Though he thinks that Paul's being pigheaded and unreasonable. "Now we have to be creative in solving this problem."

Beer bottles litter the table in various postures, standing, leaning, horizontal, so that the scene seems to be a Dos Equis re-creation of the aftermath of Valley Forge. "Yeah," Paul says. "Like, how?"

"For example," Artie says, looking meaningfully at Tomas, who has become distracted by another large party, a group of five attractive women wriggling their bodies into jackets, leaving. "Who would you take with you to pick up your father at the airport?"

Tomas returns his consciousness to the table, as if just finished with a very demanding form of astral projection. He shifts his gaze as if moving a refrigerator from one end of the dining room to the other. "Yeah," he says, joining in, "like, brothers, sisters, cousins?"

Paul laughs. "Yeah, I've got a brother. Who looks nothing like either of you guys. You can bet on it."

"Another blondie," Tomas says.

"Yeah. Blonder than me."

Artie remains undeterred. He's got an idea, and is leading up to it, developing a sound foundation for its presentation, making his audience pay attention to it. He's creating a subtle philosophical argument, as if the awarding of his Ph.D. depended upon this. "You might take a girlfriend with you."

Literal-minded Paul has no understanding of imagination. "My dad doesn't know about Linda moving in with me yet. I thought I'd wait until this whole deal went down before I told him, you know, just to keep everything cool."

Artie perseveres. "You would not have to take Linda with you. You could take someone else, who your father would think was your girlfriend."

"I'll go in drag," Tomas says, and then does his patented gay voice, that he usually reserves for his Rudy-Nureyev's-masseur-persona's stories. "Your father will simply adore me, Paul, darling."

"Great," Paul says, stacking one empty beer bottle on top of another. "Dad always thought I had terrible taste in women."

Now Artie's ready to reveal his idea, its gestation period having worked up sufficient interest in what it's going to turn out to be. "How about Tomas's old lady?"

"Wait a second, man," Tomas says. "She's furious with me as it is. I don't want her involved in this anymore. I don't even want her to know that this is still going down."

"Hey, that's kind of a cool idea, actually," Paul says.

"It's not a cool idea, man," Tomas says, louder.

"We could ask her if she would do it," Artie says. Reasonable, introducing new aspects of his concept in steps and stages.

Paul says, "She's pretty. My dad would be impressed, seeing me out with an older woman."

Now Tomas is really pissed off. "She's not that much older than you, chump. You make her sound like she's over the hill. I don't hang out with old bags."

"That is not what he meant," Artie says, holding his hands up, flat, palms out, like a dog trainer trying to teach a rambunctious pup to stay. "He meant that his father would like it. We are making progress here."

"Okay, okay," Tomas says, nodding, losing the mass and bulk he instantly put on in his anger, chest resuming normal size, everything on the surface for him, overt, nothing hidden. "I get it."

"It's a deal?" Paul asks. Artie and Tomas look at one another, then nod. "Because, I'd still rather go alone. But if you guys are going to be weird about this, I kinda like the idea of taking your old lady along as the peacekeeping force." He stops, considers. Tomas can see that Paul's picturing Sasha, remembering her, maybe even imagining her without clothes, certainly the limits of Paul's fantasy abilities. The little asshole, Tomas thinks, he better watch out. Artie kicks him under the table.

"Good," Artie says. "We are very pleased."

Tomas says, "We've still got to ask her."

In the kitchen, Tomas sees his cooks doing no work, lounging like men at the racetrack. They stand to attention when they see him, make lame attempts to appear to be cleaning up. Pablo scrapes the grill with a knife, and Paco bangs one pot into another. Noise must indicate busyness.

But Tomas doesn't seem to notice. "Where's my *novia*?"

"Out back, taking a break," Paco says in syrupy tones. Indicating, she's loafing, but here we are sweating and slaving for you.

"Who said she could take a break?" Tomas says, joking.

But Pablo feels some spirit of individualism and anarchy rise in him. "She was right! She said you were a fascist!" Tomas walks right through the kitchen into the alley, as Paco slugs Pablo in the arm for being such an *estúpido*.

Sasha leans against Tomas's truck, slumped, arms lax, not the usual posture of someone who wants the world to take notice of her. "*Corazón*," he says, "are you tired?"

In a dull voice, energy-less, she says, "Why do I always get worried these days when you call me that?"

He leans next to her, puts his arm around her. "Can't I even call you by a pet name?"

"And when you're concerned about my welfare," she continues. "Then I know something's up."

"A guy has to be careful about everything around you," Tomas says, working up his ire so she'll have to feel bad, have to acquiesce. "I hear you're calling me a fascist in front of my workers."

"Yeah, I'm their hero," Sasha says. "Simón Bolívar."

"You'll have them mutinying before long," he says, and moves in front of her to kiss her, but the moonlight glints oddly in her pale hair, and he stops to examine what seems to be a too-white, rather than yellow, strand.

"What is it?" she asks. "What'd you see?"

He moves her around by the shoulders, trying to get the light to catch her hair in exactly the same way, as he puts his nose to her forehead so he can get a close-up look at her scalp.

"What's going on?"

"False alarm," he says, and kisses the top of her head. "I thought I saw a gray hair."

"Jesus Christ, haven't you ever heard of Clairol? So what if I had a gray hair?" She pushes at his shoulders, then pulls him to her. "You can trade me in on a newer model if you're tired of me."

"Fat chance," he says, and kisses her, leaning her back again onto the truck. He can feel her body go rubbery, melt into him a little as he encircles her with his arms, puts his hands in the middle of her back the way she likes to be hugged. All the manipulative tricks of intimacy. Her mind goes black, blank, filled with only him, for a moment, and then, as always, the wonder comes back. Why does he affect her this way? What does this mean, this spark that never seems to go out, even though it might occasionally waver, or turn from passion to anger and back again?

"Babe, I need your help," he says at the end of the kiss, and she knows she's been had.

"You didn't tell them you were out of it, did you," she says softly, sadly.

"No. I'm still in."

"Okay," she says. "I'm in too. But I'm not a smuggler. I'm an actress, and a damned good waitress. And that's it. I don't think I have an ounce of criminal instinct in me."

Tomas is enthusiastic now, and she wonders what she said that was right, was what he wanted to hear. "Yeah, that's great," he says. "All you have to do is act." He kisses her again, with a slightly different kind of passion, as if she's being rewarded rather than desired. "This is terrific, babe, You won't be sorry."

But she thinks: big trouble. We're really in for it now.

Twenty-one
SASHA

I hate Los Angeles International Airport, because I'm never the one flying off somewhere, or just coming home from vacation. I'm always the one with the car, picking up or dropping off. Dropping off is no fun because friends about to go on vacation have already left you behind, mentally. You're like a checklist of bathroom items they made and then crumpled up after packing each item. Useless, now. They look at their watches a lot, worry about whether they brought enough suntan lotion or hair mousse. As if you can't buy that stuff on vacation. What fun is that for you? Picking up is even worse, though. Friends who you pick up are on vacation standard time. Slow. The freeway's crowded? No problem. They're not the ones who have to be at work at six. They're still on the beach at Tahiti in their heads, frying their skin and drinking cocktails with itty bitty paper parasols in them. I hate picking up tan people in Hawaiian shirts. Even worse if those people are wearing leis. I hate the airport.

I wonder how I can use this hatred in my performance today. Hating the airport is not a good thing for my character. Maybe I could funnel it into the probable anxiety at meeting new in-laws.

But anxiety does nothing for this part either. Quiet, watchful friendliness is what I need, which demands a different kind of acting than I usually do. I usually work hard at putting out energy, giving myself a kind of glow. Because of my type. Big blondes aren't supposed to look pensive. We don't play Ophelia, we don't play Lady Macbeth, we don't even play Eliza Doolittle. We play health. This can be more demanding than it sounds, because most days I'd rather be in bed reading magazines, or with Tomas, than out trying to shine. But we do shampoo commercials, and granola, and suntan lotion. I did a Coke commercial once, too. I glowed as I roller-skated down the Venice boardwalk wearing nearly no clothes. I'm trying to talk myself into liking this part, into believing this really is a part rather than kind of scummy real life, as Paul and I wait at a crosswalk in front of the Pan Am terminal. Paul glows, though he probably doesn't know it. And I don't even like Paul. He looks healthy as hell, and he's the little creep who's gotten Tomas into trouble again.

No. Correction. Tomas has gotten Tomas into trouble. Again. And me along with him. But I still don't like Paul.

The afternoon doesn't give us a break. It glares, the kind of heat that makes you sweat under your clothes. As if smuggling gems weren't sticky-making enough. And all these people headed for the international terminals, crowded onto the curb with us. Everyone's got too much luggage. Traveling light a completely abstract concept, something Jean-Paul Sartre invented one day when he'd had too much absinthe. One guy's got three bags loaded onto a steel contraption perfectly fitted to his suitcases like a custom-made torture device. A lady has little wheels on her two bags, and walks them on leashes as if they were Afghan hounds. Don't they know the rest of the world isn't neatly paved and organized? Haven't they heard of cobblestones? I've got to calm down and pay some attention to Paul, who's been talking nonstop, on the ride over, since we parked the car. He's into this, worked up about getting the scam under way, and about having me along as Tomas's and Artie's agent. An excuse to unload the story of his life, like

I'm his shrink all of a sudden. He needs to learn the same cosmic lesson as the lady walking her bags and the guys with the perfect steel contraption.

"Okay," Paul says, "here's the info again. Dad's name is Jim." I stare at the flashing "Don't walk" sign as if it's a bad drug experience. There's an approach to this role for me: hallucination. "My brother's name is Jim, Junior. Don't mention my mother at all. Dad hasn't seen her since the divorce five years ago, when she really stuck it to him for heavy community property." DON'T WALK, DON'T WALK, DON'T WALK. One of the bags on wheels nudges my calf like an anxious Seeing Eye dog. Paul goes on, "We've been seeing each other for two months. That means our relationship started just after Dad left on this last trip. It's perfect. He'll really go for it."

I look up into his squinty eyes and say, "How romantic," trying to keep this adolescent under control. His baby-sitter. But my stomach jumps. I'm nervous. Anything might go wrong in this kind of living theater, and here I am used to playing healthy. Used to acting as if I never even get a cold, never perspire, never blink. "So, how do you usually act toward your girlfriends?" This is one of those amazing streetlights that never changes. We'll miss Jim, Sr.'s arrival. Something bad is going to happen.

"Whatya mean?" Paul has no interest in theater.

"You know, do you keep your arm around them all the time, or are you just a hand holder, or are you one of those guys who likes to pretend he doesn't know the woman he's with until another guys comes on to her?"

Now the light changes, and WALK glares down green at us. Paul and I get bumped and pushed into the street first by the overpacked tourists and the rolling suitcases. A policeman on the other side writes out tickets for cars illegally parked as he sizes up all of us. Paul says, as we walk toward the cop, "I guess I'm a hand holder."

"And how do you like your girlfriends to act toward you?"

Paul squints down at me suspiciously. "Were you a psychology major?"

The cop is much more interested in the guy with the guitar case than in me and Paul. Traveling with a guitar must mean drugs stashed somewhere in the luggage, a sure thing. The cop takes a walkie-talkie out of his pocket and signals to someone about this potential bust. Paul's too oblivious to the world, wrapped up in his spy-novel life, too cool now, like he's sleepwalking, like he does this every day.

"Do you think actresses can work on nothing?" I say, playing good and cranky to get him to pay attention to what's going on. "To play a part well, you really have to understand your character. In this role, I'm just a supporting part, so I have to play off you. You're the main character here. I have to understand you."

Into the terminal, through the robot doors that sense our presence. We're magnetized by one of those TV monitors that list all the arrivals and departures. As if there could be twenty flights coming in from Burma. I don't even know any cities in Burma. Where is there an international airport in Burma? Where do connecting flights connect?

"I like," Paul says, studying the little green letters and numbers which are posted just a touch too high and far away, "affection, I guess. I want to be treated nicely."

"Even in front of your father?"

"Nothing outrageous. But you could act like you liked me a lot."

"There's strong emotion to play off of," I say as we walk toward the metal detector. "You want to be liked. Great parts have love, passion, romance in them." Paul's getting irked, wrinkling his forehead at me, diluting the glow, but at least his eyes look awake now.

"Hey, we're just picking my dad up at the airport," he says, and pushes me up to the metal detector first. I lay my purse on the conveyor belt. Maybe Paul's tinny little heart will set the machine off, and this whole scam will fall through painlessly.

The waiting area by the arrival gate looks like a movie studio's commissary at lunchtime. Men in fezes and business suits cruise by with Arabic newspapers. Sheik types in full Lawrence of Arabia regalia. Indian women in saris. A few pale Swedes with that Johnny Winter albino look, washed-out and rat-eyed, my people, my heritage. At least the dark types look alive. Bergman must use special tinted lenses on his cameras to make all those Nordic actresses seem so lush and sexy. With a pink lens, a white mouse could look like Brigitte Bardot.

Every language is being spoken and, standing still while this international hodgepodge flows by, it feels as if I'm remote controlling through TV stations. A spurt of guttural German, blending into melodic Danish, into nasal, sexy French, into clipped Cuban Spanish. I've studied every accent, I can pick them out, I can do them. I just can't understand a word of any of it. Paul leans, like a seasoned lounge lizard in Vegas, against a railing, his eyes focused on something far away that I can't see. Acting as if he doesn't even know me. We wouldn't convince anyone we were lovers. I step up next to him, take his hand, and he stands up straight, like he's been reprimanded.

"Just practicing," I say.

The little creep winks at me, and does this long lazy smile. "Feels fine," he says. Tomas might have to beat him up, later.

"Oh, yeah?" I say. "You're clammy. Nervous, kid?" I'm doing my bit, pretending I'm the heroine of some Howard Hawks tough-guy/tough-gal film. But I'm terrified. This is not my life.

"I just hate waiting for anybody," he says, reptilian. "About ten more minutes. Wanna sit down?"

I wish I had some gum to crack in my mouth. Help me believe I'm hard as nails. "What a cheap date," I say. "You're not gonna buy me magazines, or candy bars?"

Something strange happens to Paul's face. It goes human. It looks young, and hurt, and real. "I spent my whole childhood in fucking airports," he says. "My family was always going overseas. Before I was ten I was in Japan, Russia, Yugoslavia, Hungary, France, Kenya, and Bolivia. Probably some others, too. And all I remember is airports. Some airports had guys standing guard with guns, you know, soldiers, bad-looking dudes who either wanted to kill us or wanted to kill someone else. Some didn't have any guys with guns, which was scary too. Some had welcoming receptions for us, some had angry mobs with placards. You'd think my dad would get sick of airports and stay home for a while. But he loves it. He's a walking ad for American Tourister and Brooks Brothers. The guy could be president."

Here's where I stop Paul's life story. Only because behind him, thirty feet, at one of the candy counters, I see a big black vampirish figure. The weird hat. Like a shadow unattached to any body, it slips behind a magazine rack. I grab Paul's arm. "I thought I saw Benny Mohammad. Behind you. Don't look around! By the candy counter."

"That's impossible."

"How many people look like that?"

"I'll check it out," Paul says. At least he understands basic logic and trends in fashion. Paul goes to the magazine rack, steps behind it, disappears for a moment, then steps back out into the open with the shadow. Having animated conversation with the shadow. Paul points to me. Benny Mohammad nods in my direction, smiles, holds one big hand up in the air, fingers spread, like a magician about to make a coin appear from someone's ear. Then he sweeps his black jacket away from his black shirt and pants with this hand, to reveal, stuck in his pants waistband, a very silver, shiny pistol, small but so mean looking. Nothing looks as mean as a gun. Mean without passion, mean from afar. I'd rather see a rattlesnake than a gun, any day. Benny smiles some more as he lets his jacket fall back into place, matinee over. Benny Mohammad then points one long lean finger at a large bulge in his jacket pocket which is directly over the gun. Paul and Benny walk up to me, and for the first time Paul looks really frightened.

"Benny's been tailing you," Paul says. Tomas talked about shadows in the alley, and I thought he was hallucinating. There are times when I should believe in Tomas.

Benny Mohammad is just a-quiver with delight and amphetamines, a bundle of trembly glee. "What a surprise," he says, "to see Tomas's old lady holding hands with little Paul here. Tomas would love to hear about this, I'm sure."

Now I know what role I've been preparing for. My instincts were right. Get tough. "Charming to see you again, too," I say. Back straight, shoulders and hips slanting, one hand on hip, chin down. I'm thinking of that great tough girl in that old film *Key Largo*. Claire Trevor, with her whiskey voice. That's me.

"What kind of triple cross is going on here, bay-bies," Benny Mohammad asks, suddenly serious, equally repulsive. This guy doesn't grow on you. Paul's weirded out.

"There's no triple cross, man," Paul says, and I understand how fear and weasely lying sound the same in the tone of his voice, how he must have been punished a lot when he was a kid for things he didn't do.

I put my arm around Paul's waist, cuddle up close to him. "It's love, Benny," I say. "A subject you obviously know nothing about. We're running off to Tahiti together, to start a new life."

This makes Benny Mohammad unhappy. No compliment to my acting ability. "Cut the shit, bitch," he says. "I got a friend tucked in my pants that makes tougher types than you shut right up."

Now, I know I'm playing a role, but what about Benny? Benny continues to send weird tuning fork vibrations into the airport insanity. I feel his quivering intensity, the unhearable sound of his anger, somewhere deep inside of myself. But should he be taken seriously? Should Paul and I be terrified, or should we laugh this off as drug-induced dementia, as anomaly, and offer to buy the guy a drink so he can mellow out? Paul's face has an Oreo caste to it, a paleness under the caramel tan which indicates to me something deep-seated and real going on. Paul says, in amazement, "How'd you get that gun past the metal detector?" Paul believes in authority, and in science. And also, clearly, that only blond, cute, college-educated people should be allowed to commit crimes, a real Germanic sensibility that should have gone out of fashion with Leopold and Loeb.

Benny Mohammad likes this question. He does a twitchy thing

with his hat, pulling it down low on his forehead, then tipping it to one side raffishly, but all too speeded up for any charm or grace. "Old Benny Mohammad's a pretty smart dude," he says, nodding, agreeing with the statement he just made. "It's a system, you know? You gotta be cool. I walk through once and set the thing to ringing and clanging, and then I look real confused. 'Who, me?' The security dudes ask me what I've got on me. I shrug, pretend to think for a minute." He pretends to think for us—and it's a scary imitation. When Benny Mohammad pretends to think, he's up to no good. His face goes dark, shuts down into mystery, like someone remembering his worst childhood nightmare for his shrink. But he snaps out of it, opens his eyes wide in imitation of someone having a good idea, inventing the light in the refrigerator. "I feel myself up," he says, doing so, "and then I give them my keys." He reaches into his bulging jacket pocket, and takes out a thick tangle of maybe twenty keys scrunched together onto one tiny key chain that also has a little pocket knife on it. Benny Mohammad holds these up for us, jingles them. This guy is walking dissonance, noise on the hoof. Just being near him makes my spine tingle in that way that fingernails on a blackboard do.

He continues, "So I deposit the keys in their laps, sincere as shit, and calmly walk through again. And I set it off again. 'Whoo, me-ee?' I'm heavy into consternation at this point. They've got a line of thirty people about to miss their flights behind me, all wanting to get detected for metal. The security dudes ask me what the problem might be, starting, by now, to sweat like Nixon, you know? I think and think." More nightmare memories. "Then I come up with the answer." He pulls up both trouser legs, to show us enormous Pilgrim buckles on his boots. Like walking around wearing leg weights. I think, this guy must be strong, must have piano wire muscles under all that heavy black clothing. "Maybe fifty people lined up by now, and some of them are shouting and whistling. One guy even tries to push through the machine, you know? And one of the security dudes has to grab him and, like, detain him." Creating pandemonium makes Benny Mohammad so happy. "At this point, the security dudes are so hassled, and so bored with me, that they hand me back my keys and send me on my way. And I get to keep my little friend."

Paul and I slump together, awed by this superior show of criminal wit. "Man, you got a future with the PLO," Paul says, demoralized.

"Now I want to know what's going on," Benny Mohammad says. "Pronto."

But Paul's tan returns, and his eyelids grow aware of gravity. His version of quick thinking. I feel like I'm getting the world's best acting lesson right now, though I'd be more pleased about it if I were on stage in front of a workshop rather than in one of the international terminals at LAX waiting for pigeon's blood rubies with a beachboy and a speed freak. Paul says, earnest, "We're just here to pick up my dad. He's been overseas for months. That's all, I swear."

Benny's face registers information like a lie detector. Assess the possibility of truth here. "So what's she doing with you?" Find the logical flaw, probe. The question that I expected, and so was already working on.

"We're in love," I say. "Paul wants me to meet his father right away."

"We've been trying to keep all this from Tomas, but it's pretty difficult," Paul adds, getting into the spirit.

"Makes me want to puke," Benny Mohammad says. "Lo-ove, and families. And double dealing."

"It's true, Benny," Paul says. He holds my hand tightly in his. Like two sweaty toads trying to hug.

"Okay," Benny says. "There's still something funny going on. You can't fool old Benny Mohammad. I'll stay out of the way of romance, if that's all this is. Just be cool. Show me you've told me the truth, and nothing bad happens. I'll be watching."

Benny goes back to his magazine rack, where he can hide while still peering through the stacks of *Playboy* and *Penthouse*. Hard for me to figure the seriousness of all this. But it seems a good idea to convince Benny Mohammad we're just two misguided, confused lovers. I turn to Paul and give him a big, wet, gooey kiss on the lips, feel his momentary surprise. But he's smart enough to know the right score on this play. He embraces me, kisses back. A real high school make-out scene, all for Benny Mohammad. This is not what I had in mind when I decided I wanted to be an actress.

So we get as far away from this vampire as possible, which means crowding up to the window as if we're anxious as hell for Paul's father to arrive. All the international types crowd with us as the 747 pulls up. Surrounded by the music of foreign languages, by exotic dress and many skin colors, I feel safer, relaxed. Paul puts his arm around me again, as he glances over his shoulder. That's right. We're supposed to be lovey-dovey, continue the live sex show for Benny Mohammad. The accordion tunnel gets attached to the jet, the international types mill in closer to the gate. Everything's happening now, my real entrance into a life of crime, as various official-looking passengers, men in business suits, all American, get greeted by the ethnic types. Is everybody smuggling gems? Dope? A world of business going on in airports, of in-flight commerce, that I know nothing about. That Tomas knows nothing about. Meeting flights from Burma can be very instructive. It makes you aware of how stupid, unprepared you are for criminal activities. It makes me very angry at Tomas.

"There he is," Paul says, and points to a distinguished-looking man indistinguishable from the other distinguished-looking men disembarking. The guy's got the requisite silver hair and properly debonair minor-league receding hairline. He's got the dark gray three-piece suit and the slightly loosened rep tie. He's got the industrial-strength briefcase. He's got the look of thoughtful anxiety, like the flight's been long and trying, and his flaky son might be late to pick him up. He scans the crowd, frowns at fezes and saris as his eyes light upon them, then sees Paul. Doesn't smile, just nods. Then sees me. Very unhappy look. This guy knew Paul would fuck up in some way, and his expectations are always correct, and fulfilled. Twenty years in the State Department must make you very good at predicting possible modes of behavior, possible courses of action, possible messes. He's primed for disappointment. Jim, Sr. walks right up to Paul and stops, about a foot in front of him, and holds his hand out for his son to shake. Paul doesn't seem to expect a hug. Like a couple of Gary Coopers, they woodenly shake hands.

"Son," Jim, Sr. says. "How are you?" Warm family dialogue. I stand there feeling invisible, because Jim, Sr. works so hard not to look at me.

"Just fine, Dad," Paul says. Then remembers me. "This is Sasha." I'm ready to shake hands with him, a quick study.

"How nice," Jim, Sr. says, in total discomfort. "I didn't think there was going to be anyone but you here to get me, son."

"How do you do, sir," I say. Striking just the right note, polite friendliness, clear deference to the senior statesman. I am ignored.

"I wanted you to meet Sasha, Dad," Paul says.

"This is very unprofessional of you," Jim, Sr. says. I think, this guy talks just like Artie. I make a note to ask him, later, if his favorite book is *The Great Gatsby*, and why.

"Dad, this is my girlfriend," Paul says. A little too whiny. If this fact were real and true, I'd be mighty upset that my guy had to whine about my existence.

"Okay, okay," Jim, Sr. says. "Let's just get out of here in a dignified fashion. We can discuss our business arrangements later."

"Can I help you carry anything, sir?" I ask, and, without thinking, reach for the briefcase. Which does not go over well. Briefcase whiplash. Jim, Sr. jerks it away from my touch, hands it to Paul instead, with significant eye contact between the two of them.

"Everything's okay, really, Dad," Paul says. He doesn't convince me of this, but, then, I know that the creature from the black lagoon is watching.

"Okay," Jim, Sr. says. "I'm sorry. I'm just a little jumpy." And for the first time he makes eye contact with me, and turns on what must be diplomatic charm. Those blue eyes heat right up, look into mine with meaningful intensity, as if he wanted to get me to sign a treaty. "Long flight, you know?"

"I understand, sir," I say. "You must be exhausted."

Jim, Sr. leaves his eyes glued to mine for a bit, then glues them to my other parts. "Fine-looking young lady, son," he says, making me invisible again, but in a different way. I understand Paul much better, his weaseliness, his needy drive. Jim, Sr. says to me, "What did you say your name was?" But my answer gets delayed for a moment, because I catch sight of a large dark shadow sidling along just a couple of feet behind us, a shadow that pulses anxious waves out into the universe like a gloom-rock radio station.

We collect Jim, Sr.'s luggage and begin the trek to the car. The shadow of Benny Mohammad cutting the afternoon's glare, making sunglasses unnecessary. I know he's there behind us as we wait at the crosswalk, as we cross the busy airport street, as we make our way into the tomblike parking structure. Paul carries one enormous suitcase and the briefcase, while Jim, Sr. carries the other, smaller bag. Because I'm a girl, I carry nothing, but it's my job to amuse Jim, Sr., or at least to give him all the information he desires. The burden of entertainment and disclosure, a lousy role.

"How did you meet Paul?" Jim, Sr. asks as we walk. You can tell Jim, Sr. is a professional traveler because of the inconspicuousness of his baggage. Brown leather, a whole herd of cows probably had to die to transport his gray and dark blue and pin-striped suits, but completely unflashy, weathered looking. No wheels, no contraptions. Jim, Sr. knows about all the unpaved streets of the world. Wherever Jim, Sr. goes, he's had native schleppers to carry his bags, and here he has his son. No one would take Jim, Sr. to be an international criminal because of his excessively good taste in clothes and luggage and his realistic outlook about human transportation of bags, a really heavy defense mechanism, impenetrable by police.

"We have some mutual friends," I say, as Paul pretends to be a deaf-mute Himalayan Sherpa guide.

"And you've been seeing him for just a short time," Jim, Sr. says, encapsulating like a news commentator on television. "Since I've been gone on this last trip."

"Yes, that's right."

Now Jim, Sr. gets conspiratorial, though he speaks loudly enough so that Paul must hear. "He's been in trouble since he was little," he says. "I don't know how many times I've had to bail him out—literally, you know."

This pisses Paul off. Amazing, the ability parents have to transform us into cranky nine-year-olds, shrink us as if we were new Levi's in a hot wash. "Dad, this isn't what you should be telling my girl."

"Don't whine at me," Jim, Sr. says. "I hate it when you whine."

Paul whines, "You see? He hasn't seen me in months, and he has to start in right away with this shit."

The gloom of the parking structure, ahead, connects with the gloom of Benny Mohammad, behind. I dread stepping in there. "Listen to the way you talk in front of this lovely young lady," Jim, Sr. says, unaware that we're about to go into cold storage. "You should be ashamed." And to me, "I apologize for my son. I thought I'd raised him better than that." We pause inside the structure, scan the painted letters and numbers on the pillars and walls, hoping Paul's little silver car will materialize. Before Benny Mohammad bumps into us.

"You never raised me at all," Paul says, "you were always at conferences and meetings. I was raised by stewardesses and secretaries."

"Aren't we nearly at the car?" I ask, to make forward motion happen again. I've seen Westerns. I know that Indians never stand still when they're being chased by John Wayne and a posse of Texas Rangers. Forward motion, at all times, and a neat diversion or two if at all possible. Dragging the horses through shallow streams, separating into smaller groups that will meet later, rigging up branches that sweep along behind you, obliterating all traces of hoof-marks. This is what you do out in the open, in Monument Valley. In a cement and steel parking structure, cold and dank on this hot afternoon, I guess all you can do is keep moving toward where you assume that fast little car to be.

"It's over there," Paul says, sticking his chin out in the direction he wants us to go. We move toward that row of neatly parked cars, one set of footsteps behind us. I know who it is, marvel at the serious regularity of those steps. Benny Mohammad follows us with an intensity I've seen only in films of those Hindu mystics who walk barefooted over hot coals and then pretend they haven't been burnt. Benny Mohammad could do that, even though he dresses like a freak and acts like his brain has been chemically treated to make it glow in the dark. His monomania turns into a spiritual force, like at that same point out in the far reaches of the universe where, scientists say, physics becomes poetry. Or vice versa.

Making the turn out of the airport and onto Century Boulevard, with my knees in my teeth because I gave up the front seat to Jim, Sr. Couldn't imagine him jammed up in this make-believe space, and he couldn't imagine it himself. State Department gallantry only goes so far. Even so, I feel lighter, like a prison escapee. The tight little silver womb of the Porsche seems safe. Benny Mohammad isn't here with us. We shoot down the curling ramp, the car low and straining to give the impression of maximum speed even at thirty miles per hour, when we hear a gunning engine, loud, needing a tune-up, hauling alongside. And there's Benny Mohammad, in this enormous, souped-up, low-riding black Chevy Impala, scrunched over the steering wheel in maniac concentration.

"People like that shouldn't be allowed behind the wheels of cars," Jim, Sr. says. Paul turns around for a second to shoot me a look. The he pats the dashboard of his car, like a jockey readying a thoroughbred for the Kentucky Derby.

"That's the kind of driver that doesn't have a penny's worth of insurance," Jim, Sr. continues. "Am I right?" No answer from Paul, who's having some type of psychic communion with his car's motor, willing it to obey him.

"Oh, you're absolutely right," I say.

"You see," Jim, Sr. says. "This young lady knows how to engage in conversation with people." But Paul doesn't let this bother him. It's him and his machine against the world now, very separate and male. We cruise down Century at normal speed, making what seem to be normal lane changes, but I know Paul is testing Benny, watching him in his rearview mirror. Because of my sideways crouch, I can watch too, and I see that whatever we do, Benny Mohammad's big black car does, tailing us like a whale behind a silvery guppy. At the San Diego Freeway on-ramp, Benny pulls right up behind us, throws his car into neutral, and revs. Then, he honks three times, just to let us know he's inescapable, indefatigable, ubiquitous. All those high school vocabulary words designed to put a fear of adult fate into kids. I remember every one of them. They all made me not want to grow up. How did I know they were merely preparing me for a life with Benny Mohammad in it?

Jim, Sr. says, "Paul, do you *know* this person who insists on following us?"

Paul answers without moving his mouth or ungritting his teeth. "Just relax, Dad."

"You know how many crazies there are in southern California," I say, cheery.

"Yes, and Paul knows all of them," Jim, Sr. says. "We have important business going on right now, son. You know what I mean. Should I know anything about our current situation?"

The light changes, we're at the front of the line-up of cars waiting to get on the freeway. As he throws it into first, jamming the accelerator, Paul says, "This car can outrun anything on the road."

This does not make Jim, Sr. happy. "Thank you for telling me that. I should have known better than to involve you in something important."

Someone's got to lighten things up here, and, of course, it's me. "Don't worry, Jim. Paul is a wonderful driver." I imagine I can hear the sound of two sets of artificially straightened, very white teeth grinding from the front seat, though it's probably only some standard feature of the Porsche engine.

Paul does some virtuoso creative driving on the freeway, finding holes in traffic O. J. Simpson couldn't run through, changing lanes with pure, thrilling, horizontal motion. I bounce in the back like a basketball, my head hitting the car's roof, my teeth chattering.

And each time I think we've lost Benny Mohammad, when there are normal, tinny, whirring Japanese cars all around us, from nowhere the whale pulls up, one or two cars back, or just to our left or right, and Benny looks over and glares at us, his mouth stretched taut with concentration and effort. Paul pulls all the way to the left, then onto the shoulder of the freeway where there's clear sailing, stomps the gas, screeches back into the left lane in front of a frightened, hypnotized Toyota driver.

"If you get us killed and my body is found with this stuff, my career will be ruined!" Jim, Sr. yells. He's got himself jammed against the seat and door to keep from loosening his fillings. But Paul pays no attention. He tries another move, a two-lane horizontal switch that really scares me, because of all the noise outside it creates—honking, tires screeching.

I can't help myself. I say, "Tomas will beat the shit out of you if I get hurt." I say it softly, my lips behind Paul's left ear, just for Paul, but of course Jim, Sr. hears it too.

"Who's Tomas?" Jim, Sr. asks. No answer. I feel stupid as hell, so I keep quiet. Paul wishes he had an eject button to help him deal with the old man. Jim, Sr. says, "Paul, are you involved with Mexicans?"

We're just about to the Long Beach Freeway cloverleaf when one of those magical changes in freeway density happens. Everyone in the world's going to Long Beach. No one's staying on the San Diego Freeway like we are. Ahead of us, wide open space, four lanes free of traffic for at least half a mile. Benny's caught a few cars back, behind a bunch of daydreaming late lane changers all trying to get over for the Long Beach ramp.

"Time for hyper-space," Paul says, and floors it. I'm plastered against the back window from the momentum, Jim, Sr. shuts up because he's flattened into his seat. This car flies, grinding away over the concrete as if acceleration were infinite, as if we could go to the moon if we wanted. "All right! One-hundred-and-ten!" Paul says, laughing and hooting. Under an overpass that leads in to the Long Beach Freeway, still nothing ahead of us. But no time to slow down because of the black and white Highway Patrol car sitting there in the shade. The cop peels out, turns on all the lights and the siren, and his voice, like the voice of God, booms out over some infernal speaker device. "Pull over to the right-hand shoulder. Pull over! Pull over!"

"Shit!" Paul says, and slows down to just under the speed of light to consider his next move.

"This boy's been getting speeding tickets since he was fourteen. And then he was driving illegally, in stolen cars," Jim, Sr. says.

"I was trying to save your ass," Paul says, cruising in the next-to-right lane, as if there's still some question about how to deal with a California Highway Patrolman with control over flashing blue and yellow and red lights on his hot little Mustang, and with a gun on his hip.

"Don't talk to your father that way," Jim, Sr. lectures.

"Just pull over," I say. "Let's be cool about this."

Amazingly, Paul listens to me, and we do pull over, the CHP car right behind us. Jim, Sr. clutches his briefcase on his lap as Paul opens the car door to deal with the cop.

Jim, Sr. and I hear the cop say, "Someone in this car better be about to give birth to triplets or save the free world from the Soviets."

Jim, Sr. turns to me, and says, with Republican despair, "Whatever happened to where's the fire? Nothing in the world ever stays the same. There's no place for traditional values anymore."

Not that I have any answer for that one. But as soon as Jim, Sr. finishes his complaint, I feel the presence of the shadow. I turn, and see Benny Mohammad's black behemoth go speeding by on the clear and empty freeway. He turns his head toward the stopped Porsche, his mouth opens in some foreign, obscene expression of rage. He shakes his fist at us. And continues on down the freeway. I don't even want to imagine what his destination might be.

Twenty-two
SASHA

We drop Pop off at the new Hilton complex, and negotiate the driveway you can get into but can't get out of. It's all over unless you're a guest of the hotel. Guests get to go in, present a major credit card, head for the elevator banks and then for their king-size beds. Unsuspecting drivers assume everything's cool.

With Jim, Sr. being helped to the door of the hotel by two valets carrying his luggage, with the rubies in Paul's glove box, stashed there by Jim, Sr. when he thought I wasn't looking, Paul takes one deep breath, expels it, closes his eyes for a full beat, and floors the Porsche. To get to where we are now—three possible ways to go, all of them wrong.

If we turn right, we get chewed-up tires from those metal shark jaws they imbed in parking lot chutes. Ahead we see oncoming traffic coming straight toward us, and every manner of STAY OUT, DO NOT ENTER, CAUTION—WRONG WAY, and DANGER sign imaginable. To the left, an expanse of more pale gray concrete blocked by pale concrete buoys. All we can do is circle back to the hotel.

"Fuck!" Paul says, loud. As we circle back, I sink into my seat, thinking cool thoughts, the usual litany. But the temperature inside the Porsche continues to rise, and nothing cools me. I rely on my ultimate cool thought: a trio of ballerinas standing in front of an open refrigerator. One of them holds the freezer door open as well. Inside the freezer, they contemplate, rather than eat, a lone carton of Häagen-Dazs chocolate-chocolate chip ice cream. I actually saw this scene on a hot New York day when, as a new teenaged runaway, I visited a friend who was a member of the corps de ballet of the New York City Ballet. Those girls could not get thin enough. Competitive late night games of count the ribs among the three roommates. And there's robust Sasha, watching this insanity, feeling ravenous. After a couple of days of watching them starve, I hitchhiked to the West Coast, where, when women don't eat, you know it's anorexia or cocaine. In New York, ballet explains all female deprivation.

I like this cool thought best, save it for particularly trying times, because it's a cool thought about a cool thought. Like looking at a TV picture of yourself looking at yourself looking at yourself. It feels artistic to me, like a real creation. I see the three ballerinas in their pink leotards, in front of the refrigerator, and I feel a little bit like Edgar Degas. Better. I look at Paul as we circle back toward the smirking valet. Paul's face turns pink, furious pink, as the car pulls up and I roll down my window, knowing Paul will remain silent, cement.

"How do we get out of here?" I ask the valet who puts his face up close to the open window.

"You see the parking lot?" He pauses. Come on, creep, I think. We've had enough drama for one day. "Take a right before it." Paul snorts at this. How could a street have grown in a place where there was nothing before? We circle again and, sure enough, there's a little turn-off before the lot, and it takes us out to the real world.

"A scam to get tips for the valet," I say.

"I hate that old bastard," Paul hisses. We wait for the light to change. "That international spy routine. Give me a break. All he had to do was hand me the stuff. But no. All that fuss, just to get him to put the stuff into the glove compartment." We speed into the intersection a millisecond before the light changes to green, daring bigger, slower cars to hit us. "He makes me feel like I've got leprosy or something," Paul says. "Like I'm some scum of the earth criminal. Like I'm Bennie Mohammad or something. For Christ's fucking sake, I'm his own son."

I touch Paul's shoulder, compassion, feel the knobby bones of it through his shirt. At the same time, he shifts into a higher gear, the car engine modulating its purr into something keener and sharper. Paul looks at me, a glance really, a quarter turn of the head so he can keep his eyes on the road. And this strange thing happens. Desire. The meaning of the hot pink air inside the Porsche changes. Everything changes. I haven't desired another man, aside from Tomas, for three or four years now, not even in fantasies, not even at the movies. Now here I am, with Paul, because of Tomas, involved in illegal activities, and I'm turned on. You are a sick person, I think, as I feel the rev of the car all over my body. Like I'm in one of those vibrating motel beds in sex jokes. I am in my body, in this moment, in Paul's Porsche. How much clearer can things get? In five minutes we will be at Paul's house.

"You've been really cool with all this shit," Paul says, both hands on the steering wheel. Large, knuckly, masculine hands. Claire would think he was cute.

"We did okay," I say. Is this seduction? On whose part? If Paul would say that he wanted to make love to me, or that I was beautiful or irresistible, I'd be his for the rest of the afternoon. I'm not a subtle person. Don't like what I can't see and hear and taste and feel and smell. This teenaged come-on is too roundabout, too much a dance, for me. I can feel desire begin to drain out of me, just like Paul pulled a plug in my big toe. Leaving me light-headed, with the beginnings of disappointment and headache.

But then he reaches over to downshift and overshoots his mark. (Which he reaches for a zillion times a day, right? I saw him on the freeway. The kid's a pro. This car's his baby.) So that his fingers graze my left thigh, just the tips of them, and then they jerk away as if they've been too close to flame. My thigh white-hot, emanating sex X-rays. And I get the old electric charge, the blue spark up to brain and down to feet, bride of Frankenstein.

"Sorry," Paul says, but doesn't look at me.

By the time we reach his house, we've both been struck dumb, and we have pulsating auras that could give anyone in the vicinity a sunburn. We crackle. I reach up to smooth my hair, and it sticks to my hand, shivers in the air, fans into straight edgy wisps. When I take the rubies, in their flannel pouch, from the glove box, the world stands still, re-evaluating its most basic principles. Gravity, rotation, revolution. I, Sasha, have got to be considered as a strong contender for the position of center of the universe right now. Then the feeling's gone, grandiosity lasting, for me, only as long as I don't blink. Some actors can sustain that puffed-up-ness, and either ruin their careers, or convince others. Mostly the former. But, right now, Paul believes that I am the magnetic north pole. He looks at me as if I'm the only live female thing he's ever seen, or the first. We sit in the car for longer than we have to, both of us facing straight ahead looking out the windshield. Maybe because the quiet street presents nothing for our eyes to fix upon, Paul has to talk. If there had been a kid on a tricycle or a car wreck, we might have sat here, silent, forever.

"So, are you gonna come in?" Paul asks. Voice curiously flat.

No, I think, I'm gonna sit here in the car for a week and a half. Have pizzas delivered at mealtimes. "Sure," I say, "we've got business to finish up."

Soon as I speak, we each reach for our door handles, open the doors, step out and up. Like that group of Air Force speed freaks flying in perfect formation at redneck shows out in the desert. This is what lust does to you: turns you into one of the Rockettes. We float up the sidewalk to his house like a science project in magnetic attraction and repulsion, keeping a consistent distance of a foot between us.

"Are Linda and your roommate home?" I ask as we near the door. Important information to have, with my body zinging like a tuning fork, sending coded messages to Jupiter.

This throws Paul off course. He stops, looks at the curb with serious intent. I stop next to him, a little ahead of him. "Their cars aren't here," he says. I think about counting cards to win at blackjack. When you keep track of all the high cards and low cards that have already left the deck, you have a better chance, mathematically speaking, of predicting what the next card you'll be dealt will be. Helps you make the correct bet. Paul and I start toward the house again.

Then I feel the way astronauts must feel in that moment when someone at Mission Control turns the capsule gravity off. We see, at the same time, that the door to the house is about two inches ajar. Not the way boys dallying on the criminal fringes operate. Paul pushes the door all the way open with his foot, and we peer in. And I realize that what I previously thought about Paul's lack of housekeeping was completely wrong. Paul's house was pin-neat compared with the tornado-wrought mess now inside. Natural catastrophe has struck this living room, and the sight of it cools sexual desire the way Gatorade quenches athletic thirst on those TV commercials.

"Jesus fucking Christ," Paul says as we walk in, stand like over-stimulated zombies next to what was once a couch. Alligators have been let loose in here, or amok ticker-tape machines. Everything's been shredded, newspapers and furniture and record albums, some great equalizing force set free that turns all matter into primal tatters.

The primal tatters are not nearly as frightening as the blood gluing the tatters together in crucial spots, so that the living room looks like a road map indicating all the highways into and out of major cities, and also centers of population density.

The crucial spots are not nearly as frightening as the words scrawled in blood on the walls. The words are fat enough that they seem to have been painted with a large, vulgar paintbrush. Only the palm of a hand could have done it. "Kill the pigs," one wall says. "Fascist insects feeding upon the people," another says. Whoever did this is into Charlie Manson and the Symbionese Liberation Army. Yesterday's headlines and passé counterculture jargon become very powerful news when written in blood. Still in some kind of synch, Paul and I look up at the same time. Bullet holes in the ceiling—maybe fifteen of them, a neat, clustered re-creation of the solar system.

"Paul," I say, softly, more of a frightened animal whine than I would like. I feel my knees start to go liquid, as they do when a small earthquake happens and everything turns slow motion so that, before you can get to a safe doorframe, the rumbling and shaking are over, though your body doesn't believe it.

Paul makes a quick turn toward the kitchen, and I follow right behind him. The same shredding monster has been set free in there, but the refrigerator door is clean and white. With a note affixed to it, held in place by a magnet hidden in a little papier-mâché birthday cake. The note is written in such big, childish letters that I can read it from a few feet away, and realize, as I read, that a different person wrote it than the creature who graffiti-ed the living room.

The note says:

> Paul,
> Benny Mohammad was here, and he was like crazy. Linda's gone, and I'm splitting too. About the living room—Benny carries a can of red house paint in his car. Sorry about Kelly.
> Josh

"Kelly!" Paul yells. "Kelly!" The setter doesn't come. Paul's shak-ing all over now, his hands in his hair, his head wobbling. Together we go back into the living room and look over the mess. And see, in a corner, behind one of the massive stereo speakers like chil-dren's coffins, the dog. Curled up, where she must have gone to hide from crazy Benny. We move to her, together, until we see that she's surrounded by a pool of what looks like red paint. She has a single, mean bullet entry hole on the side of her head we can see. Her eyes stare at nothing, like marbles, stuffed animal eyes.

Twenty-three
SASHA

This must be, Sasha thinks, the longest day in the history of the universe. Because she is East, in the Los Angeles sense of East, the sky is merely pale gray instead of flamboyant flamingo colors. Over Santa Monica, Venice, her home which she is afraid to go to, over the Pacific Ocean, pink clouds dapple the sky like the work of an indecisive impressionist painter. But here, east of La Cienega and south of Melrose, no sign of night approaches as Sasha knocks on Claire's door. Claire must be home, Sasha thinks. This is prime pre-waitressing time, relaxation time. Sasha looks out onto the street, noting the nuances in the nearly identical, squat, two-story apartment buildings. She has not made a mistake. This is Claire's street, Claire's building, Claire's door, which Claire better answer fast. Sasha fears the imminent arrival of the Benny-mobile, fears anyone who would kill a dog and destroy a house as part of his day's work.

She pounds on Claire's door until her knuckles feel bruised. In fact, she realizes her whole body hurts. Great, she thinks, I'm coming down with the flu. Though she does not believe it. She knows her body hurts because of the emotional whiplash of the day, very like what a car crash creates, only no one to sue in this case, no way to collect.

The sound of an eight-cylinder, American-made car motor rumbling down the street makes Sasha plaster herself against the apartment wall, then peer down and onto the street to see if Benny's found her. American cars can't sneak up on anyone, she thinks. Like a herd of elephants. But it's just a big old Chrysler looking for a place to park. Sasha listens to her heart thumping in her chest, loud and efficient as eight cylinders newly tuned up.

"Claire!" Sasha yells. She pounds some more, yells again. "Claire!" A neighbor across the courtyard peeks out of his window at her. Then the door opens, Claire there with her hair standing up crazily, happy to see her.

"I was blow drying my hair," she says, "that's why I didn't hear you." She pauses, looks at Sasha's poor posture and tight face. "What the hell's going on?" she asks. "You look terrible."

"Let me in," Sasha says, and follows Claire into the tiny apartment. Where she sits, and cries silently, and lets Claire make her a cup of tea while Sasha evasively tells part of the story: trouble with unnamed hoods, chasing all over Los Angeles and Orange counties, fear of reprisals, a dead dog. It all sounds pretty foolish.

"When did you get into international espionage?" Claire asks, incredulous and confused. Sasha does not get upset easily. But, also, Sasha does not keep secrets. A little irony has always eased them through the most difficult auditions, but it does not seem to help there.

"This isn't funny," Sasha says, "believe me. I just can't talk about it."

"Okay, okay. I get it," Claire says, watching Sasha sink into her old floral sofa with invertebrate ease. Sasha, who always remembers more cool thoughts than she herself can, appears to be melting, turning smaller and smaller. "Make yourself at home," Claire says, and strokes her friend's arm. "I've gotta go to work."

Sashs sits up slightly. "I need another favor."

Dashing into the bathroom for her hairbrush, then returning

with brush and barrettes and near-empty can of styling mousse, Claire sits next to Sasha on the couch. She sets down her paraphernalia, then puts her arm around Sasha as she smooths down her own unruly dark hair. "At your service, Mata Hari."

"Get Tomas for me. Tell him to come here fast, but to take the goofiest route he can think of. And to make sure no one's following him."

"So he's in this too." Claire has never trusted Tomas, though she finds him very sexy in a seedy and dangerous way. Other people's sex lives are always incomprehensible. Chemistry, Claire calls it, this palpable and exotic tension that exists between Sasha and Tomas, as if they're always communicating on some band of radio waves that no one else can completely tune in on. It's irritating, makes you feel left out, and a little envious that someone else has this kind of access to your friend.

"The whole world's in this," Sasha says wearily.

Claire wants to be breezy, cheerful for Sasha. She's certain nothing really bad is going on here. "Okay, I'll stop at the restaurant on my way to work. No problem."

Claire rushes into the bathroom again, comes out this time with a tube of lipstick which she applies to her lips on the run. "Gotta go," she says as she grabs her purse up off the motel-style coffee table. Sasha grabs her own purse too, clutches it to her chest. Claire stops because of this gesture. Sasha looks like a very disturbed child for a moment, a lost child in a supermarket at closing time. Things are wronger than Claire suspected.

"I want you to look at something with me," Sasha says, and Claire sits down again. Sasha fishes a six-inch square of soft gray felt out of her purse, and hefts the purse in her hands. Then she spills the rubies, perhaps two or three dozen of them altogether, onto Claire's coffee table. Claire gasps, and waits for Sasha's explanation.

"In case anything happens to me," Sasha says slowly, in a dead flat monotone. "I thought you should see this. You can tell the police that I had the goods. And that it was probably Benny who did it." Sasha starts to collect the rubies off the table, slipping them back into the little pouch, where they whisper against the felt and crackle and click against one another.

"Did what?" Claire's scared now, as she watches Sasha scoop rubies off the table as if they were Halloween candies collected in one night of trick or treating.

"Anything," Sasha says, not looking up, concentrating on two dazzling little red stones that have scooted under Claire's June issue of *Vogue*.

Sometime between the time Claire leaves and when a knock sounds on the door, night arrives. But Sasha misses the transition, as if she has taken a half-hour nap with her eyes wide open and her purse plastered to her chest. Her arms ache from holding the purse so tightly. The room goes bright orange when she hears the knock, a tensed synapse stimulated into explosion, the visual and the auditory one in nervous exhaustion. Seeing the color of a sound is one thing. Having that sound look like the moment after an atomic bomb has been dropped on the corner of Melrose and La Cienega is quite another. Another knock on the door.

"Coming," Sasha says loudly. Then shakes her head, amazed at the instant and normal response to stimulus. She reaches up and under Claire's table lamp for its on-switch, feeling like a cat burglar. With the light on, she can put her purse down next to the sofa, and answer the door.

Of course it is Tomas, looking suspicious and sympathetic and concerned, and anxious to be back at the restaurant. She falls into his chest, her face against the collar of his shirt and his warm neck, where she can feel his hot, steady pulse. When his arms go around her, she feels an unstoppable sob rise from her heart, and the tears start again. Without warning she is shaking and whimpering like a child just awakened from a nightmare of monsters and boogeymen.

"What is it, babe?" Tomas says gently, as he steers her back into Claire's living room. He pets her hair, her neck, her shoulders, sits her down, gathers her against his sturdy body. If anything in the world can convince Sasha she is safe and loved, it is Tomas, Tomas's body. Yet it's Tomas who got her into this whole mess, she thinks, Tomas who arranged for her to go speeding around Orange County with an angry rich kid in a Porsche and the kid's father, with Benny after them, all ending with one poor, dead dog. She grabs his shoulder, shakes it, frees herself from her gluey and lachrymose attachment to Tomas's side, like some disgusting little marsupial baby, she thinks, and picks up her purse again. Finds the pouch.

"Here," she says. She shoves the pouch at Tomas, and he takes it, as he takes most other things that are offered to him, joints, white powders, money. Women? she wonders for a moment. He looks inside, and makes a low whistling noise through his teeth.

"Chihuahua!" he says. He looks at her slyly, appreciatively. "How'd you get Paul to give you the stuff?"

At this, she starts sobbing again, gasping out words. "Paul's hiding out," she manages. "He's afraid Benny's going to kill him. He killed Kelly. It was terrible." Snuffling, gulping, she holds her hands and sleeves to her nose, breathes through her mouth. Control, she thinks, enunciation. But posture and poise just don't seem to matter anymore.

Alarmed, Tomas grabs her again, rocks her on the couch, saying, "Baby, baby. What are you talking about? How'd Benny get involved here? Who's Kelly?" He holds the pouch with the rubies in both of his hands behind her, against her back. This sobers her, the pricking of the many tiny stones through the felt and through the jersey of her top.

"Benny followed us from the airport," she says, half-whispering, pausing after each word as if she has not spoken English for years. "Then we lost him. So he went to Paul's house, and ripped the place up. And shot Kelly."

"Holy shit," Tomas says. "Is Kelly that skinny little roommate of Paul's?"

Before she can answer, she feels herself caught in the middle of another attack of sobbing. But this is different. She's light-headed, giddy, these sobs could turn to frightened laughter. She takes more deep and even breaths and then says, "Kelly was Paul's dog. Benny shot a dog." Tomas's face struggles with this idea, with a re-adjustment of the scene he had already pictured. She says, "Benny totally destroyed the house, just shredded it. He wrote things on the walls with red paint. Then he shot this poor cowering dog in the head." She pauses, closes her eyes, sees the events she's just described taking place in a kind of underwater slow motion. "I don't ever want to see Benny Mohammad again."

Tomas stands, she thinks he's about to pace around the room in a male and decisive fashion before coming to some decision as to what's to be done. Instead, he hugs her once more, and says, "I've got to go back to the restaurant."

She stands too, though feeling wobbly, feeling as if gravity just increased tenfold. "Don't leave me!" she says, sounding so female and forlorn and in need of protection she can't stand her own voice. More controlled then, "What are we going to do?"

"I'll talk to Artie," Tomas says. "Artie will know what to do with all of this." She notices that Tomas has crammed the ruby-pouch into his shirt pocket, where he usually carries whatever percentage of a lid of marijuana he has left in a plastic baggie. The rubies have become a part of his domain.

"I'm coming too," she says. "I want to talk to Artie too."

Thinking, maybe that macho little nut will understand her story better than Tomas has, will get the menace that Benny intended, the maniacal and rather literary point of trashing Paul's house. Artie reads novels. Artie has some bizarre sense of style. She's sucked back into the intrigue without realizing it, the dead dog's eyes forgotten for a moment. She thinks of the rubies as hers, and there they are, in Tomas's pocket.

"Okay, *corazón*," Tomas says. Then he bends to her, kisses her. "I'm sorry about all this shit. I never meant for you to get mixed up with crazy Benny and murdered animals." He kisses her again. "You know that, don't you?"

"I know," Sasha says.

"I can hold my liquor," Sasha says to nobody as she surveys the eight empty wine glasses on the table in front of her. She sits in the back booth of El Caballo Blanco as the last customers finish their meals and prepare to leave. Closing time, but Tomas and Artie remain invisible in the kitchen or alley, conferring about what may have gone wrong in their scheme to get rich, and how they can remedy it. Julio brings a full carafe of white wine to Sasha's table, and prepares to fill one of the glasses, but she grabs the carafe from his hand.

"Just give it here," she says.

Julio clucks his tongue in a grandmotherly fashion. "Too much to drink," he says.

"Get lost, Mac," she says to him, then fills each of her eight glasses half way.

Then Artie appears next to her without warning. Either he walks very quietly, or she is drunker than she knows, she thinks. But she is prepared to behave in a surly fashion to him, too. He's too spotless, evidence of no work done, on a day when she's been through so much. With his hair slicked down, his gold Rolex, his white starchy shirt and pressed jeans, he looks like he should be hanging out on a *West Side Story* streetcorner doing some midnight theatrical business in someone's illicit dreams instead of supposedly bussing tables at a greasy little Mexican restaurant.

"Having a party?" Artie asks.

"Fuck off," she says, smiling, or trying to smile. She finds that her mouth wants to say and do things she's unaware of, or at least unprepared for.

Tomas appears behind Artie, then slides in next to her and puts his arm around her. "*Corazón*, you're gonna feel like shit tomorrow morning."

"I already feel like shit," she says.

"Sometimes getting drunk is not such a bad thing," Artie says, "in terms of dealing with unpleasantness and time." He sits down across from Sasha and Tomas. Suddenly, with eight glasses of white wine on the table about to be consumed by Sasha solely, after she has already consumed nearly that many, a powwow is happening.

"So what are we gonna do?" Tomas asks, looking at Artie though he keeps his arm tightly around Sasha. His pocket still bulges, with rubies, she wonders, or pot? Then she thinks, they're taking me seriously. Something has already been decided about the danger here. A victory. Artie thinks I've got credibility. But these thoughts slosh around in her head and become fuzzy. She really doesn't want seriousness right now.

"I'm gonna get much drunker than I am," Sasha says. "That's my plan."

Artie ignores her. "We better arrange to get rid of this stuff quickly. Even if we have to take a worse deal than we originally expected. Benny is too great a threat to security and to general functioning."

"Right," Tomas says. Sasha can feel that his hand is clammy through the jersey of her top, right down to her shoulder and arm. "We're cool. No problem."

"I will put out feelers on the street, see what is really going down with Benny," Artie continues. "Maybe we can make peace easily."

"He's got a gun!" Sasha says, her voice carrying a little too far, too high. People at a table in the front of the restaurant turn to look at her. Tomas smiles, waves at them, shakes his head to indicate nothing's wrong.

Artie says, "We will not cut him in. No matter what."

"I don't know man," Tomas begins, the compromiser, but Artie interrupts, clearing his throat.

"He will not hurt us," Artie says. "He does not deserve a cut—he has not acted in good faith. He is not a good businessman."

Sasha drinks one of her glasses of wine quickly, then sets it down on its side on the table, a dead Indian. She's losing interest in this talk. Patrons of the restaurant should take up a collection and send old Artie to Harvard business school, she thinks. Or buy him majority shareholdership of some movie studio. Let him apply his code of ethics to real business. Any business in which she doesn't have to face crazed Arabs and dead animals. Until Tomas speaks again, in a low voice, as if she is a child so enraptured in her own fantasy world that she won't hear.

"I say we talk to Granny about this," Tomas says.

"You talk too much."

Sasha is shocked. "Sure, get your sweet old grandmother involved in crime. Just like you got me involved in crime. Sic Benny Mohammad on your grandmother. Send your grandmother to the pen." The people at the front table turn around again, then get up and go to the cash register, waiting for Tomas. Sasha feels proud of herself. She knows how to clear a joint. Actress's skills are good for something.

"You should not have said anything about La Señora, man," Artie chastises.

"Fuck you," Tomas says. "Granny has a say in what we do next."

Sasha feels much more sober now, the sobriety that comes of focus and incomprehension, of mystery. "What's going on?"

Artie relents, sighing, though he keeps his voice menacing, low, unable to be picked up by any tape-recording bugs placed under the table by who knows whom, a voice that defies surveillance, should surveillance happen. "Okay. I guess it does not matter anymore who knows what. We will go talk to La Señora."

Twenty-four
CONCEPCIÓN

When my greatest fear in the world was that harm would come to the General, too young to realize the power and fascination of inevitability, I would yell at him about that white horse. "*Estúpido*," I would say, "only an idiot gringo in a cowboy movie rides such a horse." It is to the General's credit that he did not hit me at such times. "The white horse is a symbol," he would say, and then say nothing more, only light a German cigarette to make the room smell so bad I would have to go elsewhere, or open one of his many dusty books about strategic warfare. What did I care about symbols? Between bullets and symbols, in those times, I understood only bullets. But only because I was young and female. And thought that any harm coming to the General was the worst thing in the world that could happen. I thought nothing of myself, of harm to myself, though I faced bullets and cutthroats and scheming politicians too, with him. As well, I seemed to have lost my memory at such times, because I did not remember the first moment I saw the General.

Because the first moment I saw the General, the white horse wore spatters and dapples of the General's blood. Like a flag, that horse, like a map, like the paintings of those modern artists who throw their paints onto their canvases with the abandon of warfare. I do not listen when other old ladies say that spatters of paint upon a canvas is not art, because I know better. Though then, when I worried about harm coming to the General, I had forgotten my first look at the General and his white horse. Now I know that those paintings are about violence and danger, the peril of continuing to live instead of only waiting to die.

The white horse, too, might have been bleeding. Men's blood, horses' blood, it is all the same in war. But the horse's blood stained its head in clumps, as if it had streamed from the horse's nostrils in the fury of tempestuous breathing and running. The General's blood made patterns, demonstrated the vulnerability and tenderness of the General toward his horse. Where his wounded arms embraced the horse's neck when he leaned forward to whisper in the horse's ear, to ask the horse to run more, faster—there were stripes of blood there, recording this plea from man to animal. Where the General's knees had gripped the horse's flanks tightly, urging the horse on—more blood, in hot stripes. And then the worst. The spattered droplets of the General's blood on the horse's hindquarters, marking the horse's response, despite the fact that it was drowning in its own body's fluids streaming from its nose—the flying paint of the General's blood, the horse his canvas, the painting about velocity, about fleeing, about clinging to life.

Only a white horse could demonstrate all of this, could show one's troops that in the face of danger one might be an artist of death. The other men in the General's small troop rode dull brown and black horses that panted from their exertions but showed nothing of the art of war, of the ways in which men mark the territory of death as their own. They looked at the General, bandaged, half-alive, on his white horse, as if he were each of their own souls. The best part of their souls, where cowardice did not live, where fear of death did not live.

I believe that the first moment I saw the General, I learned more about the power of art than I would for the rest of my life, though I was only sixteen at the time, and thought I was merely falling in love. Life and love and art may not be such separate creatures—but that is the thinking of an old woman. To a young woman, seeing a handsome, wounded man astride a bloodied white horse, all things blur, all ideas. Her heart beats faster. Tears fall from the corners of her eyes. She wants to comfort him, and make love to him, and own him, and protect him, all at the same time. Who cares about art then?

But memories are valuable. The thoughts of an old woman are valuable. One perceives the power of a symbol through many viewings and re-viewings in one's memory. Feelings are stupid and true. Memories are smarter and, though they may be artificial, are not necessarily false. My desire, when I first saw the General, to hold him, to heal his wounds, and to make love to him was exactly what he had in mind when he purchased his first white horse. If blood must be shed in war, at least young girls could be moved to want to offer him their bodies—the General must have thought this. Ultimately, I think this is what I loved in him. He always had many reasons for everything he did, always considered and enjoyed all the many possibilities that dangerous life would offer him if he tempted it enough.

To be able to make art of your life—this is something men can do, and women can watch. I was lucky, because the General saw the power of yet another symbol. Not only the white horse gave him his self-created heroism. The General realized that a handsome and courageous young general, on a white horse, with a pretty young wife right there at his side, as courageous as he—there was the stuff that gringo photographers wanted to immortalize in their daguerreotypes, there was the stuff that inspired wives at home to wait faithfully for their husbands to return from war. And that inspired the husbands to leave home with confidence. I can imagine the number of unfaithful wives for whom I was held up as an example. "If you cannot make war like Concepción, at least you can keep your legs closed while I risk my life for our country," the men must have said. So I too became art, part of the canvas the General's whole life was. But not the artist, not me, not a woman. The General created this vision of me that I loved, just as a portraitist might paint his mistress dressed up as Athena. I loved it so much that I lived it my entire life, well after the General had succumbed to his own vision of himself. The artist dies, the work of art lives on. Now I am a tough old woman who has spent too much time alone with gringo daguerreotypes on the wall. With only my grandson for company. And he has heard all the stories about the General too many times, though he was always a polite boy who listened and nodded and smiled.

Here is where I become confused. Because Tomas, somehow, though he has the same blood as the General, is not an artist of his own life. Tomas has no vision of what the canvas of his life should be filled with. I wonder, is there something wrong with Tomas, some grave flaw that prevents him from seeing symbols, art, much as I was prevented as a sixteen-year-old girl by my sex and my age? Or is it the nature of our time? There seems to be no arena for artistic heroism, for pure courage. The very canvas itself must be created before the symbols, the spatters of paint, can be placed. This is a mighty demand, too much for a boy like Tomas who always enjoyed pleasure better than work.

I do not worry about this for myself. Because I am an old woman, I am used to the idea that I will never know the end of the story. I worry about this because I love Tomas. I fear that a life without vision will lead him into foolish dangers masquerading as true chances to create his own heroism. He might then lose himself in these foolish dangers, in a false sense of his own stature, in artificial vision. Or he might lose himself in a much more literal sense. Arturo tells me about the boys with knives and guns and their gangs' names tattooed on their arms, these boys on drugs that make them feel powerful and great. Arturo tells me about this Benny Mohammad. And I see the men who mistake the petty dangers of drink and drugs for the real canvas of life. My own son was one of these. The boys with the weapons, the lure of false heroism and dissipation, may kill Tomas. Mostly, this is what I worry about.

Whether it is the fault of the time, or the fault of some frailty in Tomas that I cannot quite understand, he can end up equally dead. As dead as the General, who created his own vision so perfectly it no longer needed him to continue to exist. It had taken on the true life of its own that artists frequently speak about when they discuss their creations: the greatest mystery of art.

I hated the General when he died, because he left me too early, too young. Imperfectly created, so that I had to try to figure out, for myself, what the vision demanded of me, what he would have wanted. But at least he left me with that. If Tomas should die of his frivolous undertakings, what will he leave me? Nothing memorable, except for a grandmother's continuing love. What will he leave his *novia*? Nothing. She will move on to other *novios*, a strong and healthy girl like that. Tomas must live through this foolishness, for both of us, the *novia* and I. He must defeat our times, which seek to turn men into worms, art into nonsense.

Okay. Maybe I go too far. Tomas may have the General's blood, but he is not the General. Even if he does not create a historic figure for himself, he must stay out of real danger, must live. Because he is the last bit of the General left to me, aside from the gringo daguerreotypes and my stories. An old woman left with nothing more than pictures and tales would be the saddest creature on earth.

With Tomas and Arturo sitting in my living room as if their spines were steel poles, and the *novia* looking smaller, fragile, droopy, and confused, at midnight, I feel twenty years old. Here is trouble, here is dissension, here is drama. Men at odds, women trying to be brave. And, even if this is not exactly the case, I have memories to transform it, to make the scene larger, grander. Only now, I am the General. I take my proper seat, pull my old chenille bathrobe closer around me, wish my feet reached the floor more firmly. A leader of men should be able to sit at a war conference with his feet planted—all portraits of generals show them with both feet on the ground. This may be why little old women do not lead armies into battle.

"We had agreed not to mention your involvement in this business," Arturo says, "and I want you to know that I was not the one to break that agreement, Señora."

I nod, wait, hold my words. If you speak last, you sound the wisest.

"Yeah, Artie's pissed at me," Tomas says.

"I do not like doing business with amateurs," Arturo says in a voice that is close to a shout. I have never heard Arturo shout before.

Tomas shouts back, "Man, I was smuggling tons of dope across the border when you were still *thinking* about smoking your first joint."

"Mama, what's going on?" the *novia* asks from her spot on the floor, next to the piano bench. The first time I have seen her around Tomas when she has not been affixed to his side like a Siamese twin. Many things are changing, and I must work to comprehend what this means.

"*Querida,*" I say in the voice I reserve for speaking to small dogs and cats, "I'm the one who hid Tomas. He was not kidnapped or disappeared."

Now Tomas and Arturo watch me, wait for me to proceed. So— none of this has yet been revealed. I feel my power growing.

"Why?" the *novia* asks.

Again, softly, carefully, in a voice that would not wake a sleeping infant. "Arturo thought there might be danger to him, that it would be better if he disappeared until the gems arrived. But because you wanted him to come back so much, you were endangering everything."

"And that is when Benny Mohammad got involved!" Arturo says, triumphantly.

The *novia* rubs her eyes with her hands, shakes her head. "Are you saying that the dead dog and the trashed house and all these people on the run are my fault?"

Arturo is relentless. "Benny Mohammad never would have known anything was going down if you had kept quiet instead of insisting on going to see Paul."

The *novia* rubs her eyes again. *Dios mio!* She's crying. This big strong gringa girl can let a little insect like Arturo Vega make her cry!

"I only wanted to find Tomas," she says through swallowed sobs.

Tomas stands now, and puffs out his chest like an ape. I have seen films of gorillas protecting their young on television, on the educational station that puts me to sleep with its public interest stories and travelogues. Tomas looks like one of the educational station's gorillas now as he swaggers over to where the *novia* sits so small and pathetic, as he puts his big hand on her yellow head.

"Cut it out, man," he says, menacingly, to Arturo. "This is getting serious."

Now the *novia* does something interesting—she tosses her head, like an angry stallion, to send Tomas's hand fluttering off of it. She glares up at him. Confused, he appeals to me with his eyes.

"This kind of arguing only strengthens one's enemies," I say. "What we must do now is decide what path to follow." I smack my right fist down onto my chair's arm, strain my legs toward the center of the earth, down, down. Authority is so hard to acquire.

"I say we sell quickly, even if we must take less than we wanted," Arturo says, the only real rival for power in this room, though even he probably does not know this.

I nod my head, making a wise old owl face. Slow, unspoken agreement is no agreement at all. I see that Arturo begins to doubt his own wisdom. I say, "And what about this Benny Mohammad?"

"I wanna get a gun, Mama," Tomas says, still stung from the *novia*'s bridling at his protection, at his touch. *Cómo no*: A big gun will make her love you again. *Pobrecito* Tomas.

The *novia* leaps up, pushes Tomas's chest so that he must sit right back down onto the couch, stands with her hands on her hips. Like feeling the rotation of the earth, or suddenly finding the magnetic north pole—the shifting of power in this room is mysterious. Tangible. With Tomas, I have watched the game that white gringos love to see black men playing—basketball—and the hard, focused magic of the bouncing ball, and whoever has it in his large hands, can give me bird bumps on my skin. That ball makes it possible for those black men to escape gravity at times, because of its intense power. Here, now, we play a similar game. Now the *novia* has the magic and power, and she is good at it. She shimmers with anger, like miles of hot and furious desert which you need to ride across to reach your destination. I have never seen her act, though Tomas tells me she has talent. For the first time, I believe this.

"Jesus Christ, Tomas," the *novia* says. "This isn't a game. I can't believe we're all sitting around here discussing life and death things as if they were simple. As if we controlled them. Benny's a dangerous maniac, for God's sake."

I speak in my tightest voice, soft, a snake-voice. "The General was assassinated by his enemies just when he was in a position to do some good for all the poor people in Mexico. When that happened, I saw that others do control our lives and deaths."

She turns to me now, her blue eyes imploring and angry. "That was politics, Mama. This is crime."

"*Querida*, the two are very close cousins."

"Sell quickly, Señora?" Artie asks, exploding to his feet in his impatience. Now I feel very small, sitting here, little in my old cat of a chair, amid the large, straight, standing young people. I sigh. Power is easily seduced by the young.

"Yes, Arturo. We sell quickly, and at the same time we look over our shoulders, all the time, for this Benny Mohammad."

"I have a feeling we won't have to look for very long," Tomas says, smug. Now he stands too.

"*Chihuahua!*" I say, clapping my hands. "Look at all of you, dancing about like fleas. When what we need is a real plan."

They sit, in a neat row on my couch. "What do you mean, Mama?" the *novia* asks. Did she think I was going to put a stop to this—just when things are getting exciting?

"First," I say, "it will be my job to get this Benny Mohammad's life threatened. I still have my ways of doing this, and of making sure that he knows about it, without his knowing exactly where the threat is coming from."

"Listen to my granny," Tomas says with pride. "She's such a tough old lady."

But Arturo looks stern. "Señora, there is no need for extreme measures right away."

Now I stand and, to appear larger to them, walk right up in front of them. I stretch my old spine as straight as it can go, and hope that they do not hear the crackling coming from it. "As if your hands are so clean, Arturo Vega! You could arrange the same thing if you chose, much closer to home."

But this Arturo, he has considered the situation much more seriously than I have thought. He says, "But that would be dangerous for me right now, respectfully, Señora. Trying to sell smuggled gems while trying to get a contract out on someone at the same time is a very stupid thing to do."

The *novia*'s eyes go wide, blue china dishes. Does she think we are playacting? Or not? "I am not talking contracts, Arturo," I say sweetly. "My friends are not gangsters. Frequently, threats alone will scare off vermin like this Benny Mohammad."

"Okay, okay," Arturo says. "The sooner we get rid of the goods, the better. You can do so many things with cash that you cannot do with rubies."

Tomas rubs his hands together in gleeful anticipation. "I used to be able to lay off a pound of coke within a couple of days," he says. "I should be able to do it with rubies."

"Tomas!" the *novia* hisses. "How can you talk that way in front of your grandmother?"

The ways of gringos always amuse me—how they hide everything they can from those closest to them, as if whole pieces of their souls were unacceptable to others, unknowable. These WASPS, like those snub-nosed *maricónes* on television late at night, make their livings telling jokes about these secret things, as if they were the most evil sins. Is this what families are for—to teach you what you must hide to be loved? I say, "I know all about his past. He may not have been a good boy all the time, but I have always loved him, and understood him."

The *novia* looks at me, at Tomas, and at Arturo with her mouth hanging open. She understands nothing right now. Standing in front of them still, in this moment of quiet, I feel a strange exultation, making me shiver. I tremble with aliveness for the first time in decades, for the first time since the General died and I escaped from Mexico with my own life. I look at the glum and confused *novia*, and know that I feel younger, more alive, than she does. Perhaps this is only crime, not noble, not courageous. But I feel wonderful!

The *novia* rises from the couch, walks a few steps as if sleepwalking, looks back at Tomas. "I feel sick," she says. "Can we go home now?"

Of course, Tomas wants to join her. But I put my hand on his shoulder, sit him back down. "*Momentito*," I say.

Then I go into my bedroom, open the top drawer of my bureau. Sort through my collection of old-lady flannel nightgowns in faded pinks and blues, old-lady underwear gray from too many washings. And extract one of the two pistols I keep there, cleaned, loaded. I have been an old lady, waiting for excitement, for too long. But I have always been ready for its return to my life. When I come back to the living room, I embrace Tomas warmly, and slip the little gun into his pants waistband. He covers my hand with his, feels the gun, pulls his denim jacket closed across it—all during the embrace, so that neither the *novia* nor Arturo see this exchange. These are the true and appropriate secrets of families, the secrets that protect them, make them strong, distinguish those of your own blood from those who might harm them.

We part, and I can see that Tomas is moved. He is my boy—he understands the secrets of blood. He comes to me again, and kisses me warmly on the cheek, holding my head in his large hand.

Twenty-five
SASHA

I'm angry, and I'm drunk. I want to break something.

And he leans against the kitchen sink, smoking a joint and flicking the ashes into the drain, relaxed as hell, even happy looking. What is with this family? I feel like I've just discovered that my inlaws are the Barrow Gang, relocated by the FBI Secret Witness Program, with changed names and an ethnicity transplant. Tomas stares out the kitchen window, into the depthless blackness of the yard, blissed-out on dope and crime. The yellow-brown smoke curls up to the ceiling, spiraling softly around him, and the smell of it makes me gag way down in my throat. I pull my legs up closer to my chest, dig my chin into my knees. I will not let him hear me swallow my nausea, my disgust. From where I sit, on our sofa, in our messy, ratty living room, this looks like any other night after the restaurant has closed. But I feel like I'm watching Tomas through the wrong end of binoculars—like he's a million miles away, though I know I could walk ten feet and hit him over the head with a frying pan. I might do that.

I want to kill him.

"I don't understand this death culture of yours," I say, as if I'm saying it to myself, kind of musing.

Tomas turns toward me, I can see his whole face now—serene. He's pleased with himself, Mister Bigshot. "Whatya mean, babe?" He thinks I'm just making conversation. He thinks he'll get laid tonight. Fucking asshole. I'm getting closer to breaking his head.

I keep my voice under control—there'll be time for shouting and shaking soon enough. "Your grandmother loves talking about how the General got assassinated, like it's her fondest memory. You want a gun. Artie's into putting out contracts on people." I pause, look up as if I'm checking off items on a shopping list I've memorized. "I felt like I was in the twilight zone at your grandmother's house tonight. You didn't see that dead dog. I saw the dead dog."

But Tomas's face doesn't change. In his philosophical voice, the voice he can usually get into after a few brandies and much more weed, he says, "Look, death is just a part of life." Gimme a break. He continues, "Granny understands this shit. She was only in her twenties when the General got killed."

I'm still under control, still testing him, his seriousness. He says lots of crap in his philosophical mode, makes him feel thoughtful and smart. "Don't give me that. She's really into this, even more than you are."

A long, pensive toke, the smoke held, exhaled in a thin lazy curlicue. There he is—the man I love, just like in some Billie Holiday song—and he doesn't have a clue about what's going on inside me, this tight knottedness that is a combination of too much wine and too much fear.

He says, smiling, "That's my Granny. The old broad still loves an adventure."

Snap—that's it. I feel something crackle in my head, some blue spark of bad chemicals putting me over the edge, past control, into the place where sonic booms come from. "Your fucking Latin culture!" I yell at him, and get up slowly, thinking about making my hands into hard fists, putting my hard fists, in combination punches, on his chin and chest. "Your fucking macho ethic! Even women have to be macho! Even your little old grandmother has to be macho!"

My brain goes into pinball/emergency functioning. Between the couch and Tomas I see nothing, bump a table with my shin, a doorframe with my shoulder, and reach him with tears streaming from my eyes and my fists limply defused. What happened? He holds me, speaks to me gently.

"Hey, you're upset," he says. "*Corazón*, I'm sorry. We shouldn't have gotten you into this."

Wrong approach. Some kind of internal, gyroscopic energy spins me away from him again. "Yeah, that's right. I don't have the blood of warriors in my veins. I'm weak. I'm not one of you."

"What is this 'one of you' bullshit?" When he throws the end of his joint into the sink, it sizzles.

"You," I begin, knowing this is going to be a doozy. This is where the real argument starts, a demarcation line, a border, a no-man's-land. I dare you to cross. And I know Tomas—he'll always take you up on a dare, always cross any line that's put in front of him. "You people, with your guns, and your putting contracts out on people, and your demented business contacts, and your smuggling." He takes his baggie of marijuana out of his shirt pocket, throws it onto the sink, opens it, sorts through it for some leaves he doesn't have to clean, always too lazy to clean his dope of seeds and stems, always wanting everything to be easy. "And your drugs," I finish triumphantly, putting a stop to his ability to focus his attention on his dope, focus anywhere besides me.

He yells, "If I'm such a bad influence, what are you doing with me?"

"And just the other day, we were talking about maybe having a baby. I can't believe it. Imagine thinking about having a baby in the midst of this. With you." Low blow. This kind of guilt-tripping hysteria enrages him.

He yells louder, "I said, what are you doing with me if I'm such a rotten bad-ass influence on your clean white life?"

A chair is the closest item around. I pull its back cushion loose and throw it at him. Something breaks in the kitchen, but I don't care. I'm full steaming to the bedroom now.

"Shit," Tomas says, wrestling with the chair cushion, I imagine. "You are the craziest gringa I've ever met."

I stop, turn. "You're just lucky there wasn't anything hard and heavy and sharp in my immediate vicinity."

This cheers him up. Now we're in violence-and-passion-ville, and that reminds him of sex. And sex reminds him of drugs. I can just see the freight train of his brain on its single track. He goes back to rolling a new joint, smiling a little. Which makes me even angrier.

"Where are you going?" he asks when I turn away from him, stomp toward the hall.

"To pack."

"Sure." He doesn't look up from his leaves and papers and baggie, the chump.

"I'm leaving," I scream from the bedroom door, and, as I say it, and realize it's true because of the power of the spoken word let loose, the tears come again, and my whole body trembles. "I'm scared, Tomas," I scream, "I'm scared all the time. I've gotta get away from you until all this blows over. I can't stand this."

"Yeah, yeah," I hear Tomas say from the kitchen, smug, sarcastic. Cocksure.

In the bedroom, I drag my beat-up old Sportsac out from under all of Tomas's and my shoes, from the bottom and back of the closet. My exciting life—no travel for, what, two years now? Waitressing and actressing don't leave you much time for jetsetting. Hardly the life of an international gem smuggler. What am I doing in this role? I make certain lots of shoes smack against the closet walls, throw the Sportsac down onto the bed as heavily as possible, throw clothes around. No way he can mistake the weight of my resolve, no way he can ignore my noise. I've got the suitcase half full before he appears leaning on the bedroom doorjamb, still Mister Cool.

"So where are you going?" he says, as if he couldn't care less. As if he might, some time in the next decade, want to talk to me or see me. I control myself, throw more clothes in the bag.

"Claire's," I say. "You can call me there if you want to talk." More clothes, and more, making it clear, with the help of props, that this leaving is serious business.

"I thought we'd be in this together," he says, a real George Raft line.

"So I'm not much of a moll," I say, stuffing into the bag my down jacket that I wore once to the snow with a boyfriend who skied, ten years ago. A boyfriend who was supposed to get me a part in a major motion picture. Fill in the rest of that story yourself. I will never wear that down jacket in Los Angeles, but I am a packing machine now, a packing maniac. "But I'm scared something horrible is going to happen. I just don't want to see it. Hearing about it will be bad enough."

Now the monumental task of zipping up the bag. It's bumpy enough, from the outside, to look as if it might have body parts stuffed inside. This is a thought that I would never have had a week ago, or a month ago, a thought that grows from the grief that Benny Mohammad has brought to my life, thanks to Tomas. My breath gets short, puffy, panting. Tomas just stands in the doorway.

"Corazón," he says, his syrupy voice. Doesn't he see what I'm doing? "I'm still short a waitress," he says. Not moving from the doorjamb. Only now, as I heft the bag, do I realize how efficiently he's blocking my way out the door. The bag is plenty heavy. If I hit him squarely in the chest with it, I could be out of the house before he can stand up.

"Not this time," I say.

"Okay. When we lay off this stuff, will you come back?" Still sweet, the Tomas who can get me to do anything in the world for him, at any other time than this.

"It's not that easy. You're not the person I thought you were."

Tomas moves very quickly when he's angry. In a moment, he's shaking my shoulders, hard, until my head wobbles on my neck, and yelling, his breath hot on my face before I can make sense of his words.

"Maybe you thought wrong," he yells. "I'm the same, I'm me.

I'm as good or bad as I was yesterday. I haven't changed at all."

"Yeah," I say when he lets go, his closeness still a powerful drug to me, the warmth of his body the best thing I have known in my life. How will I sleep, alone, at Claire's? "Maybe I have."

With my bag at my feet, Tomas in front of me, I have a couple of options. Scram fast, probably the smartest in terms of emotional wear and tear, but I'm not that smart. Something aches in my rib cage, and at the base of my throat, and I know that if I hesitate for very long, I'm fucked. I know this, yet I hesitate. I know this. He knows this. Up close, Tomas's chest and shoulders obscure the rest of the entire world from my view, he becomes the world, and it's kind of comforting. I can hide here. I force myself to remember what's out there. Remember Benny Mohammad fidgeting murderously in the backseat. Remember the Irish setter looking beyond dead, more like a battered old stuffed animal than an ex-pet, that one neat and clean hole in its head. Move, I think—move.

Pure will. No one can say I'm not tough as nails when I need to be. But I reach my mouth up to his first, kiss him. And find him to be made of stone, the warmth deceptive, something he has turned on to fox me. No response. I breathe twice, a good trick to keep in mind before going on any stage, heft the bag, and walk around him. I don't believe he turns around, or moves, at all. I concentrate on feet walking, arms carrying, making the body do the work until it all becomes unconscious, the mind and body one set of smoothly meshing gears, a wristwatch, an action toy.

I don't cry until I'm on the Santa Monica Freeway, and a black pickup truck passes me on the left, another black pickup, with a couple of teenagers in it drinking beer and laughing.

Twenty-six
SASHA

"Not bad," Concepción says as she wiggles her fingers in the air. "An eight-hundred-dollar night." As Tomas stuffs the wads of bills, piles of coins, few checks, and the stack of receipts into the grimy cloth bag, she reaches for her remote control wand, and zaps her TV awake. David Letterman is interviewing a famous movie dog, which goes through its repertoire of cute tricks as if in response to his questions. Concepción shakes her head sadly at the obvious demise of Western culture going on before her eyes. "At least this silly gringo likes animals," she says, holding the wand aimed at the screen.

But Tomas isn't paying attention, to her or to David Letterman. He says, softly, again, what he's already said throughout the evening, and which Concepción has patiently tried to ignore. "Everything's gone so smooth," Tomas says. "It's incredible, you know? The big time is easier than the penny ante stuff. My buddy Jerry, the slimy lawyer, turned us on to these rich dudes. All with empty safe deposit boxes just breaking their hearts. Like empty Christmas stockings, you know? Got to fill them up with goodies."

"You want to see this *maricón* talk to this dog?" Concepción asks. But Tomas still fiddles with the bag, shaking the paper and metal inside it as if he's making a very dry martini for James Bond.

"We've only got a few stones left," he says. "This deal is so close to being over. I can't believe how simple it's been."

Concepción points the wand at him. "Don't trust it."

"Are you beaming me up?" Tomas laughs.

"What about this Benny Mohammad?" Concepción asks, keeping the wand trained on Tomas, as if it will keep him as safe and contained as David Letterman inside her television.

"Invisible!" Tomas says, and goes into her kitchen. She hears him open her refrigerator, clink and clank things around, close the refrigerator door. She thinks, if anything happens to Tomas, if anything goes really wrong, I will learn a new lesson about life, one I am too old to fully comprehend. This cannot happen: I am too old for a new kind of broken heart. Tomas returns with two bottles of beer, one for each of them, opened.

"*Salud,*" Tomas says, and gulps his. Concepción takes a long drink too, then waits for Tomas to speak. She knows he is too full of himself and this deal to contain himself for very long. He says, "Benny hasn't shown up at all. It's great. But I've been carrying my gun in the car, just in case."

At this, Concepción hoots, "that will do you a lot of good."

Tomas looks up, alert, interested. "Whatya mean?"

Concepción puts the wand through its paces, watching milliseconds of "Magnum, P.I." repeats, two cheaply made, black and white, '50s horror films featuring slimy things creeping out of the ocean and blondes in bathing suits, "Honeymooners" repeats, static, standard late-night fare, all of it used, dated, irritating. Back to David Letterman, for whom the dog is now sitting up and waving. "You will certainly be attacked by this Benny Mohammad while you are sitting, waiting in your car."

"Come on, Mama," Tomas begins, but she interrupts him, pointing the wand for control.

"Here is what will happen to you while you're in your car. You will be stopped by a policeman for driving after drinking too much wine or beer. You will reach into your glove box for your registration papers. The gun will tumble out. Then the worst that will happen to you is that the policeman will shoot you dead. Just another dead Mexican who tried to pull a gun on a cop."

"And the best that'll happen?" Tomas enjoys this tough-talk with his granny.

"You will be arrested for carrying a concealed weapon, and your poor old grandmother will have to come bail you out, because you no longer have your *novia* to help you." This is a low blow. Tomas looks stricken.

"Yeah," he says, and takes a long pull on his beer. "I guess you're my only old lady now."

"A dubious honor. I liked things much better when you had your *novia* to look after you. I didn't worry so much about you then, because at least she had some sense."

"Maybe that's why she left me," Tomas says. Concepción looks carefully at his strong-featured face, trying to separate irony from real feeling, banter from the emotion it deadens and conceals. She and Tomas have always spoken this way to one another, because she never felt she wanted to hide anything about herself from him, and because she has always enjoyed dealing with adults much more than coddling children. She knows she has always been hard-boiled, but she also thought that the great amount of love she felt for him would balance this out, would make him feel appreciated and give him a healthy sense of humor and distance, make him into a man more quickly. For the first time, now, she thinks she may have been wrong. Perhaps children do not need humor and distance at such an early age. Perhaps these things make them into dangerous adults. Maybe she didn't do such a good job of raising her grandson. This frightens her, and forces her to say something real to him.

"Do you want your *novia* to come back to you?" she asks, no edge in her voice.

Tomas says, proud, haughty, "If she doesn't want me, I don't want her."

She laughs one dry, hard laugh that sounds like a cat spitting. "That's certainly a mature outlook."

Now Tomas is earnest, downcast. He looks straight at her, his deep brown eyes without irony now, his large hands limp upon her coffee table. "Mama," he says, "she hurt me last night."

"And you have never, ever, in the whole time you have known her, hurt her?" Concepción asks, in a harsh voice Tomas has never heard before.

A flurry of plant activity in Concepción's front yard turns both of them into alert animals, listening intently, experiencing sound like bats, like dolphins, whose worlds depend upon noise for moment-to-moment navigation. They sit absolutely silently. The crackling and whooshing continue for a few seconds, then disappear. Perhaps only a snoozing cat awakened by a bad dream, sent sprawling into the night by a neighborhood dog, or the scent of rodent. Perhaps an owl in the willow tree, descending upon an unwary lizard. A crazed prowler? But both of them think, Benny Mohammad. As if they've conjured him by talking about him, by the mere uttering of his name. Concepción feels that she has electricity running through her veins instead of blood. When Tomas starts to rise, his eyes trained on her front door, she stands too, grabs his arm, stills him. No more sound from outside. No car engine revving and speeding off, no furtive footsteps.

"Sit," Concepción commands, after silent seconds pulse through her body, and he does. He swigs what is left of his beer, shoots a look at the front door once more. Then they both watch, without seeing, the commercials on the television.

"Mama," Tomas says, finally. "Why didn't you ever re-marry?"

Concepción takes a long breath, exhales, and nods her head at the sagacity of the question in this moment. "Sure," she says, "there were other men. But it was never the same. With the General, there was always the danger, the risks, the noble goals. Even if the means of reaching those goals weren't always so noble. In a life like that, every little thing seems extraordinary and exciting. Love is even better when the third partner is history. Or what you imagine will make history." She pauses, thinks. "Maybe, even if what you experience together, you imagine will make thrilling memories, just for the two of you, to talk about in your old age. If the General were alive, and had started the restaurant with me, and we could sit here like two normal old people, we would talk about old times. Why would we talk about anything else?" She pauses again, looks at Tomas, and imagines she can see his body relaxing after the shock of some predator at the window. He gradually turns into the day-to-day Tomas, his face softening, the surface of his eyes changing from black reflecting pools to dark marbles, like the eyes of stuffed animals. She continues, "After the General, there were other men, certainly. I am not a saint, as you know. But none who could give me history. So I ran the restaurant, and raised you."

Now that she has calmed herself by talking, Tomas knows he can get up, go to the door to look out to make sure the night is in order. She admires him as he strides to her front door, admires the decisive, foolish, courageous way he steps out onto her stoop to survey what he must consider to be his territory, as he is the only male around. Two generations removed from herself and the General, yet she sees the General's heroism in him now, twisted and bent by the time, the place, and by her own mythologizing. But there, just the same.

Satisfied that his surveillance has turned up nothing dangerous, just the impregnable, vegetable darkness of his grandmother's front yard, Tomas returns, sits back down, plays with the wand.

"Mama," he says, "what should I do about Sasha?"

Concepción considers this carefully, because she knows that Tomas will probably do whatever she tells him. "Wait until your business with Arturo is complete," she says. "Then assure your *novia* that you will never do anything like this again."

Tomas throws the wand down onto the coffee table. He yells, "But what if I'm like you? What if I'm not capable of living everyday life?" She holds one frail hand up to him, to assure and quiet him, but he continues, softer, "I like thrills, Mama. I like living close to the edge."

"Even so," Concepción says, carefully, wanting to be understood. "You must tell her that." The old woman pauses, nods, glances at the television, then speaks again. "I didn't say it had to be the truth."

Twenty-seven
SASHA

Amidst Claire's unmatched, pastel print sheets, in makeshift pajamas of a T-shirt and sweat pants, her hair uncombed, Sasha sits curled up in genuine dishevelment. What used to be Claire's living room couch now resembles an elaborate nest. Sasha rubs her eyes, disoriented. Up late last night, being comforted by Claire, and now it's late morning, the sunlight already too bright and direct, nearly afternoon light, to allow her to feel anything but genuinely vampiric. Her eyes too feel terrible, from all the crying—old lady eyes, dry skin hardening into papier-mâché around them, squinting mechanism turned up high because of the wear and tear of emotion when it turns to water and salt. This kind of thing takes five years off your career, Sasha thinks—ages you instantly. No such thing as an ingenue with red eyes, or black circles, or crows'-feet. Either wake up fast, or decide to waste the day. And both seem equally disgusting right now, equally evil, as today is that rare, nearly extinct creature, a day off. Claire makes the decision for both of them. She comes into the room carrying, under one arm, an already-opened bottle of white wine, and in each hand a glass. The appropriate breakfast on such a day, when emotional hangover feels just like the real thing. A hair of a different dog.

Claire pours into each glass, offers one to Sasha, then proposes a toast with her own.

"To lying about your age forever," and Claire sips. Sasha nods, then sips, and the wine tastes downright salubrious, like orange juice full of vitamin C and Florida sunshine. Claire sits on one corner of the opened-out sofa, looking thoughtful and concerned.

"Y'know, most people live these calm, boring lives, and read mystery novels to keep their fantasy lives of crime and sex and glamour healthy," Claire says. "I bet you're the only person in the whole world who has crime and sex, and just wants to sleep on her best friend's couch and be bored."

"You don't bore me," Sasha says. "Never." She raises her glass in another toast: "To friends." The two women sip in silence.

"So," Claire says, "what're you gonna do about things?"

Sasha leans back into the fluffy nest of the couch, shaking her head. "I don't know. I don't mean to move in on you indefinitely. I've just gotta decide about some important issues. Like what I'm doing with my life."

"I know. You can stay here as long as you want."

"Thanks," Sasha says, in true gratitude.

But Claire continues, barely giving her time to speak her single syllable: "But life goes on, you know? You've got a man out there in the real world, and a life of crime and romance. Can you desert all that?"

"This is the scary thing," Sasha says, holding her wine glass in one hand, a strand of her very yellow hair, yellower in the bright sunlight, in front of her face. With her other hand, she examines it instinctively for split ends or other signs of damage that might be correctable with cream rinses and conditioners and moisture packs. Actresses must have thick and perfect hair. "I'm not sure I can. I've been happier with Tomas than I ever have in my whole life. I have these bad, violent thoughts, about breaking things, about killing him, but they don't seem to really indicate anything bad. The bottom line is, most of the time I'm happy."

Claire nods in agreement. "You sure seemed happy."

"But what does that say about me?" Sasha tosses her head, sending the one hank of hair flying. A little out of control, the hand with the wine glass whips around too, and some wine spritzes across the bed. Claire pretends not to notice.

"That you fell for this very interesting guy," Claire says slowly, and Sasha appreciates her friend's attempt at positive thinking. And good acting: Claire's face looks earnest as a Girl Scout's, her measured voice could only be uttering an absolute certainty, the Pledge of Allegiance, wedding vows, a wish upon a star. "He's a sexy, charming, dangerous man. That's not so bad. Like with tall, dark, and handsome—you settle for two out of three."

Sasha stands, walks to the living room's only large window, looks out, as she materializes a rubber band from a sweat pants pocket and ties her hair up into a ponytail. Without makeup, with her hair up, she looks much younger than all her cosmetic special effects for auditions ever make her look. She says, "If you could only delete the dangerous part. Like, if you could say, a sexy, charming attorney. Or a sexy, charming dermatologist."

Claire downs her whole glass of wine, to strengthen her resolve to tell the whole truth. "But that's not Tomas," she says. "You take all of him, or you take none of him. You wouldn't like it if he said to you, 'I want you, but I don't like this actress shit. Get a nice job as a secretary, and then we can really settle down.' You'd wanna murder him if he said that."

Sasha, looking out the window, hears the wistfulness in her own voice as she speaks, making her eyes go liquid with self-pity and self-loathing. "I always wanted to be an actress," she says, "ever since I was a little girl. So I could pretend to be a heroine, have adventures that were make-believe. Safe thrills, and a guaranteed happy ending." She pauses, then continues, "If not happy, then at least glorious."

"Poor baby. You've sure gotten some heavy real life therapy these past few days."

"Yeah," Sasha says. "It really makes me sick."

Sasha returns to the couch, and pulls the covers up to her neck as she sits and sips her wine. She keeps the glass, in one hand, behind the covers too, so that when she bobs her head to drink, the sheet hides half her face, as if she is in purdah. Claire pours herself another, visible, glass, conversation stymied by the Great Unspoken.

"You cold?" Claire asks. Sasha shakes her head, even as she pulls the sheet and blanket up around her tighter. Then Claire asks, "Do you still love him?"

"Yeah." Sasha feels an enormous, nauseating, tidal force of verbalized truth washing over her, like jumping into a bright blue, pellucid David Hockney swimming pool, so beautiful, and only then remembering you can't swim.

Claire is relentless. "So what does that tell you?"

Now, for the first time this morning, Sasha smiles. "You would have made one hell of a psychotherapist, you know?"

"I was a psychology major in college," Claire says, sheepish. "B.A. in psychology from UCLA. And here I am, waitress to the stars, the movers, and the shakers."

"What happened? Where did you go wrong?" Sasha asks, good humor returning as the focus of the opprobrium of the cosmos shifts from herself to Claire, surely what friends are for: to remind you, when you're making a mess out of your life, that they have made just as much of a mess of theirs.

"I wanted to be a heroine too," Claire says, nodding guiltily. "The idea of watching self-indulgent jerks lying on a couch while they blabbed out their problems to me just didn't seem like something Ingrid Bergman would do with her life, you know? Remember that Hitchcock film, with Gregory Peck as the nutcase, and Bergman as his shrink? Nobody believed it."

"Salvador Dali did the sets for the dream-sequence, right?" Sasha pauses. "I wanted to be Ingrid Bergman too."

Claire does Bogart: "You wore blue, the Germans wore gray," and now both of them go misty-eyed.

"Yeah," Sasha says. This time the tide of truth sweeps over both of them for a moment: Chances are neither of them will make it, neither will be Ingrid Bergman, neither will get to make even a second-rate Hitchcock film. Claire fills their glasses once more.

"So what about real life?" Claire asks.

"Well, Doc, I just don't know. I'm a trifle confused about real life. My real life has people getting threatened, and smuggled rubies, and nutty speed freaks in it. My fantasy life, right now, has settling down with a nice orthodontist for a calm fifty years or so. Everything seems turned around." Sasha pauses, her timing perfect. "Where did my parents go wrong?"

In an impeccable German accent, Claire does Freud. "Mit years ov intenze analyziz und more wine, vee may be able to cure you, Liebchen." Claire fills their glasses dangerously high, so that each must bring her lips to the glass, instead of the other way around. They look like two exotic birds drinking.

Twenty-eight
EL CABALLO BLANCO

The night is too hot for Mexican food. Nobody feels like eating enchiladas when the temperature rises above ninety during the day, stays close to seventy-five after sunset. Hot weather infuriates Tomas, because it magically transforms what should be a thousand-dollar night into a six-hundred-dollar night, sometimes even less.

The cooks, on the other hand, love hot nights. They sweat in the kitchen no matter what the weather, and so are curiously immune to seasons. Some nights, for them, are slower than others, for no discernible reason given the constant tropical heat of the kitchen, though if they were to check the weather in the newspaper, they would understand. Some nights, they make fewer enchiladas, more tostadas, but they don't care why. They get paid the same, whether they throw some pre-shredded lettuce and re-fried beans onto a crisped tortilla or have to set into motion the intricate chain of events necessary for a tamale to happen. Tamales, the heaviest food on the menu, happen more in winter, less on these hot nights.

Paco leans against the refrigerator, fanning himself with one fat hand. "Pedro Guerrero, hombre. He's the only Dodger that'll ever get in to the Hall of Fame now that they've traded Garvey."

Pablo, the skinny, older cook, stares at the wall that prevents him from seeing the diners in the dining room, and makes a disagreeable face. "Garvey—*qué gringo!*"

"Come on, man. He was a great player." Nothing gives Paco as much pleasure as baseball—a meditative sport, demanding great amounts of beer to be drunk for true appreciation.

"When Roberto Clemente died," Pablo says, sadly, nostalgic, "baseball died for me as well."

"Pendejo," Paco says, "you're living in the past."

Pablo turns philosophical, knowing he will get the last word in as they both hear the heavy footsteps of the boss, and know they will have to simulate work momentarily. "If the past is better than the present, I prefer to live there," Pablo says as Tomas enters the kitchen, with the surfer busboy, Billy, behind him. Paco and Pablo stir whatever is on the stove, pretend that the sliced tomatoes and shredded lettuce demand a great deal of their attention.

"When there's a girl you're interested in, you just can't hang around making cow eyes at her," Tomas says, putting his arm around Billy's shoulder avuncularly. Paco and Pablo exchange a look that says, here is a subject the boss knows all about.

"What should I do?" Billy asks, his dull blue eyes suggesting the possibility that Tomas is inventing, on the spot, the concept of the pick-up.

Tomas, however, has already invented it for himself. "You bring her a glass of wine," he says, "and just leave it in front of her, without saying a word. That's pretty *suave*." He pronounces it as a Spanish word, "swa-vay," which in itself is much more suave. But still Billy doesn't get it.

"Then what?" he asks.

Tomas, sighs, rolls his eyes. What he could do with a more adept pupil. Maybe he should open the Don Juan School of Social Skills, he thinks. "Then, just before she's ready to leave, and she's wondering if she's going to be charged for the glass of wine, you go up to her and ask her if she enjoyed her dinner."

"Yeah?" Billy says uncertainly. "What does that do for me?"

Tomas is on a roll now. "She asks you if the wine was a mistake.

She looks up into your eyes when she asks you, and you look down at her, looking very serious about this whole thing. That's important. She needs to know you're not making fun of her, not pulling any kind of fast one. Then you get to say to her, 'No, I brought you the wine because you have the sexiest eyes I've ever seen.'"

But Billy shakes his head, concerned, disbelieving. "No," he says, "I couldn't say that."

"It works every time." Tomas slaps him on the back, thinking, at once, how much he likes Billy, and how dim the kid is. Tomas, in fact, prepares to go on strategizing, to send Billy back out into the world of the dining room with enough flirting skill to pick up anyone, male or female, old or young. Tomas feels that he, himself, could do that. Then Artie comes in from the alley, looking perturbed, the features of his narrow face held together by tight, clenched lines like a pencil drawing.

"Hey," Tomas says, "who's out in the dining room besides the customers? What is this, the clubhouse?" Immensely good-humored: He enjoys being both funny and the boss, an unbeatable combination. Artie isn't going for it.

"May I speak to you for a moment?" Artie asks, and glares at Billy, who fidgets uncomfortably in the odd, gravitational attraction and repulsion number he's getting simultaneously from Tomas and Artie.

"Try it, man," Tomas says to Billy, sending him back into the dining room. "What's up?" he says to Artie, having forgotten about the real world of crime while enjoying his own expertise in other arenas. Now Paco and Pablo really clear out, busy themselves as far away from Artie and the boss as possible. Some things are serious, and they're respectful, always, of Artie, especially of Artie when he's in a funk.

In his lowest voice, soft and menacing, a whisper tuned up one notch, Artie says, "One of my most respected and infallible sources just told me that Benny has been seen in the area. Cruising down Sunset. Coming this way."

"Should we panic, or what?" Tomas asks, still full of himself, his prowess as a seducer. He's flirting, a little, with Artie.

But Artie has never been flirted with, nor does flirtation play any part in the transaction of business. Flirtation is activity absolutely without meaning for Artie, different from seduction, which he can understand as a principle of business, and different, even, from fucking someone, or fucking someone over. Business and sex correspond on many points, but flirtation, as a subspecies of personal charm, has no meaning in Artie's intellectual world, creates no picture for him, seems a useless endeavor, a waste of time and energy. Artie says, "I do not think panic is necessary. But we should arrange to walk out together when we close up tonight, to avoid a possible ambush of one or the other of us alone, or a hostage or ransom situation." Dead serious.

"Okay," Tomas says, his good cheer vanished. This Artie is one walking bummed trip sometimes, Tomas thinks. "I'll send Julio out to my truck to get my gun. We can at least have a gun when we close up."

"This gun talk makes me uneasy," Artie says. "As if we were asking for trouble."

"Are you chicken, Artie?" Tomas can't stop flirting sometimes, a weakness, he knows.

"I have done business with Benny Mohammad before," Artie says. "He knows I am fair with him. He has no reason to mess with me in this manner."

Now Tomas is fed up, and the vestiges of his idea of his own charm school, himself the John Robert Powers of flirtation, the Dale Carnegie of the pick-up technique, vanish. "Man, Benny is a crazed motherfucker," he says. "Benny's not a rational businessman like you and me."

Artie shakes his head, considering. Easier for him to believe that Benny has a fix on quantum physics, understands Mandarin Chinese, can convert German marks to French francs in his head using today's market figures, than to believe in complete irrationality. Complete irrationality does not compute for Artie. Again, Tomas knows this is a weakness, this time in his business partner, a weakness that he fears could get him into the realm of physical pain. Tomas says, "Man, Benny takes drugs." Not, of course, alluding to the smoking of marijuana, which even Artie partakes of. Alluding, old conservative Tomas, to that shit the kids take, that makes them feel five stories tall and indestructible. Tomas has tried it: He knows.

"You take drugs," Artie says, interested in what this angle might mean.

"Benny takes *more* drugs," Tomas says.

Artie holds up both hands, an international gesture of fed-upness. "We leave together, tonight, as quickly as possible. We go straight to La Señora's house, divide up the money we have right now, divide up the remaining merchandise, and split up this partnership."

This hurts Tomas's feelings. "We might as well finish up what we've started, don't you think?" he says sullenly, resentfully, realizing, as he says it, that this was the United States' tactic in Vietnam.

"Hey, man," Artie says, raising his voice enough to make Paco and Pablo look over in apprehension from their green sauces and rellenos. "This gig has been unprofessional from the start. Dealing with dangerous amateurs is not for me. I want to go back to the regular underworld—some dope, some counterfeit bills, the usual. I got in over my head, thinking I could be big time. I committed the sin of grandiosity." He smacks himself on the forehead with one open palm, hard, so that his small head jerks back on its skinny neck. Tomas makes the sign of the cross in front of him.

"Say ten Hail Marys, my son, and I absolve you," Tomas says. Artie looks like he's about to punch Tomas. Paco and Pablo creep toward the door to the alley with their eyes glued to the boss and Artie. "I got a feeling we're just gonna sail outta here tonight, no problema," Tomas says, full of cheer, scared to death of Artie.

"One of the first rules of business is, never resort to false optimism," Artie says, wagging one finger at Tomas.

"You read that in *Gatsby*?" Tomas asks.

"No," Artie says. "I just made it up. But it is still true."

Nothing is quieter than a restaurant that has just closed. The cash register rings louder. Chairs scrape more heavily against the floor. You feel the clatter of a pot falling in the kitchen at the base of your spine, the noise intruding into your being like a knife. Like a real dud of a party, that all the guests have left too early, forcing the hosts to reconsider their choices for food, drink, music, and friends.

"See you tomorrow," Julio, the cheerful waiter, calls out as Tomas unlocks the front door for him, watches him walk down the street. Julio does not think of questioning the boss's judgment. If the boss wants him to leave by the front door tonight instead of the back door, fine. The bus stop is around the front, down on the corner, anyhow—closer, though Julio never feels frightened by the alley, feels at home in it, like a lizard whose protective coloration makes the jungle a safe and snug habitat.

Tomas carefully re-locks the front door behind Julio, sighs, looks at Artie, who lounges near the register. Tomas feels glad that Sasha isn't here tonight. If he should have some failure of nerve, does he want his girlfriend to see it? Of course not. Artie is the perfect witness for such an event, because of his complete discretion. If Tomas should quiver or falter, or get hurt, Artie will never tell. And, if Tomas should behave heroically, still Artie will never tell, but he himself can spread the story, humorously, transformed into one of his funny monologues complete with Artie-imitations and Benny-imitations and even Granny-imitations. Except for the fact that Benny Mohammad makes tonight truly dangerous, this would seem like a no-lose situation to Tomas. A rush of adrenaline—he straightens his posture as he has seen Sasha do so many times as he walks toward Artie, throws his head back a little, like a spirited and unbreakable stallion.

"Now we play cowboys and Indians," he says to Artie.

Artie doesn't move, a small, thin statue depicting tensile determination, man against the universe. In a soft voice, he says, "I never saw myself as an underworld type, you know? I saw myself as an executive. A man who told other men what to do. A man who kept up with financial trends."

"The life of Arturo Vega," Tomas intones in a TV anchorman voice. "Sounds like your whole life is flashing in front of you, bro'."

"I am scared," Artie says.

Tomas slaps his hand down hard on the counter by the register, making Artie jump like a nervous cat on the Fourth of July. "I've got the blood of warriors in my veins, man," Tomas says loudly, though a tiny tickle in his head makes him wonder if he's been saying this too much lately, if this has become old news. "I've got the gun."

"I have heard rumors that people with guns sometimes get hurt," Artie says, "statistically speaking," shakes himself into the aisle of the dining room, and begins to walk toward the back. Tomas pulls his pistol from the drawer under the register where he has it cached, sticks it in his pants waistband, then puts on his denim jacket, effectively hiding the gun, but also impairing his access to it.

"Hey, wait, man," Tomas says to Artie, who is already at the door to the kitchen. Artie looks back, but does not stop. "Sometimes you are one depressing dude, Arturo Vega," Tomas says, and scurries after Artie like a large, unwieldly, detached shadow.

Twenty-nine
SASHA

I'm beginning to think I'm morally defective. Like, there's something missing in the ethics department, something in my character that never evolved as it should have. I mean, I've always thought of myself as a good person. Someone who wanted the best for others as long as it didn't mean that they got roles I wanted. Someone who didn't want to hurt other people's feelings. Someone who voted. Even when Tomas did weird things and I went along with them, I never thought passivity indicated I was a sociopath. I suppose that's what the girlfriend of that guy Norman Mailer wrote about, the guy who got executed by the firing squad in Utah or some other such place where they believe in hands-on experience with death, thought, too. What a fun guy, she must have thought. Or maybe she thought nothing. I have indulged in both of those paths, but when the coin comes up heads, heads, heads, it must indicate something. For me, right now, it indicates I'm a sicko. And it's hard to figure where it started.

I'm thinking, now, of the time, right after Tomas and I moved in together, that he brought home the bricks of Afghan hashish. This was during what you'd call a transitional period in my love for him. Because we had just started living together, I was experiencing my first pangs of real, angry jealousy when he wasn't home by eleven-thirty at night. Before, I had been easy and loose about the power of my connection with him, didn't realize that deep in my being I believed we were spiritually handcuffed together, for life. I could be cool. But when we moved in, my love changed, from cool love, to deeper, furious love, jumping every stage in between.

So this one night, he comes home, on time, and pulls something odd out of his jacket, hidden between his jacket and his shirt. Something in a linen bag tied up top with a string, maybe a small breadboard or cheese board?

"Come here, baby," he says, "look at this." As if he's brought home gold. I'm a good girl, plus I'm just so pleased he's home early, instead of out drinking with the boys or doing God knows what. What I hadn't yet given a real name to, in my mind, though I would soon enough.

"What is it?" I say, pleasant. Tomas smiles at me, kisses me, holding, with one hand, this odd-shaped Ping-Pong paddle wrapped in cloth. Then he unties the cloth bag, pulls out of it a smooth, even, perfectly manufactured rectangle of what looks like molded dog shit. I'm still smiling, pleasant. A pungent aroma fills the room, not bad, just strong, almost like the smell of coffee grounds, that rich and full. And here I am, I think I've been around, I think I've seen it all, but I have never before seen a whole brick of hashish. I'm innocent enough to think the stuff comes, organically, in pellets, or wads. Nothing that looks like this.

"Afghan," he says. "Look at this." And he points out, stamped into the actual body of the stuff like bas-relief, what must be the Afghan seal of approval—a round, embedded something, with curling letters and maybe even a little picture of something that would have meaning in Afghanistan, like Betty Crocker or Mr. Clean or the Pillsbury Doughboy here. "I'm just holding this for a couple of days, for friends who will make it worth my while." He gets his wicked little-boy look, which I have, up till now, found irresistible, and says, "But we could break off a tiny little bit and smoke it up."

All of a sudden I get the picture. Not that I'm an angel, not that I'm against having substances for recreational purposes around the house. But what Tomas is showing me here, now, is one gigantic walking felony, is a real prison term, because not even the smartest lawyer in the world could convince a judge or jury that this cheese board was for our recreation alone. This has commerce written all over it, maybe what the Afghan seal is all about.

I say something like, "What the fuck do you think you're doing—bringing this into our home? Where do you think you're going to put this?"

He puckers his brow, looks up at the ceiling. "The closet?" he asks, maybe being funny, but maybe not.

"Oh, come on, sure, and stink up all our clothes," I say. "No way. No fucking way." And, probably, I start to cry.

He hugs me, says, *Corazón,* and probably *Querida,* still holding the brick. Gradually I start to calm down. I think, no big deal, he understands. We're kissing, getting kind of serious, but he breaks away from me, looking all bright and sexy and alert, an unusual combination.

"Just a sec, babe," he says. "I've got five more of those in the car, I wanna bring them up," and he disappears out the door, leaving it hanging open as if he's collecting a six-pack of Bud from the trunk. I'm left standing there with my mouth hanging open.

But here's the thing. I put up with it. I let him store this shit in the closet, under shoes and suitcases and some weights Tomas carted around with him from some other time when he was into weight lifting, I guess, or maybe some old girlfriend of his was. The stuff stayed in our closet for three or four days, I'm not sure, really, because at some point I came home from work one night and it was just gone. Though the smell lingered in the closet for weeks. And for a long time, we had hash to smoke, little rolled-up balls of the stuff, looking like some baseball player's chawing tobacco. Tomas had hidden it all over the place, could produce it, like a magician, seemingly out of nowhere—the way magicians make quarters and lit cigarettes come out of kids' ears.

And somehow, I still thought he was cute. I always think he's cute. It's a real disease. There've been other incidents like this one, though none so tangible. Six bricks of Afghan hash in linen bags in your closet is as real as you can get in the morally defective category I'm considering, the scam category, short of murder, worse than lying. Most other scams are much more insubstantial, making them seem more like part of Tomas's endless verbal riffs, which are so cute, than like real life. I guess I've never known exactly what was real and what he was inventing to amuse me, to keep me laughing, keep me loving him.

I had those rubies in my hands, though. I carted them around Los Angeles and Orange counties. I was not just pissed off, not just passive, not just amused. I was a courier. An accessory. I saw the dead dog.

Here I am, in bed on Claire's sofa, and I miss him. If he came to the door right now, this minute, and would not even apologize, not even promise me anything, but just smile and hold out his arms, I'd be his all over again. This is a real weakness, a characterological disorder I don't know what to do about. I feel like a wimp, a wuss, the chick who buys a Cartier watch knock-off for full Cartier price and doesn't know she's been taken.

On the other hand, I also feel good and tough. Feeling good and tough has gotten me through most of my life, at least since I became a teenage runaway. Tomas has made me stronger in that department, or at least allowed me to hold on to that adolescent brashness, curried it and praised it instead of telling me to grow up. And now, maybe it's too late to grow up. Maybe I just missed growing up, completely, and, like a missed bus stop or train station, a missed connection at an airport, it's hard to backtrack and pick up.

All I know is, I feel hard and small and alone, a single coconut on a deserted beach. I haven't felt that way, either, since I ran away from home and started getting tough. But I don't want to be tough, now, without Tomas around to appreciate it. Being tough and alone is a pretty thankless chore.

Thirty
TOMAS

"Wait just a minute there, bay-bies," Benny Mohammad's voice cuts clear and sharp through the shadowy, grimy black night of the alley. Emanating, it seems, out of nothing, perhaps broadcast live via satellite from the corner, or maybe Benny hides, in his werewolf-persona, amid the garbage cans, having eaten the next-door Doberman for dinner.

Tomas can't see him. Artie can't see him. But they both feel prickly cold all over, the itchy sensation you have when you awaken from a very bad dream, or when you think seriously about death.

"Shit," Tomas says, deeply earnest.

"Benny?" Artie says.

The Benny-voice comes closer. "Ver-ry clever, Artie, my man, I always knew you were one clever dude. And into noo-tri-tion these days, too, is my bet. You been eating your carrots, man, make you see in the dark like a tiger."

"Whatya want, asshole?" Tomas asks the alley.

"Ooh," Benny squeals. "Ver-ry tough. Ver-ry macho. You wouldn't be so tough if you'd been eating your carrots like your pal Artie. If you'd been eating your carrots like your pal Artie, you'd see that I've got a cannon pointed right at your chest." Benny talks even faster than usual, his voice marked by a musicality, an oddball trilling up and down the scales that has nothing to do with the content of the speech.

"Come out where we can see you, man," Artie says. Now, swallowed up by the alley, Tomas and Artie cannot see one another.

"Why, I'm right here, Artie, bro'," Benny says, and steps out from in front of Tomas's truck. They can see him only because, as he takes his first step, he also turns on a flashlight he holds in his other hand, the hand that does not hold the gun. Tomas and Artie cringe, shield their eyes, cower, do the entire *Stalag 17* pantomime, making Benny very happy.

"Yeah," Benny says enthusiastically. "Mr. Gestapo, Benny Blitz-krieg Mohammad, at your service." He clicks his heels together in Germanic, military fashion, as proper as Erich Von Stroheim in *Grand Illusion*, except for the fact that he's dressed as always, and, as his heels click, the wings of his black bat-hat flutter, and his black leather jacket looks liquid, silvery in the flashlight's glow. Benny's skin looks phosphorescent, shimmery, unhealthy, Day-Glo, as if he's just taken his minimum daily adult requirement of plutonium. "Now," Benny says, pleased, "why do I get the feeling that you two are in the mood to have a lo-ong talk with me tonight."

Tomas and Artie, pupils constricted into four comic strip dots in Dick Tracy's hair, behave properly too. They put their hands up in the air and wait until Benny finishes speaking and being proud of himself, though Tomas can feel his own gun, hidden under his jacket, alive and burning into his waist, giving Tomas the sensation, momentarily, that he knows what it's like to be eight months pregnant. Be cool, be cool, Tomas thinks, knowing he only gets one reach for the gun, unless Benny decides to feel him up for hidden weaponry. But Benny seems too far gone, into his own power and glee, and Tomas decides to wait him out. To play smart, for once.

"We've always had nothing but the warmest feelings toward you, Benny, man," Tomas says in an Eddie Haskell voice.

Benny nickers like a horse, pulling his thick evil mouth into a straight line which must be evidence of having his funny bone tickled. "*Très amusant*, bay-bies," he says through this frozen mouth. "You guys hate my guts. Artie forces himself to tolerate me, because I can do him some good every so often." Benny pauses, looks down at his two-gun stance, spins the flashlight a little so that the light wildly illumines various parts of the alley, real POW effect. "I could waste both of you guys without thinking twice."

Tomas feels his own gun, hotter, angrier, stuffed against his side.

"Benny, man, this is business," Artie says, in a completely normal voice. "This is not necessarily a life and death matter."

"That," Benny says, "depends entirely on you, bro's. Let's get into the truck. Artie, man, you come around this side with me. Let's see how much you're worth to your partner and good pal, Tomas. We'll just give him the chance to get into his truck and peel out. Leave you and me behind to play post office."

Tomas sighs, thinking that Benny is making this all much more tiresome than it needs to be. Speed talk, coke talk, grass talk—it's all too much talk. Then, he wonders, am I ever this out of control and dull when I smoke a little? And then: How does Sasha put up with me? All in the time it takes Benny and Artie to walk around to the other side of the truck, for Tomas to get in and slide across the seat to unlock the door after a moment's hesitation. What if he should leave Benny and Artie behind, in the alley, to fight it out? Intelligent men entertain all the possibilities before ruling them out, Tomas thinks. Artie, given such a choice, would think about it seriously.

Inside the truck, Tomas is a little sorry he didn't split. Three adult males in the cab of a truck is one male too many, especially when one of them wears a large, black, Flying Nun hat that obscures everything behind them. Before starting the engine, Tomas looks in the rearview mirror, as he always does when he's not too stoned or drunk, to check out the alley, and sees black, flat and smooth and perspectiveless. A moment of claustrophobic nausea ensues before he realizes it's just Benny's hat blocking the rear view, and not a symbol for the state of his existence, or a prophecy for his immediate future. Then he starts the truck, deciding to pull out over whatever is back there, and discovers he's got no room to maneuver inside the cab. Tomas is a big man, his shoulders so broad they extend halfway across the car seat. Artie sits scrunched into Tomas's right shoulder, Benny's left shoulder, ducking Benny's hat. Benny sits crunched against the car door, like a human letter "c," with the posture of a bird of prey. He balances the gun on his thighs, aimed at Tomas. When Tomas swings his body around to try to look out the back window, he whacks Artie hard in the ribs with his elbow, and shakes the whole truck so badly he fears the gun might go off. The perfect hostage, Artie winces but makes no noise.

"Sorry, man," Tomas says.

"Okay," Artie says, softly. Benny glows malevolent, green, against the car door and window, their own little lighthouse.

Tomas's truck evolved in the pre-power-steering era. Tomas tries, now, to turn the wheel hard enough to angle into the alley, but this time he dislodges Artie, violently, from his niche against Tomas's shoulder, sending him thwacking into the car seat, then hits him in the ribs with his elbow once more. Still the truck hasn't moved.

"Okay," Artie says, not waiting for Tomas's apology, wearily.

Benny's eyes light up like a pinball machine. "Okay, okay, I get it," Benny says. "You two are talking in some kind of code. Am I right?" He raises the gun up off his legs, brings it closer to Artie's prominent jaw.

"Jeez, no, man," Tomas says, fed up. Tomas wonders, where was this phenomenon in all of the Patty Hearst literature, this complete boredom with one's captor? If Benny were the dreariest, laugh-tracked sit-com on television, Tomas and Artie couldn't have been more disaffected. Yet Benny is the one with the gun. How can anyone with a gun not be the life of the party? "I'm beating him up," Tomas says.

The bat-hat wobbles in the rearview mirror. "Yeah, good idea," Benny says. "He always used to be a fair guy. Always a fair deal from Artie Vega. Then he decided he could screw the little guy, like me. Screw old Benny Mohammad and get away with it."

"Little guys do not have sawed-off shotguns," Artie says.

"Ma-an," Benny says, "listen to this dude here. Al-ways rational. Is that why you figured you could get away with fucking me over, Artie, man? You figured, that Benny Mohammad, he's some weak link, and he won't have any firepower. I can step on him like an ant. Oh, this causes me great con-ster-nay-tion."

"That is not what I figured," Artie says, with dignity.

Now Benny gets really jumpy, begins bobbing and weaving with his shoulders, ducking his head, bouncing his knees, all manners of hand and body jive, a real live wire. "Come on, man," he whines, "let's get this wreck moving. My hand's getting itchy from holding this hunk of metal here."

"You wanna drive?" Tomas says, classic retort to all backseat drivers, with or without weapons, and punches the accelerator. In neutral, the car revs and coughs.

"Ver-ry clever. No, I don't wanna fuckin' drive. If I fuckin' drive, who holds the fuckin' gun? You?"

"Yeah, sure, I'll hold the gun for you. You can trust me," Tomas says.

"Sure, just like I can trust Artie here," Benny says, perpetual motion.

"Even more," Tomas says, revving again.

"Aww, man, let's cut the baby talk," Benny says, and puts the gun to Artie's temple. Artie does not flinch, cringe, or moan. "Like, I wanna go to wherever your stash is, and I wanna go there now. Anything else is bullshit, and, right now, bay-bies, I tell you true, I ain't got no patience for bullshit."

"Okay," Tomas says, and throws the truck into reverse gear, hits the accelerator, and elbows Artie, who bats his head against Benny's gun. The truck raises a cloud of dust that makes alley visibility about six inches, and hits something metallic and bounce-able behind it.

"Okay what?" Benny says. "Okay what? Where're we going? I don't like this un-known des-tin-ay-tion business, makes me nervous, and you don't want me nervous. I know Artie doesn't want me nervous. Where you taking Benny Mohammad?"

Artie sighs, looks at Tomas. Silence, except for Benny's knees hitting the dashboard in a little Morse code samba, Benny's feet shuffling on the floor mat, Benny's elbow hitting the metal of the truck's door in syncopation to his other bodily percussion. Finally, Tomas speaks. "My granny's house."

Benny blows a long, ballpark whistle from between his teeth. He hums a little tuneless song, maybe just talking to himself. Gradually all his body parts subside into stillness. "Yeah, yeah," he says. "I should've guessed. The old lady is the brains of the outfit."

"La Señora is merely holding the money for us," Artie says, impressing Tomas with his quick-thinking, protective impulse. The gun on Tomas's hip seems to be interfering with his thought processes, intercepting thoughts, just like those copper bracelets they used to tell you to wear to improve your game of tennis. "She is not involved in any other way."

"Yeah, yeah, yeah," Benny says, tapping his gun against Artie's head with each syllable. "You little *hijo de puta madre*. All along I thought it was you out to get me. You skinny little small-time motherfucker. I should kill you just for being such a mistake, such a mote in my eye. But it's the old lady. Yeah. What'd I ever do to her?" Benny, every bit of him jangling, sending radio waves to Jupiter by merely being alive and angry, taps and weasels and fidgets and quivers, but remains silent now.

Which is even scarier than when he talks. For once, Tomas too is at a loss in a conversation. He wishes he could think of something to say, some way to defuse this collection of humming, furious voltage sitting in his truck cab, but his mind remains absolutely and recalcitrantly empty, a movie screen with nothing projected onto it. Finally, when a thought comes to him, it is a long-lost leftover from a college literature course.

He thinks of Dostoevsky, with his gambling bills and various other illegal activities held against him, being taken before a firing squad, dragged out to face the rifles, in the middle of Russian winter (Tomas imagines this scene as he drives; he never paid that much attention in any class; and Dostoevsky, in his daydream, looks remarkably like Tomas). The rifles point at Dostoevsky, at attention, ready. Then some little clerk runs out to announce the execution has been stayed for a day, a week, a month. Details are unimportant, Tomas thinks, everybody makes them up anyhow. For a moment, he entertains the notion of telling this story to Benny and Artie, just to fill up the silent space they drive through. This, he decides, is a terrible idea, given the present circumstances. They all remain quiet as they cruise through Hollywood, to Concepción's house.

By the time they get there, the silence becomes so great and weighty it resembles underwater—pressurized, thick, unbreathable, palpable, put it in a glass and you could drink it. Even Tomas, normally so aware of anything new and different in the universe, is hypnotized by the silence, so that he doesn't notice, parked across the street from Concepión's house, a gunmetal gray Ford with Mexican, Sonoran, plates. Usually, his truck is the only car parked on the street, everyone else tucked safe and neat into driveways or garages. Tomas does think or imagine that he hears Artie's teeth chattering under and near his right ear, but it might be Artie's watch ticking too. Or Benny's brain working.

Tomas scrapes his front tires against the curb, throws the gearshift into neutral and revs loudly until the truck backfires, cranks his parking brake up as hard as he can. Anything to warn Granny about what approaches. Without looking at his two passengers, he gets out of the truck, slams the door, and walks around to the other side where Benny and Artie, dark Siamese-twinned shapes, wait.

Artie doesn't speak until Tomas stands next to him, a backup, a second. "Really, Benny, man," Artie says. "If you will allow me to go in and negotiate the release of our moneys and merchandise, we can go elsewhere to settle this, and spare La Señora any difficulty."

Benny turns all his snarling attention onto Artie. "That old bitch," he says. "She's sitting in there laughing at me." Benny takes a few steps up Concepción's walk, nearly disappearing into the fecund growth that surrounds the house, only his glimmering, greenish pallor visible in the moonlight. The lights are on inside Concepción's living room, and Tomas thinks he can see the pale bluish light of the television pulsing.

"*Órale*, Señora," Benny whispers obscenely, loud enough for Tomas and Artie to hear. "Come out, come out. Don'tcha wanna have a party with me, bay-bee? I'm the man for you, I know what to do. All you gotta do is share your booty with me." No response. No open door. The only changes happen inside Tomas, who feels like a boiling teakettle. His skin goes hot, red, his stomach tightens into a small knot under his lungs, his throat constricts. Benny says, throwing his hands wide for Artie and Tomas to see, the gun dangling from one hand like an earring, "That old bitch just doesn't like me. What's a man to do?"

Tomas's voice surprises everyone, because of the sincere and evil menace in it. "Hey, man. Don't talk about my granny that way."

"You're forgetting one it-ty bit-ty thing here, bro'," Benny says, nonchalantly bringing the gun up to his waist, pointing it at Tomas and Artie and the truck. "I'm the one with the deadly weapon. I can say anything I want about anybody I want. That's the right of the person brandishing intent to kill, kids. I talk, and you listen."

Tomas unbuttons one button of his jacket. Then the second. "No, man," he says. "You got it wrong." He unbuttons the last button, so calm, and pulls his pistol out of his waistband. Artie sees it all in slow motion, the underwater effect still working, but for Benny, everything's speeded up. His head snaps back as if he's just been in a rear-end collision, and he looks like one of those car accident mannequins that are used in films warning you about the dangers of not wearing seatbelts, those dummies that always suffer, at least, severe neck and head trauma, though they usually die for the sake of insurance statistics. Then Benny chuckles, a sound like someone gasping for breath from the bottom of the deep end of a swimming pool.

"I'm a Latin, man," Tomas says, snake-voice. "You don't say anything bad about a Latin's mother or grandmother. You can say anything you want about me, man. But you talk about my granny that way, you pay." Tomas points his gun at Benny. Ten feet of dead night air separate them. Everything is too quiet.

"Wait a minute," Artie says, in a strangulating voice that tries to resemble his regular speaking voice, but flies into a higher register on the last syllable, like a young boy's voice cracking during his attempt to master his bar mitzvah speech. "We can negotiate here. This is a situation in which we all have to remain calm."

Benny finds all this risible. "I think you Latins have a name for this," he says, and laughs maniacally. "Yeah, yeah. I think what we got here is your typical Mexican standoff. *N'est-ce pas?*"

Tomas can still hear Artie ticking, irritating as he tries to concentrate on the bizarre and aerodynamic outline of Benny on his grandmother's walk, tries to figure where he should aim to cause Benny the most pain and suffering.

"What is so funny?" Artie asks, voice still out of control.

"Think about it, Mister Doctor of Philosophy Arturo Vega," Benny says. "What happens next? Ooh, yeah." Benny's delight is uncontrollable. His shadow sways to some fast, uptempo, imaginary song only he hears.

"We get sensible," Artie says. "We figure it all out."

"No, man," Tomas says. "There's nothing sensible about this." Tomas and Benny, statues, still lives, mirror images with guns pointed, with Artie in the middle as the hyperactive trained chimp, a child's game. The vegetation behind Benny rustles briefly, and they all shiver into alertness. But the trees and bushes emit no other communiqués.

This break in the flow of impending death has not calmed Benny. Instead, it seems to have fueled him, the rush of organic chemicals caused by the sound from the trees mixing, explosively, with whatever inorganic substances he stoked up on earlier. His skin goes vampire silver, his hat quivers, he raises the gun to chest height in front of him. Tomas, breathing loudly, deeply, mimics Benny's movement.

"Hey, Tomas, man," Benny says, words running together now, until his weird urge to re-direct the rhythms of speech takes over and he pauses for small, convulsive puffs of air. "You always pretended to be one *vato loco*, man. Yeah, one tough vaa-to lo-co. Hah! You're soft now, bay-bee, you settled down. You've mellowed, man. But not me. Not Benny Mohammad, motherfuckers. No. I'm cray-zi-er than ever."

Tomas stays still, waiting. Which impresses Artie, who feels his body to be full of insect life, the amphetamine high of pure fear. "Calm down, Benny, man," Artie says, unconvincingly, not a model candidate for poise himself. The ticking of his own Rolex sounds metronomic, loud enough to dance a waltz to it.

"No way, José," Benny says. "There's a big difference right now between old crazy Benny and Tomas there. The difference is, I *like* this. I *love* it. This is what makes me feel aah-liive. But Tomas there—he wants to live to be an old man. He's thinking about his old lady. He's thinking about his grandmother. He's thinking about the restaurant. He's thinking about too-mor-row. Too many thoughts weigh you down, man. He doesn't have a chance."

"I'll kill you, man," Tomas says in perfect, natural Clint Eastwood-ese, a growling monotone that means business. "I won't let you in there with my granny."

Artie involuntarily takes some steps back, away from Tomas, as he waves his hands in the air like an NFL referee and says, "Let's talk about this."

"This is it, man," Benny says, and laughs like a happy demon. He holds his gun up in front of him, looks at it, looks at Tomas, then back at the gun. Tomas raises his gun too, but it feels dead in his hand, his whole hand devoid of sensation, and though he wills tightness, wills his finger to pull back on the trigger, he experiences a floatiness, a detachment, that makes him unsure just what his hand has in mind at that moment.

Time becomes a rubber band as, for a fraction of a second that takes an hour, Benny enjoys the good tight fit of his finger and trigger and Tomas, ten feet away from him, yet part of this whole immediate synchronism. He enjoys, as well, a visionary moment, as he foresees the hole his gun will blow in Tomas's body, Tomas staggering, bloodied, opening to the world like a flower blooming.

In that same fraction of a second, a very old, very tall man dressed all in black, visible only because of his thick white hair, steps out of Concepción's front yard foliage, with Concepción right behind him. The old man is graceful and swift, and carries an enormous and efficient-looking rifle. In one quick step he is behind Benny Mohammad, swinging the rifle butt into Benny Mohammad's head. The crack of butt into head sounds so much like a muffled gunshot that, across the yard, seeing only the unidentified flying object of the old man's hair, Tomas and Artie remain unsure of what has just happened. They see the light go out in Benny Mohammad's face, see him crumple to the ground until he turns into a black mass under his bat-hat, a disappearance similar to the Wicked Witch's in *The Wizard of Oz* when Dorothy pours water on her, Tomas thinks. All his flaming craziness extinguished just as easily as one blows out a match—what a world. As Tomas and Artie run toward Benny, they see Concepción daintily step up and take the old man's arm, murmur to him.

Tomas and Artie stop, short, in front of these odd models for the toy bride and groom for the top of some geriatric shotgun wedding. The old man smiles, showing gold canine teeth. Concepción smiles.

"Alfredo," Concepción says, "*este es Tomas, el hijo de mi hijo. Y este es Arturo Vega.*" The perfect hostess, she continues, as if at a party, "*Tomas, Arturo, este es Señor Alfredo Guzman, el mejor amigo del General.*"

"*Dios mio,*" the old guy says, looking at Tomas. "*El mismo del General.*"

"*Lo siento mucho, pero no,*" Concepción says, wry, patting Tomas's cheek.

Now that they are close, Tomas and Artie can see that the old guy came slickly dressed, gigolo-style, for his role as an ambusher: black suit, black shirt, black tie, newly shined black shoes. His whole outfit looks perfectly tailored, made to order for his elongated and youthful body. Gradually, they see, too, that a diagonal line bisects his face into two triangles, crossing from the left side of his forehead to the right side of his jaw, neatly cutting across the bridge of his high, Spanish nose, interrupting the flow of wrinkles. The old guy smiles and nods some more, then points his gleaming, state of the art rifle at the prone form of Benny Mohammad.

"*Por La Señora*," he says proudly.

"*Muchas gracias*," Tomas says. Artie's teeth chatter now, grinding together as rhythmically as his watch ticks.

"*De nada*," the old guy says.

"Alfredo is a very important man in Mexico," Concepción says. "After the wars, not all of the General's compatriots went straight, or opened restaurants. Alfredo turned his soldier skills—he was a general too, you know—to a successful career in organized crime. He has been my adviser over the years, in many little matters."

Artie finally manages speech. "I am impressed, Señora." She acknowledges his compliment with the slightest inclination of her chin.

The old guy pays no attention to conversation, as he focuses, like a possessive dog with a very desirable bone, on Benny. He kicks Benny over, so that the unconscious ghoul-face shines silvery again amid the ruins of the bat-hat, the eyes rolled back and open so that no iris remains, just more slivered silver.

"*Él está muy borracho, no?*" the old guy says, laughing good-naturedly. He picks Benny up, throws him, limp, over his shoulder in the posture of a fireman rescuing a child from a burning building.

"*Sí, hombre*," Tomas says. "He's drunk out of his fuckin' mind. You better take that fucker right home before he gets into any more trouble."

The old guy carries Benny Mohammad to the gunmetal gray Ford across the street, balances him while he opens his trunk, tosses Benny into the trunk and slams it shut. Then he opens the car door and casually throws his rifle onto the backseat. He turns to Concepción, Tomas, and Artie and, lifting one hand in a large,

Santa Claus-y wave, calls out, jovially, "*Adiós, Conchita!*" And blows a kiss to Concepción. He gets in his car, secures his seat belt in the tinny, slimy, refrigerator-light glow of the car's interior, turns on his headlights, and slowly drives away. They can see him fit spectacles onto his nose as he drives.

Smug, Concepción says, "That *pinche cabrón* Benny Moham-mad will wake up tomorrow morning in a Tijuana jail with quite a headache. That *pendejo.*" She clucks her tongue in her mouth, sorry and superior.

Tomas puts his arm around her, hugs her to him with fierce affection, pride, and relief. "Listen to my Granny talking dirty." Artie, looking at the two of them, suddenly feels that he's in a movie. Not a character in a movie, nor an actor, but watching and deeply involved in a movie, when, all of a sudden, the camera pulls back. You were a foot away from suspense, danger, drama a second ago. Now you're three football fields away, in a shot that couldn't even be filmed by cranes, must be done using a helicopter and a Steadicam and great personal risk to a cameraman. Artie feels that alienated, that far away, from the two of them. And at the same time the profound longing to be back in the action, involved, close, to zoom back in on this real life of Tomas and Concepción which seems so charmed, symmetrical, a world in which everything that is broken can be fixed. He reaches instinc-tively for the book he keeps in his jacket, touches the place where it resides, as one does an amulet. Life has not been like that for Artie Vega, and he would like to study this phenomenon much more, figure out how he, himself, can fake it.

Thirty-one

CONCEPCIÓN

Most old people die of boredom. This is a known fact. Sitting around listening to their bodies groan and squeak—what could be more tiresome? I am sure that the last two weeks have added years to my life. All this scheming and planning, all this action. Wonderful! I may well live to be one hundred and twenty. Tomas is safe, and richer, and wants to buy a new stove for the restaurant. The General would be proud of me for my superior poise and intelligence. And that Benny Mohammad is *desaparecido*, for which I feel no guilt. Human beings who live like *cucarachas* deserve to be treated like *cucarachas*.

But, for this one thing, I am filled with guilt and unease. And, I am not prepared for this guilty thing. The General never thought about this, or he could not have made war so well. Because of me, because of my encouragement in this endeavor, my help in this endeavor, Tomas has lost his *novia*. This is bad enough. But, even more than this is my fault.

I raised Tomas to be proud and tough, a combination that I thought would protect him from many of the difficulties of life. When I raised my own son, the other Tomas, I made the opposite mistake. Because I had seen so much war, so much suffering, I raised him to appreciate only physical pleasure, to be soft in the face of the demands of the world, to give in, to value sensation for its own sake. I encouraged him to become a sybarite, as if this would protect him from suffering, and then lost him to his plea-sures, and was given another chance with his son.

And this son, this second Tomas, was already a bad boy, so I manipulated his bad-boyness. I taught him to be proud of what he was, to think of himself as a warrior in unheroic times, to be foolishly, foolhardily brave, to take chances that would trick him into thinking himself courageous, when actually they were only adolescent pranks. I know that I flirted with him, loved him as a sweetheart should have. A teenaged sweetheart, at that. But, then, I wanted the General back, as desperately as I still do. Though with every passing year my vision dims, both in life and in memory. And though I miss the General, I forget what exactly it is that I miss. His name, the sight of him on his horse, the first time we made love: These are clear and liquid memories, but the space around them seems ill-defined, or empty, like canvas waiting to be filled in by a painter, pages waiting to be written on by a writer. I try to pretend the General is as alive as always, within me, like a child always about to be born. Will never be forgotten. But this is my own foolish pride. The truth is, when I try to picture him, all I see is his face as it looks in that one portrait on the wall behind my piano. The truth is, I raised Tomas to be the mortar that patches the cracks of my monument to the General, holds the crumbling edifice together. What a lousy thing to do to a child—*cómo no*!

Now he mopes around, my Tomas. He sighs like a schoolgirl. His eyes look dull as a stupid dog's. He has called me on the telephone three times already today, to talk about business, about re-painting the restaurant, laying down a new linoleum floor, hiring another waitress. All the excitement and aliveness of the past days about to be overtaken by the tremendous dullness of Tomas's broken heart. For what is duller than melancholy? The General never became melancholy. When the General was depressed, it had a romantic grandeur to it. He threw whole sets of imported china out of windows. Fired rounds from his favorite pistol out into the night trying to shoot out the stars. Tore his own clothing upon his body. Once, he slapped the face of his favorite lieutenant, almost causing a duel between them. In that night, and unknown to the General, I went to his lieutenant and pleaded that this duel not take place. The revolution would suffer from such pettiness, I told the lieutenant. The loss of either one of them would be too great and ridiculous a loss merely because the General was in a bad mood, I said. In the morning, the lieutenant sent his servant to our quarters to announce that he was profoundly sorry for the incident. The General got drunk, before breakfast, to celebrate. Then, as it was a slow day in the war, he went out hunting for mountain lions, hoping to kill something.

And with the blood of warriors in his veins, the blood of generals, Tomas calls me up to talk about the new stove and, in the middle of a sentence, sighs as if he is breathing the thin air of heartbreak.

I am angry at myself, for helping to create this new Tomas, who seems to have no interests in life outside the most boring and redundant rhythms of his own body, his shallow breathing, his quickened heart, the conscious litany of tasks to be achieved in the world, the unconscious imaginings of conversations he would have with his *novia*, if he could only overcome his pride. Nothing very heroic about any of this, I am afraid I must admit. And I am angry at Tomas, because he behaves like a different person than the one I raised him to be, yet I see how this behavior is the inevitable outcome of my stories and flattery. I regret my mistakes with him, yet I still expect him to behave as the General would have behaved. What this confusion indicates to me is that I must take certain steps.

Besides, already I am bored with my ancient life, because my life of crime has for the moment been terminated, been so successful that it is finished. So, like a child bored with a new toy, already longing for an even newer toy, I will invent a new scheme, this time in the realm of love instead of smuggling. I will call the *novia*, and ask her to come visit me. No one can refuse the request of an old woman—it may be her last, they always feel. Old women, if they play their cards right, can be spoiled rotten, worse than the most spoiled child. Being old has its rewards, is not so bad if you retain your imagination and your desires.

The *novia* comes to my door looking small and tired. This big strong girl, with her shoulders slumping, her yellow hair hanging limp, dirty. I feel that, if she sighs, I will have to slap her.

But she seems happy to see me, takes my hands in hers when she comes in, kisses me on the cheek. Looks at me, with those gringa eyes, in expectation. I wonder where she got her pride, without an old granny to tell her tales. Stronger, and probably smarter, than Tomas, this *novia*, because she invented her own version of foolish pridefulness, without benefit of Generals in her family history. As soon as she sits down on my couch, she starts to cry. I know I can convince her of anything. Young people are so simple to comprehend.

"Mama, I'm so confused," she says, after I sit in my chair, waiting, silently, for her to speak first. Tears stream down her pale cheeks.

"I miss him and I'm afraid of him and I don't know what I want in my life," she gushes. Forfeiting her power by exhibiting her soul so quickly. She trusts me.

"*Querida*, these are three different issues," I say, in a tiny, old, sage voice. "But this I can tell you. He misses you too, and is so very sorry he has hurt you."

"But how can I ever believe in him again?" she asks, sobbing. A little dramatic, this *novia*, I think at first. Then, when her weeping continues, I think: She does love him. This will be very simple.

"Believe in him?" I ask incredulously, as if I have never heard these words before. "Do you believe he loves you?"

"Yes." The tears continue, but no more of this gulping sobbing. A good sign.

"Do you believe that he wants you back, and wants to make you happy?"

"I guess." Still the tears raining down her broad, pink cheeks.

"*Entonces,*" I say, triumphant, my hands spread wide before me.

"I want a real life, Mama," she says, and sobs again. *Dios mio*, how this *novia* reveals herself. "What if I want a home, a baby? Tomas scares me."

"Okay," I say, get up, bring her a glass of water from the kitchen, which she sips like an obedient child. Of course, I have never believed that drinking water in any way soothed one out of crying and grief, but this kind of action is expected of grandmothers and, right now, I am playing a part. I am playing a grandmother, instead of a brilliant criminal, though I prefer the latter. As the heaving in her chest becomes controlled, so she can concentrate more on what I have to tell her, I say, "What is real life? Safety? Hah! Do you want to turn dull and fat and mired in real life? Danger is better than safety, better than real life. If you have any tiny bit of larceny in you, if you think that ever, in your whole life, you might get the itch for adventure, and look at your husband and child and home and think, 'What have I done?', you had better think twice about this notion of safety." I pause, for the effect of carefully thinking about what I have just said, though I know exactly where I am heading.

"Now, Tomas is young, and loves the thrill of adventure. But he also loves you, loves your life together. If the two of you work at it, you can have both comfort and danger." This is something I have heard on talk-radio, read in "Dear Abby," something young people believe in these days: that one must work at a relationship, that if it isn't hard work, it must be superficial and meaningless to be with another person. The General and I never worked at our relationship. The wars were enough work, staying alive was enough work. Life was grander, bigger, harder. The relationship, as they call it these days, was easy. We were comrades. Today, with nothing grand in the world for young people to be engaged in, they create struggle with one another, conflict in relationships, war in love.

"Yes," the *novia* says. "I'm willing to work at it. I want to make it work."

"Good," I say, and clap my hands together, as I would for a dog that had just performed the trick I had requested.

"But," and her lip quivers again, her chin wrinkles up toward her mouth. *Pobrecita*, she tries to be strong. "He was involved in all this"—she pauses until the correct word comes to her—"awfulness. He got me involved in this awfulness."

If only she knew about last night, with Benny Mohammad and Tomas pointing their guns at one another like two boy-children playing at gangsters. I will never tell her, and I will warn Tomas that he too must never talk about this incident.

"Now, honey, you're sounding like a gringa," I say, frowning. "Don't you understand? This is what makes Tomas full of life, it makes him sexy, it makes him loved by many people." I stop, pretend to consider some more. In making serious talk in which you want to convince someone else of your point of view, especially in an emotional disagreement, pauses become very important. You must seem to dig deep into your soul for the truth, present this well-considered truth in slow words. "This dangerousness. It is essential to Tomas. Why were you first attracted to him?"

She stops, thinks, shuts her eyes. I can tell that she runs a movie in her head, the movie of when she and Tomas first met. "Because he seemed so alive," she says, making big cow eyes at the vision in her memory.

This is a test that always works, should you desire to test love in others. If they can reminisce about their first meeting with the one they love while looking in your eyes, if they can make the memory part of the flow of conversation, their love is not real. Not, at least, their love for the other. In my experience, people like this love themselves, love hearing themselves talk. But they do not love the one they are talking about. Sometimes, if you use this test, you can determine that somebody actually despises the person they pretend to love. Their lips will curl as they talk about the loved one, their eyes will dart to the side, the muscles in their necks will become stiff, rigid, and knotty as a trick rope used to make magic.

I ask the *novia* this question, so that I can base the rest of my scheme for Tomas's life on how she responds. And still the cow eyes. In spite of the fact that Tomas has introduced her to a life of crime and danger, she loves him. Or, because Tomas has introduced her to a life of crime and danger, she loves him? Neither is absolutely true, as human beings are much more contrary than any single sentence can communicate. Nor does it matter why she loves him, in terms of my continued scheming. Still, as other people continue to interest me, because I see so clearly, as an old woman, how my study of others has so often saved my life and the lives of my loved ones, I will think about this, and try to position the *novia* in either the "because" or "in spite" camp. I am, essentially, an old soldier. In war, there are always two camps, two armies, with different ideas about how the world should work. Just a simplified version of the human soul.

"You see?" I say to the *novia*. But she flaps her long eyelashes twice, blinking away tears, perhaps, or maybe making clarity. She nods absently, plays with the ends of her long yellow hair. For a moment, watching her think this way, I feel as if I am a visitor to a zoo, and she is one of the exhibits, one of the animals. How can she be a member of the same species I am? I try to remember charity and kindness. But I never looked like that, even forty or fifty years ago. Certainly, I was pretty. And I was strong. But small, compact, hard, dark. I never opened my eyes so wide, wide enough to see the whole world at once, like those special lenses they put on cameras that record the curvature of the earth. Me, I looked to the horizon, squinted at points far away where a single horseman would prefigure the arrival of an entire force of men. To see this soon enough meant survival. The General valued my eyesight. But this girl, this *novia*, looks, now, as if she has the eyes of a big china doll, seeing nothing, eyes as decorative and as useful as sapphires. Of course, I know that this reflects introspection. I know she is not a stupid girl, this *novia*. And yet, I could not feel more foreign, could not feel farther away from another person.

Her eyes snap back into focus. I see them emerging from the forest of thought after two more blinks, see that she sees me again. And now I know her again, feel that she has returned to the human race. I have learned something from her, this minute, and it makes me feel happy and young. I have learned that watching someone in the midst of despair, watching this person trying to decide an important issue in her life, is very intimate. This person becomes naked before you, hides nothing, is vulnerable to your scrutiny in a new and perilous way. Again, as when I first saw her today, I realize: What the *novia* has displayed before me is her trust of me. My heart pounds harder, so that I hear it in my ears, feel it in my arms. That trust should not be betrayed.

The *novia* says, "Mama, I'm just not sure I can live this way." She stops, thinks again, makes a sheepish little smile. "If I can't live with him and I can't live without him, how do I decide? Either way, I'm not really living."

Now I feel old, with the weight of responsibility. With wanting to make Tomas happy, and wanting the *novia* to make the correct decision. Where is the possible intersection of these two desires?

"Okay," I say to the *novia*. "When you say this, the answer becomes clear to me. Can't live with. Can't live without. Which is better?" I stop, look at her, but she makes doll eyes at me, thinking hard, the confusion of despair. I can put her out of her misery. "Can't live without is better. You have something then, something to work with. But, can't live with—you have nothing." I stop again, hear something echo, resound, in my head, the collision of languages. "Think with your heart, *querida*, instead of with common sense. Your heart tells you you can't live without Tomas. Your brain tells you you can't live with him. The heart is what breaks. The brain is strong, like a mule."

She cries, tears collecting in her big eyes and flooding out, and then sobs into her hands, hair falling all around her face like a waterfall. I know I have done the right thing: Tomas will get her back, she will have a good life with him. He loves her, and he holds nothing back from her but, occasionally, truth.

What echoes in some big, empty place in my head, though, is what the *novia* said. Do you live with or without? *Con o sin?* What a choice. I realize that, no real consideration necessary, I have chosen to live my life without. Since the General died, I have lived my whole life without. I tell the *novia* that deciding to live with Tomas is correct for her, but it would not have been so for me. I am singular, and a world without suits me. *Sin amor, sin marido, sin país.* These are the choices I have made, always *sin*, without. A soldier lives without. But the *novia*, not a soldier, but an actress, has different needs, needs connection to others as I never did, needs a life *con amor, con familia.*

Dios mio, between *sin* and *con,* such a decision! Life hurts you and laughs at you and never lets you win. The only near-victory is in endurance. I am old. So I have almost won.

Thirty-two
SASHA

When there's a knock at the door, you don't think, this is going to change my life. Like that old hippie cliché—today is the first day of the rest of your life. I never went for that. Tomorrow could be shitty, the next day sunny. The knock at the door could be some guy trying to sell me a new long distance dialing service guaranteed to save me money.

I'm rambling around Claire's apartment, looking in her closets and drawers and piles of folded but not stored clean clothes on the floor for those few items that she owns and I could wear to work, feeling close to content because I've got a mission.

Your head gets on one track, it skates around that track as fast as hell, like it's in the Olympics. That guy with the bulging thighs, with the pin head, who won all those speed skating awards a few years ago, Eric Heiden? That's my head, and the sound of the skates on the ice, endlessly high-pitched humming, the one tune my brain can hum. The only movie playing in town. Tomas, Tomas, Tomas.

But that's because I've been sitting around, indulging. And Claire's been indulging me, too. It's rat-in-a-maze thinking, small thinking, that I've been engaging in. Problem is, as much as you hate yourself for it, you don't know what to do about it.

Crying, moaning, cringing, dreaming, sighing, whimpering: None of these helps one bit. These are what I've been doing for the past forty-eight hours, and I do not look like I've spent the time at Elizabeth Arden. I look terrible. Eyes swollen, skin pale and doughy. Hair hanging flat and lusterless. I look like the "before" half of one of those magazine make-overs. How do I get to "after"?

Claire's already at work, taking over somebody else's early shift and keeping her own late shift. I've got to be at work at six. So I look for something to wear. And for fifteen, maybe twenty minutes, I don't think about Tomas. The name Tomas does not enter my consciousness. I'm standing at the closet, staring at a big white shirt of Claire's that I hold out in front of me as if it's artwork I've created, I'm considering how Japanese fashion designers have made it possible for me and Claire to wear the same shirt and look equally shapeless. And this lightning bolt hits me in the forehead, like the ceiling is cloven by it, like it's Greek mythology time. Tomas! Stricken, I sit on Claire's unmade bed. This big emptiness starts to open up somewhere in the center of me, black, growing, something essential missing, what I thought was a small piece that could be discarded turning out to be more like the whole, like everything.

"Idiot," I say aloud to myself, smack myself on the forehead. But I've still got to go to work. The mission, once discovered, occupies a parallel track to the Tomas-track. It's smaller, it's less demanding, less compelling. But it's like backup singers, or the bass player's part on a record. You can force yourself to listen and, when you do, you have to admit it's not bad for a change. The white shirt, crumpled up, is still in my hand. I take off my sweats, put on Claire's oversized shirt, look in Claire's mirror. Again, not bad for a change. Now all I need is some skirt with an elasticized waist, some one-size-fits-all type of thing for my lower half, something long on Claire that will be normal length on me. The Japanese are into that too. It should be possible in Claire's closet. All right. I'm back into the groove, the slow lane of traffic in my mind, low-grade obsession better than fever, when the knock at the door happens.

I stroll out to the living room, thinking clothes, thinking a pair of Claire's tights might fit onto my bigger legs. After a couple of years living at the beach and being alone late at night, when Tomas is at the restaurant, I say, "Who is it," before I even unbolt the deadlock.

"The big bad wolf," Tomas's voice says.

I unbolt the door, the most natural thing in the world. Until I actually see him.

He needs a shave. He needs a shampoo. His shirt could use a little ironing. Nothing unusual, the way he goes to the restaurant on nights when, the night before, he's been up too late, has drunk too much. In his mind, hygiene has nothing to do with his inevitable and overpowering charm. And he's right. I see the big face, the warm eyes, the strong arms held out to hug me, and I feel a little dizzy. Instead of stepping into his hug, I take a step back into Claire's living room, sensible. He looks confused, but only for a moment.

"Come in," I say, and of course he does. He was going to anyway. We stand, like strangers, like prizefighting opponents, a few feet away from one another in the apartment, wary.

"Listen, *corazón*," he says, "Granny told me that she talked to you. I didn't want you to think I put her up to it. To put pressure on you, I mean."

Here he is, the one groove in the single record in the jukebox inside my head for the past two days, right in front of me. Nausea, excitement, desire; sweaty armpits, racing pulse in a few key body sites. I think cool, all my training necessary, I think green tea ice cream, I think gin and tonic, I think skiing down a pale blue fjord, among Norwegians speaking their very cool language of lifting consonants and sloping vowels. A deep but invisible breath. "That never occurred to me."

"It didn't?" he says, amazed. I wonder why I never get any good roles. I can see that I'm a convincing actress. We look at each other for a second, sizing up, making reality and memory and imagination come together into this moment.

"So how's the big scam?" I ask, keeping sarcasm, irony, broken-heartedness out of my voice. More Oscar material, best supporting actress in a criminal and/or love scene.

Tomas looks like he's going to cry. "Look, the scam is all through," he says.

"Yeah? What happened?"

"It all worked out, no problem."

"What about Benny Mohammad?"

"He kinda disappeared," Tomas says. "It's all finished." He closes his eyes, sighs now, the untrained actor preparing for a soliloquy like he's about to run a hundred-yard dash. "Look, *querida*. I've turned over a whole new leaf. I swear to you, no more scams. No more crime. I'll turn into the most boring WASP in the world for you. I'll make the restaurant into a real money-maker with my take from the rubies, you'll see, I'll be a real businessman. I'll only use drugs when someone at the restaurant forces them on me, or on birthdays and holidays, or nights when the restaurant breaks a thousand dollars. I'll be a born-again capitalist. I'm gonna work hard, I promise, and get real boring. I'll be Mister Straight."

As he talks, I feel his magnetism grow, like in that children's game when you're looking for something that's been hidden. The hider says, "You're getting warmer, warmer, you're hot now, you're sizzling" as you get close, and you can feel your fingers burn as they near the hidden thing. Tomas glows, like he has the hidden thing inside him, like he's swallowed some radioactive substance. He is that hidden thing for me, what I need to find, to hold, to win. Cool cool cool, I think, the pale lights of the aurora borealis over an arctic ice floe. I try to turn my eyes into those lights, but it doesn't work. I see ice cubes melting, coating the outside of a glass with a slick, sweaty, liquid skin.

"I'm a sick person," I say. "I almost believe you."

He smiles, and I'm lost. It's not that I can't distinguish between truth and fiction, honesty and dishonesty, danger and safety. It's that I don't care. He says, "I've got a present for you," and reaches into his pants pocket, brings out something small, valuable, that he holds in his fisted hand. When he touches me, takes my hand in his open one, deposits the contents of the closed fist into my palm, the jolt and buzz make an illegible sign light up in my head. I'm not sure whether the sign reads "Caution" or "Applause" or "No exit." It doesn't matter. What he's placed in my hand is an enormous ruby.

"Whatya think?" Tomas says, grinning.

"I know where it came from," I say, slowly, backing away from him.

"Artie'll never know the difference," Tomas says. "It'll make a beautiful ring for you."

He doesn't get it: He's just promised me perfect and appropriate and legal behavior as he presents me with an illegal, smuggled, stolen, filched ruby. I tighten my hand around it, feel it small and hard against my palm and fingertips. And I wonder whether the General lied to Concepción, whether she lied to him. And who knew what were lies and what were truths, and who kept quiet over the lies? Then I think, come on, how can an actress have such a lousy sense of narrative? This line of reasoning isn't what makes good mythology, good epic tales. Who cares about little lies? Love and war get passed down through generations as stories, not petty dishonesty. Maybe the stories are what matter, or should matter, in the moment too. Maybe if you take the epic view, give to the present all the allowances you make for the past, the exaggerations you accept, the choice of details that you take for granted as good story-telling, you'll be happier. I'll be happier. I can be with Tomas.

"I dreamed of you every night, real hot dreams," he says, as I step into his hug, feel his arms around me in that familiar, intoxicating embrace that turns my brain and spine into a swoony mess, defeating evolution and physiology in a simple instant. Defeating truth.

"Oh, baby," he says, right before he kisses me. "I've missed you."